LARGE PRINT EDITION

RANDOM HOUSE

PETER BENCHLEY

▲ ▲ ▲ ▲ ▲ ▲ ▲

WHITE
SHARK

▲ ▲ ▲ ▲ ▲ ▲ ▲
▲ ▲ ▲ ▲ ▲ ▲ ▲
▲ ▲ ▲ ▲ ▲ ▲ ▲

Published by Random House Large Print
in association with Random House, Inc.
New York 1994

Library of Congress Cataloging-in-Publication Data
Benchley, Peter.
    White shark / Peter Benchley.—1st large print ed.
        p.   cm.
    ISBN 0-679-75388-5
    1. Scientists—Connecticut—Fiction.
    2. Sharks—Connecticut—Fiction.
    3. Large type books.   I. Title.
[PS3552.E537W45   1994b]
813′.54—dc20   94-1755
                                                     CIP

Manufactured in the United States of America
FIRST LARGE PRINT EDITION

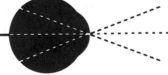

For Jeff Brown
and
in memory of
Michael W. Cogan
and
Paul D. Zimmerman
—missed men

ACKNOWLEDGMENTS

For their counsel and corrections on matters
cetological, ichthyological, chondrichthian,
ornithological, hyperbaric and cryptomedical,
I am in debt to Richard Ellis and
Stanton Waterman. Any inaccuracies
or speculations that may remain are mine,
not theirs.

And for her patience, perseverance, wisdom,
encouragement and friendship, I am,
as I have been for nearly two decades,
grateful beyond words
to the incomparable Kate Medina.

—P.B.

WHITE SHARK

PART ONE

▲ ▲ ▲ ▲ ▲ ▲ ▲

1945

1

THE WATER in the estuary had been still for hours, as still as a sheet of black glass, for there was no wind to stir it.

Then suddenly, as if violated by a great beast rising from the depths, the water bulged, heaved up, threatening to explode.

At first, the man watching from the hillside dismissed the sight as yet another illusion caused by his fatigue and the flickering light from the cloud-shrouded moon.

But as he stared, the bulge grew and grew and finally burst, pierced by a monstrous head, barely visible, black on black, distinguishable from the water around it only by the gleaming droplets shed from its sleek skin.

More of the leviathan broke through—a pointed snout, a smooth cylindrical body—and then silently it settled back and floated motionless on the silky surface, waiting, waiting for the man.

From the darkness a light flashed three times: short, long, long; dot, dash, dash—the international Morse signal for *W.* The man replied by lighting three matches in the same sequence. Then he picked up his satchel and started down the hill.

He stank, he itched, he chafed. The clothing he had taken days ago from a roadside corpse—burying his own tailored uniform and handmade boots in a muddy shell crater—was filthy, ill fitting and vermin-infested.

At least he was no longer hungry: earlier in the evening he had ambushed a refugee couple, crushed their skulls with a brick and gorged himself on tins of the vile processed meat they had begged from the invading Americans.

He had found it interesting, killing the two people. He had ordered many deaths, and caused countless more, but he had never done the actual killing. It had been surprisingly easy.

. . .

He had been traveling—fleeing—for days. Five? Seven? He had no idea, for stolen moments of sleep in sodden haystacks had blended seamlessly with hours of slogging along shattered roads, in company with the wretched refuse of weak-willed nations.

Exhaustion had become his companion and his

plague. Dozens of times he had collapsed in ditches or flopped in patches of tall grass and lain, panting, till he felt himself revive. There was no mystery to his fatigue: he was fifty years old, and fat, and the only exercise he had had in the past ten years was bending his elbow to sip from a glass.

Still, it was infuriating, a betrayal. He shouldn't *have* to be in good shape; he wasn't *supposed* to be running. He wasn't an athlete or a warrior, he was a genius who had accomplished something unprecedented in the history of mankind. His destiny had always been to lead, to teach, to inspire, not to run like a frightened rat.

Once or twice he had nearly been seduced by exhaustion into succumbing, surrendering, but he had resisted, for he was determined to fulfill his destiny. He had a mission, assigned to him on direct orders from the Fuehrer the day before he had shot himself, and he would complete that mission, whatever it cost, however long it took.

For though he was not a man of politics or world vision, though he was a scientist, he knew that his mission had significance far beyond science.

· · ·

Now exhaustion, fear and hunger had all vanished, and as he made his way carefully down the steep hillside, Ernst Kruger smiled to himself. His years of work would bear fruit; his faith had been rewarded.

He had never really doubted that they would come, not once in the endless days of flight nor in the endless hours of waiting. He had known they would not fail him. They might not be clever like the Jews, but Germans were dependable. They did what they were told.

2

A SMALL rubber boat was waiting when Kruger reached the pebble beach. One man sat at the oars, another stood on shore. Both were dressed entirely in black—shoes, trousers, sweaters, woolen caps—and their hands and faces had been blackened with charcoal. Neither spoke.

The man on shore extended a hand, offering to relieve Kruger of his satchel. Kruger refused. Securing the satchel to his chest, he stepped aboard the boat and, steadying himself with a hand on the oarsman's shoulder, made his way forward to the bow.

There was a sound of rubber scraping against pebbles, then only the soft lap of oars pulling against calm water.

Two more men stood on the deck of the U-boat, and when the rubber boat glided up to its side, they helped Kruger aboard, took him to the forward hatch and held it open for him as he climbed down a ladder into the belly of the boat.

· · ·

Kruger stood behind a ladder in the control room and listened to a blizzard of curt orders and immediate responses. The air inside the submarine was a fog. Every lightbulb had a halo of mist around it, every metal surface was wet to the touch. And the air was not only humid, it stank. He parsed the stench, and recognized salt, sweat, diesel oil, potatoes and something sickly sweet, like cologne.

Kruger felt as if he were a prisoner in an infernal swamp.

He heard a muted sound of electric motors, and there was a faint sensation of movement, forward and down.

An officer wearing a white-covered cap stepped away from the periscope, gestured to Kruger and disappeared into a passageway. Kruger bent his head to pass through an open hatch, and followed.

They squeezed into a tiny cubicle—a bunk, a chair and a folding desk—and the commander introduced himself. Kapitänleutnant Hoffmann was young, no more than thirty, bearded, with the gaunt pallor of U-boat veterans. Around his neck he wore a Knight's Cross, and when it snagged in the collar of his shirt, he flicked it aside.

Kruger liked the insouciance of the gesture. It meant that Hoffmann had had his *Ritterkreuz* for some time, was probably entitled to wear oak leaves with it but didn't bother. He was good at his job, but that was already obvious from the simple fact that he had survived. Nearly 90 percent of all the U-boats launched during the war had been lost; of the thirty-nine thousand men who had sailed in them, thirty-three thousand had been killed or captured. Kruger remembered hearing of the Fuehrer's rage as he had read those figures.

Kruger gave Hoffmann the news: of chaos in the country, of the retreat to the bunker, of the Fuehrer's death.

"Who is the new leader of the Reich?" Hoffmann asked.

"Donitz," said Kruger. "But in fact, Bormann." He paused, debating whether to tell Hoffmann the truth: there *was* no more Reich, not in Germany. If the Reich was to survive, the seeds of its survival were here, in this submarine. He decided that Hoffmann didn't need to know the truth. "Your crew?" he said.

"Fifty men, including you and me, all volunteers, all party members, all single."

"How much do they know?"

"Nothing," Hoffmann said, "except that they're not likely to see home again."

"And the trip will take how long?"

"Normally, thirty or forty days, but these days aren't normal. We can't get out the shortest way. The Bay of Biscay is a death trap, crawling with Allied ships. We'll have to go up around Scotland, get into the Atlantic and head south. I can make eighteen knots on the surface, but I don't know how much we'll be able to travel on the surface. I'll have to maintain economy speed, about twelve knots, so as to keep our range at about eighty-seven hundred miles. If we're harassed, we'll spend more time submerged. We only make seven knots submerged, and our E motors give out after sixty-four miles and need seven hours of surface running to recharge. So the best I can give you is a guess: about fifty days."

Kruger felt sweat bead on his forehead and under his arms. Fifty days! He'd been in this iron tomb for less than an hour, and already he felt as if a mailed fist were crushing his lungs.

"You'll get used to it," Hoffmann said. "And when we get south, you'll be able to spend time on deck. *If* we get south, that is. We're at a disadvantage. If we have to fight, we'll be like a one-armed man. We have no forward torpedoes."

"Why not?"

"We took them out, to make room for your . . . cargo. It was too big to go down the hatch, so we removed the deck plates. Then we found it wouldn't fit between the torpedoes, so they had to go."

Kruger stood up. "I want to see it," he said.

They moved forward, past space after tiny space—the radio room, officers' quarters, the galley. When they reached the bow of the ship, Hoffmann swung open the hatch leading to the forward torpedo room, and Kruger stepped through.

It was there, secured in an enormous bronze box, and for a moment Kruger simply stood and looked, remembering the years of work, the countless failures, the derision, the first tiny successes and, at last, his triumph: a weapon unlike anything ever created.

He saw that the bronze had begun to tarnish, and he stepped forward and checked swiftly for any signs of damage. He saw none.

He put a hand on the side of the box. What he felt was beyond pride. Here was the most revolutionary weapon not only of the Third Reich but of science itself. Very few men in history could claim what he could: Ernst Kruger had changed the world.

He thought of Mengele, Josef Mengele, his personal friend and professional rival. Had Mengele, too, escaped? Was he still alive? Would they meet in Paraguay? Mengele, known as *Der Engel des Todes,* the Angel of Death, because of his experiments on human beings, had been contemptuous of Kruger's work, proclaiming it fanciful, impossible. But in fact, Kruger's research had a very practical, and very deadly, purpose.

Kruger dearly hoped Mengele was still alive; he couldn't wait to show Mengele his achievement, the ultimate weapon: *Der Weisse Hai.*

He turned away and left the torpedo room.

3

AS THE U-boat rounded the tip of Scotland, it hit a savage westerly gale. Pitching and rolling like an amusement park ride, it inched south, west of Ireland, and made its way slowly into the Atlantic.

On May 8, Hoffmann told Kruger that a bulletin had come over the radio: Germany had surrendered. The war was over.

"Not for us," Kruger replied. "Not for us. For us, the war will never be over."

• • •

The days fell, like autumn leaves from a linden tree, one after another, indistinguishable. Hoffmann had avoided the shipping lanes, and so encountered no Allied vessels. Three times the lookout had seen trails of smoke on the horizon; half a dozen times Hoffmann had ordered the boat to submerge, shallow practice dives rather than emergencies.

For Kruger, time became a monotonous cycle of meals, sleep and work in the forward torpedo room. His work was crucial; it was the sole motivation for his own life now, and for enduring this interminable voyage.

In the torpedo room, Kruger pushed a release button hidden beneath a tiny swastika etched in the bronze. The cover of the huge box opened; with a magnifying glass he examined the thick rubber O-ring seals that kept the box air- and watertight. He applied grease to any spots that appeared to be pitting or drying out.

Kruger's superiors had immediately grasped the military applications of his experiments. What he saw as a scientific breakthrough, they saw as a magnificent weapon. And so money was lavished upon it, and Kruger had been pushed to complete it. But then, with success so close, time had run out; the empire of the Reich had shrunk to a bunker in Berlin, and Kruger had been told that the weapon would be transported, even though programming was incomplete.

· · ·

Four weeks into the voyage, Kruger was summoned to the control room. Hoffmann's arms hung over the wings of the periscope, his face was pressed to the eyepiece and he was turning in a slow circle. He didn't look up, but as soon as Kruger was in the room, Hoffmann said, "This is the moment we've been waiting for, Herr Doktor. It's calm, it's twilight and it's pouring rain. We can go topside and have a shower." Hoffmann looked away from the eyepiece and smiled. "And in deference to your station, you shall be on the first shift."

It had been more than a month since Kruger had bathed, shaved, brushed his teeth. The boat could store only a few gallons of fresh water, and that which its desalinizers made every day was reserved exclusively for cooking and for servicing the batteries. He longed for the feeling of fresh water on his stinking skin. "Is it safe?" he asked.

"I think so. There's not much traffic this far south—we're about two thousand kilometers east of the Bahamas." Hoffmann returned to the eyepiece and said, "How much water under the keel?"

"No bottom here, Herr Kaleu," a sailor at a control panel replied.

"No bottom?" Kruger said. "How can there be no bottom?"

Hoffmann said, "It's too deep for our Fathometer to get a return. We must be over one of the midocean trenches . . . three kilometers, five kilometers . . . who knows? Plenty of water. We're not likely to hit anything."

The rush of fresh air, as a crewman opened the conning-tower hatch, smelled to Kruger as sweet as violets. He stood at the base of the ladder, holding a bar of soap, and savored the drops of rainwater that fell on his face.

The crewman scanned the horizon with binoculars, called out, "All clear!" and slid backward down the ladder.

Kruger climbed up, stepped over the lip of the bridge and descended the exterior ladder to the deck. Four crewmen followed him, scaling the ladders as nimbly as spiders. They gathered on the afterdeck, naked, and passed a bar of soap among them.

The rain was steady but soft, not wind driven, and the sea was slickly calm. The long, gentle ocean swell lifted the submarine so slowly that Kruger had no trouble keeping his footing. He walked forward to a flat stretch of deck, took off his clothes and spread them on the deck, hoping the rain would rinse the stench from them. He lathered himself and spread his arms.

"Herr Doktor!"

Kruger dropped his arms and looked aft; the four naked crewmen were rushing up the ladder to the bridge.

"A plane! Hurry!" The last crewman on the ladder pointed at the sky, then kept climbing.

"A what?" Then, over the sound of his own

voice, Kruger heard the drone of an engine. He looked in the direction the crewman had pointed; for a moment, he saw nothing. Then, against the lighter gray of the western clouds, there was a black speck skimming the wave tops and heading directly at him.

He scooped up his clothes and ran for the ladder. His foot hit something, some obstruction on the deck, and he sprawled forward onto his knees, scattering his clothes.

The drone of the plane's engine sounded closer; it had risen to a yowl.

Stunned by a sharp, hot pain that shot from his big toe up through his calf, Kruger abandoned his clothes and struggled to his feet. He glanced backward to see what he had hit; one of the deck plates just aft of the forward hatch looked warped, as if a weld had popped and sprung one of the plate's edges.

He began to climb the ladder.

The engine noise was deafening now, and Kruger ducked reflexively as the plane screamed overhead. He looked up as it began a long loop into the sky.

One of the crewmen leaned down from the bridge, reaching his hand out to Kruger, urging him on.

From somewhere inside the hull Kruger heard the klaxon for an emergency dive, and as he fell over the lip of the bridge and sought footing on the interior ladder, he felt the thrum of engines and a sensation of motion forward and down.

The hatch clanged shut above him, the crewman shimmied past him down the side of the ladder, and Kruger found himself standing on the bottom rung, naked, drenched, a film of soap running down his legs.

Hoffmann was bent over the periscope. "Pull the plug, Chief," he said, "we're taking her down."

Kruger said, "On the deck, one of the—"

"Periscope depth," the chief called. "E motors half speed."

Hoffmann spun the periscope ninety degrees. "Son of a *bitch,*" he said. "The bastard's coming back."

"He didn't fire on us," Kruger said. "I think you—"

"He will this time; he was just making sure. He's not about to let a U-boat get across the Atlantic, war or no war. Forward down fifteen, aft down ten. Take her to a hundred meters."

Hoffmann slammed the wings of the periscope up and pushed the retractor button, and the gleaming steel tube slid downward. He glanced at Kruger, noted the stricken look on his face and said, "Don't worry, we're a needle in a haystack.

Night's coming on, and the chances of his finding us—"

"Fifty meters!" called the chief.

"On the deck," Kruger said. "I saw a . . . one of the pieces of metal . . . have you taken this boat to a hundred meters before?"

"Of course. Dozens of times."

"Seventy meters, Herr Kaleu!"

· · ·

At seventy meters below the surface, there was nearly a hundred pounds of water pressure on every square inch of the submarine's hull. The boat had been designed to operate safely at more than twice that depth, and had done so many times. But when the forward deck plates had been removed to take on Kruger's cargo, one of the welders assigned to replace them had worked too hastily. A few superficial, inconsequential welds had failed during the shallow dives, but all the critical ones had held. Now, however, with thousands of tons of water squeezing the hull like a living fist, one gave way.

· · ·

There was a noise forward, a resonant boom, and the boat lurched downward. Men were thrown from their seats; Kruger slammed into the ladder, bounced off and then grabbed it to keep from pitching down the passageway.

Hoffmann's feet skidded out from under him, and he clutched the periscope.

"Emergency surface!" he shouted. "Bring her up! All back full! Blow fore and aft!" He shot a glance at Kruger. "Did you dog the forward hatch?"

"I can't remem—"

There was another boom then as the forward hatch blew open, and a solid jet of water five feet high and three feet across blasted from the torpedo room through the petty officers' quarters. It rushed into the galley and the officers' wardroom.

"Ninety meters, Herr Kaleu!" a voice shrieked.

The boat continued down. Kruger suddenly felt weightless, as if he were in an elevator.

There were loud creaking noises; somewhere a pipe burst; there was a hiss of steam. The control room filled with the sour smell of sweat, then of urine, and, at last, of oil and feces.

Another boom, at two hundred meters.

Darkness. Screams. Wailing.

In the millisecond before he died, Ernst Kruger reached a hand forward, toward the torpedo room, toward the future.

4

THE SUBMARINE sank swiftly. It plummeted, bow first, to a thousand feet. There, well beyond its test depth, the pressure hull finally gave way, in a dozen places at once. Air rushed from ruptures of torn metal, the boat shuddered and torqued. Its hydrodynamics destroyed, it began to tumble.

Down, down it went, passing through two thousand feet, then five thousand. And with every thirty-three feet another fifteen pounds of water pressure forced the hull, rushed into tiny pockets of residual air and crushed them like grapes. At ten thousand feet, more than two tons of water pressed against every square millimeter of steel, and the last scintilla of air popped from the shattered hulk and drifted upward in the darkness.

The submarine descended as if it were a discarded soda can, until finally it struck a mountainside, bounced and rolled in slow motion, throwing clouds of unseen silt and dislodging boulders that accompanied it into a stygian canyon. There, at last, it came to a halt, a heap of twisted steel.

. . .

In the rubble of the bow, the huge box, cast of bronze, sealed with rubber, denied penetration to the seeking sea.

The silt settled, time passed. Legions of infinitesimal organisms that patrolled the abyss consumed what was edible.

Calm returned to the ocean bottom, and the relentless cycle of life and death went on.

PART TWO

▲ ▲ ▲ ▲ ▲ ▲ ▲

1996

LATITUDE 26 DEGREES NORTH

LONGITUDE 45 DEGREES WEST

5

ABSOLUTE DARKNESS is rare on earth. Even on a moonless night, with clouds hiding the stars, the loom of civilization glows against the sky.

In the deep oceans, absolute darkness is commonplace. Rays of the sun, thought for millennia to be the sole source of life on earth, can penetrate less than half a mile of seawater. Nearly three quarters of the planet—vast plains, great canyons, mountain ranges that rival the Himalayas—are shrouded in perpetual black, broken occasionally by bioluminescent organisms that sparkle with predatory or reproductive intent.

· · ·

Two submersibles hovered side by side like alien crabs—white-bodied, brilliant-eyed. The two five-thousand-watt lights mounted on their concave snouts cast a path of gold some two hundred feet in front of them.

"Four thousand meters," one of the pilots said into his radio. "The pass should be dead-ahead. I'm going in."

"Roger that," the other pilot replied. "I'm right behind you."

Propellers turned simultaneously as electric motors were engaged, and the first submersible moved slowly ahead.

Inside the steel capsule—only ten feet long and six feet across—David Webber half lay, half crouched beside the pilot and pressed his face to a six-inch porthole as the lamps picked up steep gray escarpments of dirt and rock that seemed to go on forever, as if descending from nowhere above to nowhere below.

Four thousand meters, Webber thought. Thirteen thousand feet of water, more or less. Two and a half miles. All that water above him, all that pressure around him. How much pressure? Incalculable. But certainly enough to turn him into a Pudding Pop.

Don't think about it, he told himself. If you think about it, you'll go apeshit. And this is not a good time or place to go apeshit. You need the work, you need the money. Just get the job done and get the hell out of here.

A few drops of condensation dripped from the overhead, landed on his neck, and he jumped.

The pilot glanced at him and laughed. "Wish I'd have seen it coming," he said. "I'd have screamed along with you, made you think we were buying the farm." He grinned. "I like to do that to first-timers, watch 'em go goggle-eyed."

"Nice," Webber said. "I'd have sent you my cleaning bill." He shivered and crossed his arms to rub his shoulders. It had been 85 degrees on the surface, and he had been sweating in his wool pullover, wool socks and corduroy trousers. But in the three hours it had taken them to descend, the temperature had dropped more than fifty degrees. He was freezing. He was still sweating, but now it was from fear.

"What's the water temperature out there?" he asked, not from genuine curiosity but because there was comfort in conversation.

"Thirty, thirty-two," the pilot said. "Cold enough to pucker your dickie, that's for sure."

Webber turned back to his porthole and rested a hand on the controls of one of the four cameras he had installed in movable housings bolted to the skin of the submersible. The boat was skimming the side of a canyon wasteland, an endless terrain of monochromatic rubble that looked less inviting than the surface of the moon. He kept reminding himself that his and the pilot's were the first human eyes ever to see this landscape, and his lenses would be the first to record it on film.

"Hard to believe things actually live down here," he said.

"Oh, yeah, there's things, but nothing like you've ever seen. There's albino critters and things with no eyes—I mean, talk about tits on a bull, what good's eyes gonna do 'em here? There's transparent things—shit, there's life of some kind damn near everywhere. 'Course, I can't speak for the *bottom* bottom, like thirty-five thousand feet. I never been down there. But, sure, there's life all around here. What's got everybody in an uproar is the idea that some kinds of life actually *begin* here."

"Yeah," Webber said. "So I hear. They're calling it chemosynthesis."

Chemosynthesis, that was the point, the reason he was here. Here, freezing his ass off two miles down in the sea, in an utter, impenetrable blackness.

Chemosynthesis: the generation of life without light; the concept that living things could be created by chemicals alone. Fascinating. Revolutionary. Undocumented.

To discover evidence that chemosynthesis was possible, to record that evidence, to prove its existence beyond all reasonable doubt—this was his assignment, a photographer's dream. A freelancer on contract to *National Geographic,* Webber was to take the first pictures ever of deep-ocean vents in the recently discovered Kristof Trench, at the bottom of the Mid-Atlantic Ridge just west of the Azores. These vents, like pustulant sores on the skin of the earth, spewed out molten rock from the bowels of the planet into the icy water. The vents themselves were mini-volcanoes, but they were believed to harbor life forms that had been created by, and fed from, the chemicals the vents emitted. In other words, chemosynthesis. Life forms created chemically, and which did not need—did not know, could be born and live and die without—sunlight.

He had been chosen for the assignment over several of his peers because he was celebrated for possessing great ingenuity with his cameras, his lenses and his housings; and also because of his youth and his courage. He had accepted the assignment partly for the money, partly for the credit in the magazine, but mostly for the thrill of being the first to prove that this oddity of science really could occur in the sea, in nature.

He hadn't thought of fear; he considered himself inured to fear. Over the past fifteen years, he had lived through three plane crashes, an attack by a wounded lioness, bites from sharks and moray eels, scorpion stings and infestation by a succession of exotic parasites and amoebas that had caused, among other inconveniences, the temporary loss of all body hair and the sloughing of the skin from his tongue and penis.

He was accustomed, in short, to surprises, to the bizarre tricks nature could throw at him.

What he hadn't suspected, had not even imagined and was amazed to discover in just the past few hours, was that he had become a claustrophobe.

When did this happen? And why? Blundering around blindly in an underwater mountain range deeper than the Rockies were high, with his survival dependent on the skills of some laid-back sub jockey at the helm of a minuscule capsule that had probably been welded together by the lowest bidder, Webber felt unwell: suffocated, compressed, imprisoned, ill.

Why hadn't he listened to his girlfriend and taken the other assignment instead? He'd be much happier in the Coral Sea, shooting close-ups of poisonous sea snakes. At least there he'd have some control; if things got hairy, he could just get out of the water.

But, no, he had to have the glory of being the first.

Asshole.

"How much farther?" he asked, eager for his voice to distract him from the sounds of his own heart.

"To the smoker? Not too long." The pilot

tapped a gauge on the panel before him. "Water temp's creeping up. We gotta be close."

As the submersible rounded a sharp point of rock in the cliff face, its lights were suddenly dimmed by a cloud of thick black smoke.

"Here we are," the pilot said, and he stopped the boat's forward motion and reversed. They descended until the lights cleared.

Webber hunched forward and gripped his camera controls. "Tell Charlie to see if he can move around to the other side," he said. "I want to get him in the frame."

"Will do." The pilot spoke into his microphone, and Webber saw the white shape of the other submersible drift through the black cloud and hover spectrally.

From this distance, the vent didn't look like much: a roiling plume of black smoke against a background of black water, with occasional slashes of red-orange flame as the belly of the earth belched molten rock up through its skin. But the *Geographic* wanted comprehensive coverage of everything he saw, no matter how mundane, so Webber began to shoot.

Each camera was loaded with one hundred frames of 35-mm film, and the strobes recycled instantaneously, so he was able to fire shot after shot as the pilot guided the submersible slowly toward the mouth of the vent.

Webber was relieved to be working now, concentrating on angles and exposures, trying to avoid the glare from the other submersible's lights, his fear forgotten.

His shivering had stopped, he wasn't cold anymore. In fact, he felt hot, as hot as he had on the surface.

"What's the temperature out there now?" he asked.

"Almost two hundred Fahrenheit," said the pilot. "The vent's like a stove, heats everything around it."

Suddenly something bumped into Webber's porthole and ricocheted away into the cloud of smoke. Startled, he jerked backward and said, "What the hell?" It had been too fast and too close for him to distinguish its features; all he had seen was a fluttering blur of white.

"Just wait," said the pilot. "Don't use up all your film. We got lots of critters out there now, might even find something brand-new nobody's ever seen before."

They were approaching the mouth of the vent now. Here, supposedly, animals fed on the vent's chemicals. There was a deep staccato rumbling sound, and flashes of red and orange, as molten rock erupted from fissures in the cliff.

Another animal sped by, then another. And then, as the submersible settled above a small mesa of newly hardened lava, a blizzard of them: shrimps. They were huge, ash white, eyeless; thousands, hundreds of thousands of shrimps, perhaps millions. So many that they filled the field of vision, swarming, pulsating like a living mountain.

"Sweet Jesus . . ." Webber said, both riveted and appalled. "What are they doing?"

"Feeding," the pilot said, "on whatever's in that smoke."

"Shrimps can live in two-hundred-degree water?"

"Born in it, live in it and die in it. Once in a while, one'll tumble into the mouth of the vent—that's about seven hundred degrees in there—and he'll burn up . . . *pop,* just like a tick in a match flame."

After Webber had fired a dozen shots, the pilot nudged the submersible forward, parting the shrimps as if they were a thick bead curtain.

Surrounding the mouth of the vent, rooted to the lava and growing like a nightmare garden, were long bony stalks, six or eight feet tall, from the ends of which protruded red and yellow feathery fingers that moved sinuously in and out of the billows of smoke.

"What the hell are *they*?" Webber said.

"Tube worms. They build those houses for themselves out of something they excrete, then send their fans out to feed. Watch." The pilot reached for a control lever and extended one of the submersible's articulate arms toward the nearest stalk. As the steel claws of the arm drew near, the fans seemed to freeze, and a split second before they would have been touched, they vanished, withdrew as if by magic into the shelter of their calcareous tubes. "Did you get a picture of that?" the pilot asked.

"Too fast," said Webber. "Let's try again. I'll set the shutter speed for a two-thousandth."

. . .

An hour later, Webber had shot more than three hundred frames of film. He had photographed the shrimps and the tube worms in close-up, wide-angle and with the other submersible in the background. He hoped he had at least twenty *Geographic*-quality images. He had no idea whether or not his pictures would verify the existence of chemosynthetic species, or would simply prove that blind albino shrimps lived in 200-degree water two and a half miles below the surface of the sea. Either way, he knew he had some spectacular shots.

For insurance, he had had the pilot use the submersible's mechanical arms to gather half a dozen shrimps and two tube worms; they were secured now in a collecting basket on the outside of the boat. He would take some macro shots of them in the lab on board the mother ship.

"That'll do it," he said to the pilot. "Let's go."

"You're sure? I don't guess your boss'll want to spend another fifty grand to send us back down here."

Webber hesitated briefly, then said, "I'm sure." He was confident that he had the money shots. He knew his cameras, sometimes he felt as if his brain were an extension of them, and he could picture now the images in his mind. They were excellent, he was certain.

"Okay." Into his radio, the pilot said, "We're outta here." He put the boat into reverse and backed away from the vent.

A moment later, Webber was making reminder notes on a pad when he heard the pilot say, "Son of a bitch . . ."

"What?"

"Look over there." The pilot was pointing at something on the bottom, outside his porthole.

Webber leaned to his own porthole and held his breath so he wouldn't fog the glass. "I don't see anything," he said.

"Down there. Shrimp shells. Zillions of them. They're all over the sand."

"So? Don't you figure these creatures eat each other?"

"Well, I dunno. I never saw it like this. I s'pose they do eat each other, but would they *shell* each other too? Maybe it's one of them deep sharks, a six-gill or a sleeper. But would *they* stop to shell a shrimp before they eat it? It don't make a lick of sense."

"Could it eat them whole and spit out the shells? Regurgitate them?"

"A shark's got digestion like battery acid. There wouldn't be nothin' left."

"I don't get it," Webber said.

"Me neither, but *some* thing's been eating these shrimp, by the goddamn thousands, and shelling 'em too. I think we better have us a look-see."

The shells appeared to taper off into a trail, and the pilot turned the boat around and followed the trail, directing the lights downward as he cruised along a few feet off the bottom.

The submersible moved slowly, no more than a couple of hundred feet a minute, and after two or three minutes the monotony of the whirring motor and the sameness of the barren landscape became hypnotic. Webber felt his eyes glazing. He shook his head. "What are we looking for?" he asked.

"I dunno, but my guess is it's the same as usual—a clue that'll lead us to something nature didn't make. A straight line of something, maybe . . . a perfect circle . . . anything symmetrical. There's damn little in nature that's symmetrical."

They had been moving for only a few seconds more when Webber thought he glimpsed an anomaly at the edge of the ring of light. "Over there," he said. "That isn't exactly symmetrical, but it doesn't look natural, either."

The pilot turned the boat, and as the lights moved across the bottom, a mass of gnarled black metal appeared on the carpet of powdery silt. It had no recognizable shape, and parts seemed to have been crushed, other parts torn and twisted.

"It looks like junk," Webber said.

"Yeah, but what kind of junk? What *was* it?" The pilot radioed his position to the other submersible, then dropped down until the bottom of his boat rested on the silt.

The mass of metal was spread over too large an area for the lights to illuminate all of it, so the pilot aimed all ten thousand watts at one end and manipulated the lights foot by foot, studying every shape and, as if constructing a jigsaw puzzle, trying to fit them together into a coherent whole.

Webber didn't offer to help, for he knew he couldn't contribute anything useful. He was a photographer, not an engineer. For all he knew, the heap of steel out there might have been a locomotive, a paddle-wheel steamer or an airplane.

As he waited, he felt fear returning. They had been down in this thing for almost five hours; it would take them at least three more hours to return to the surface. He was cold; he was hungry; he needed to take a leak; most of all, he needed to move, to *do* something. And to get the hell out of here.

"C'mon," he said. "Let's forget it and take off."

The pilot waited a long moment before he replied. When at last he did, he turned to Webber and said, "I hope you still got a pile of film left."

"Why?"

" 'Cause we just found ourselves one hell of a bonus."

6

THE PILOT summoned the other submersible and positioned it fifty yards away, across the field of wreckage. With the four lamps throwing a twenty-thousand-watt pool of light, they could see nearly the entire site.

The pilot grinned at Webber and said, "Well?"

"Well what?"

"Well, what is it?"

"How the hell do I know?" Webber snapped. "Look, I'm freezing, I'm tired, I have to hit the head. Do me a favor and stop—"

"It's a submarine."

"It *is*?" Webber said, and pressed his face to the porthole. "How do you know?"

"Look there." The pilot pointed. "That's a diving plane. And there. That's gotta be a snorkel tube."

"You mean a nuke?"

"No, I don't think so; I'm pretty sure not. It looks to be steel. See how it's oxidizing—real slow, because there's almost no oxygen down here. But it *is* oxidizing—and it's small and the wiring's shitty, old-fashioned. I'd say we're talking World War Two."

"World War *Two*?"

"Yeah, but let's try to get closer." The pilot spoke into his microphone, and, on cue, the two submersibles began to crawl toward each other at a speed barely above idle, skimming the bottom just high enough to avoid roiling the silt.

Webber's film counters told him he had eighty-six frames left, so he shot sparingly. He tried to imagine the wreck whole, but the destruction was so complete that he couldn't see how anyone could identify individual sections of the ship.

"Where are we on the thing?" he asked.

"Looks to me like the stern," the pilot said. "She's lying on her starboard side. Those pipes there should be the after torpedo tubes."

They passed one of the submarine's deck guns, and because it actually looked like something, Webber shot a couple of frames of it.

They came to a gaping wound in the side of the ship and saw on the silt a few feet away a pair of shoes looking as if they were waiting for feet to step into them.

"Where's the guy that wore them?" Webber

asked as he shot the shoes from different angles. "Where's the body?"

"Worms would've eaten him," the pilot said. "Crabs, too."

"Bones and all? Worms eat bones?"

"No, but the sea does. Deep, cold salt water dissolves bones . . . it's a chemical thing. The sea seeks out calcium. I used to want to be buried at sea, but not now, not anymore. I don't like the thought of being lunch for creepy-crawlies."

They saw a few more recognizable items as they crept toward the bow: pots from the galley, the frame of a bunk, a radio. Webber shot them all. He was readjusting one of his cameras when, at the edge of his field of vision, he saw what looked like a letter of the alphabet painted on a steel plate. "What's that?" he said, pointing.

The pilot turned the submersible around and moved it slowly forward. Looking through his porthole, he said suddenly, "Bingo! We just identified the boat."

"We did?"

"The kind, anyway. That's a *U* painted on one of the conning-tower plates. It's a U-boat."

"A U-boat? You mean she's German?"

"She was. But what she was doing this far south in the middle of nowhere, the Lord only knows."

Webber shot pictures of the *U* from several angles as the pilot nudged the submersible on toward the bow of the submarine.

When they reached the forward deck area, the pilot disengaged the motor and let the submersible hover. "There's what sank her," he said, focusing the lights on an enormous hole in the deck. "She imploded."

The deck plates were bent inward, their edges curled as if struck by a giant hammer.

As Webber shot a picture, he felt sweat running down his sides; he imagined the moment, half a century before, when the men on this boat suddenly knew they were going to die. He could imagine the roar of rushing water, the screams, the confusion, the panic, the pressure, the suffocation, the agony. "Christ . . ." he said.

The pilot put the motor in gear, and the submersible inched forward. Its lights reached into the hole, illuminating a skein of wires, a tangle of pipes, a . . .

"Hey!" Webber shouted.

"What?"

"There's something in there. Something big. It looks . . . I don't know . . ."

The pilot maneuvered the submersible above the hole, tilted the bow down and, using the claws on the ends of the articulate arms, tore away the wires and pushed aside the pipes. He angled the lights into a single five-thousand-watt beam and shone it straight down into the hole. "I'll be damned. . . ."

"It looks like a box," Webber said as he watched the lights dance over the greenish-yellow surface of a perfect rectangle. "A chest."

"Yeah, or a coffin." The pilot paused, reconsidering. "No. Too big for a coffin."

For a long moment, neither of them spoke. They just stared at the box—wondering, imagining.

At last, Webber said, "We ought to bring it up."

"Yeah." The pilot nodded. "The only question is how. The bastard's gotta be eight feet long. I bet it weighs a ton. I can't lift it with this boat."

"How about both boats together?"

"No, we can't lift a thousand pounds apiece, and I'm just guessing. It could be a lot more than that. We couldn't . . ." He stopped. "Just a sec. I think they've got five miles of cable in the hold of that ship up there. If they can weight an end of it and send it down, and if we can get a sling around the box, maybe . . . there's a chance. . . ." He pushed a button and spoke into his microphone.

· · ·

It took the two submersibles nearly an hour to retrieve the weighted cable sent down from the mother ship and to secure the box in a wire sling.

By the time they gave the ship the order to begin lifting, they were pushing the limits of their air supply. And so, as soon as they made sure that the box was free of the submarine's hull and was rising steadily, they shed ballast and began their own ascent.

Webber felt exhausted and elated and challenged, impatient to get to the surface, open the box and see what was inside.

"You know something weird?" he said as he watched the depth gauge record their meter-by-meter progress up toward daylight.

"This whole thing's weird," the pilot said. "You thinking of something in particular?"

"That wreckage. All of it was covered by silt. Everything had a gray film on it . . . except the box. It was clean. That's probably why I saw it. It stood out."

The pilot shrugged. "Does silt stick to bronze? Beats me."

7

"I DON'T *believe* this!" Webber said. "Metallur-
gists, archaeologists, chemists . . . who gives a
shit? All that counts is what's inside! What are
they *thinking* of?"

"Yeah, well, you know bureaucrats," the pilot
said, trying to be sympathetic. "They sit around
with their thumb up their ass all day, and now,
suddenly, they got something to do, they gotta
justify their existence."

They were standing on the stern of the ship as
it steamed westward toward Massachusetts. The
box was secured on a cradle on the fantail, and
Webber had spent hours mounting lights on the
ship's superstructure to create a suitable atmosphere of mystery, for when the box was opened.
He had chosen sunset, photographers' "magic
hour," when shadows were long and the light soft,
rich and dramatic.

And then, not half an hour before he was to begin shooting, the ship's captain had handed him a fax marked "Urgent" from the *Geographic:* he was to leave the box untouched and unopened until the ship reached port, so that a cadre of scientists and historians could meet the ship and examine the box and open it in the presence of a writer, an editor and a camera team from the *National Geographic Explorer* television series.

Webber was devastated. He knew what would happen: his lighting setup would be destroyed; he'd be shunted aside, given a backseat to the TV team, ordered around by the experts. He'd have no chance to shoot enough film to have ample "outs"—pictures the *Geographic* wouldn't want and which he could sell to other magazines. The quality of his work would suffer, and so would his pocketbook.

Yet there was nothing he could do about it, and worse, it was his own fault. He should have stifled his excitement and waited to inform the magazine about the discovery of the box.

Now he shouted, "Shit!" into the evening air.

"C'mon," the pilot said, "forget it. Let's go down to the wardroom; I got a friend there named Jack Daniel's who's dyin' to meet you."

· · ·

Webber and the pilot sat in the wardroom and finished the Jack Daniel's. The more the pilot groused about bureaucrats, the more convinced Webber became that he was being shafted. He had discovered the box, he had photographed it inside the submarine, he should be the one to take the first, the best—the only—pictures of what was inside.

At eight-forty-five, the pilot pronounced himself stewed to the gills, and he staggered off to his bunk.

At eight-fifty, Webber decided on a plan. He went to bed and set his alarm clock for midnight.

. . .

"That's Montauk Point," the captain said, indicating the outer circle on the radar screen, "and there's Block Island. If we had a calm, I'd anchor off Woods Hole and wait for daylight." He looked at the clock mounted on the bulkhead. "It's one-fifteen now; we'll be able to see pretty good in four hours. But with this easterly blowing like a banshee, I'm gonna take her into the shelter of Block and then go up the coast at first light. No sense getting everybody sick and maybe smashing up some gear."

"Right," Webber said, nauseated by the pool of acid coffee that sloshed in his stomach as the ship nosed into a trough and then rose askew onto the crest of a combing wave. Pushed by a following sea, the ship was corkscrewing through the night. "Guess I'll go back and try to get some sleep."

"Put a wastebasket by your bunk," the captain suggested. "Nothing worse than trying to sleep in a bed of puke."

Webber had gone to the bridge to see how many lookouts were on duty and had found only two, the captain and a mate, both in the wheelhouse, both facing forward. The stern was empty and unobserved.

Back in his cabin, he put a finger down his throat and forced himself to vomit into the toilet. He waited five minutes, tried to vomit again, but brought up nothing but bile. He brushed his teeth, and, feeling clearheaded and more stable, he slung a Nikon with an attached flash over his shoulder, picked up and tested a flashlight and walked aft, out onto the stern.

The wind was blowing twenty-five or thirty knots, but there was no rain, and the ship was moving with the wind at fifteen knots, which cut its bluster: walking across the flat, wide stern was no worse than trudging into a fresh breeze.

Two five-hundred-watt lamps flooded the afterdeck with light. The submersibles squatted on their cradles like mutant beetles assigned to guard the gleaming greenish-yellow box that lay between them.

Webber stayed in the shadows as he crossed the hundred feet of afterdeck. He crouched behind the portside submersible, checked to be sure no one was watching from the wings of the bridge, then shone his flashlight on the side of the box.

He had no idea how heavy the lid of the box was—hundreds of pounds, certainly more than he could hope to lift alone. If he had to, he could use the lifting rig from one of the submersibles, a big steel hook shackled to a block-and-tackle arrangement and powered by an electric winch. But perhaps the lid was spring-loaded; perhaps there was a release latch or button.

He emerged from the shelter of the submersible cradle, crossed the deck and knelt beside the box. Facing aft to shade the flashlight beam with his back, he followed the lip of the lid from one end to the other. On the far side, only a few feet from the edge of the fantail, with the ship's wake boiling as it rose and fell beneath him, he saw a design etched in the bronze: a tiny swastika. Beneath it was a button.

He pressed the button, heard a click, then a hiss, and the lid of the box began to rise.

He knelt, stunned, for a moment as he watched the lid move up tantalizingly slowly, rising at no more than an inch a second.

When it was about half open, he got to his feet, turned on his camera, raised it to his eye, focused it and waited for the beep signaling that the flash was ready to fire.

The light was dim; the lid shadowed the interior

of the box, the view through the lens was shimmery and amorphous. The box was full of liquid.

He thought . . . was that a face? No, not . . . but it was something, and face*like*.

There was a sudden thrashing in the liquid, and flashes of what looked like steel.

For a fraction of a second, Webber felt pain, then a rush of warmth, then a feeling of being dragged underwater. And then, as he died, the bizarre sensation that he was being eaten.

8

IT NEEDED to feed, and it fed until it could feed no more. It drank, sucking ravenously, inefficiently, until its viscera refused to accept any more of the warm, salty fluid.

Once nourished, it was still disoriented and confused. There was motion and instability and, when it rose from its box, an alarming lack. Its gills fluttered, gasping for sustenance, but found none until it submerged again.

Nerve impulses fired randomly in its brain, crossing barren synapses, unable to sort responses. It was programmed with answers, but, in its frenzy, it was unable to find them.

It sensed that sustenance was nearby, and so, in desperation, it emerged again from the safety of its box and sensed its surroundings.

There, just there. The dark and welcoming world to which it must return.

It was bereft of knowledge but keen in instinct.

It recognized few imperatives but was compelled to obey the ones it knew. Its survival depended on fuel and protection.

It had no powers of innovation, but it did have enormous strength, and that strength was what it called upon now.

Trailing streaks of mucous slime, it moved to the far end of the box and began to push. Though increasingly starved for oxygen, its brain was able to generate electrical impulses that charged its muscle fibers.

· · ·

The bow of the ship buried itself in a trough, then the stern rose. The box slid forward, pushing the creature with it. But then the bow recovered and climbed toward the sky, and as the stern fell rapidly, there was a tiny interstice when the box was weightless.

The box moved aft, teetered on the edge of the fantail and tumbled into the sea.

As soon as it felt the cold, comforting confinement of salt water, its systems responded with instantaneous regeneration. The creature soared downward through the night sea, infused with the primitive perception that it was once again where it should be.

The ship pitched and slewed its way toward the lee of an island as a blood-spattered Nikon camera rolled back and forth across the afterdeck.

PART THREE

▲　▲　▲　▲　▲　▲　▲

1996
WATERBORO

9

SIMON CHASE leaned close to the television monitor in the boat's cabin and shaded it with his hand. The summer sun was still low in the sky, and its brilliance flooded through the windows and washed out definition on the green screen. The slowly moving white dot was barely visible.

With his finger Chase traced a line on the screen, checked it against a compass and said, "Here she comes. Swing around to one-eighty."

"What's she doing?" asked the mate, Tall Man Palmer, as he spun the wheel to the right and headed south. "Been out to Block for breakfast, coming back to Waterboro for lunch?"

"I doubt she's hungry," Chase said. "Probably so full of whale meat she won't eat for a week."

"Or longer," said Chase's son. Max sat on the bench seat facing the monitor and meticulously copied its data onto graph paper. "Some of the carcharhinids can go more than a month without eating." He made the remark with studied casualness, as if such esoterica about marine biology was on the tip of every twelve-year-old's tongue.

"Well, excuse me, Jacques Cousteau," Tall Man said, chuckling.

"Don't mind Tall Man, he's just jealous," said Chase, touching Max's shoulder. "You're right." He was proud, and moved, for he knew that Max was reaching out, trying to do his part in building a bridge that, under other circumstances, would have been built years ago.

Tall Man nodded toward shore and said, "Let's go tell the folks on the beach that the lady ain't hungry. They'd be tickled to hear it."

Chase looked through the window at the rocky beach of Watch Hill, Rhode Island. Though it was not yet nine in the morning, a few families had begun to arrive with their picnic hampers and Frisbees and inner tubes; a few young surfers in wet suits were bobbing on the minuscule waves, waiting for a ride that might never come—not today, at least, for there was no wind and no forecast of any.

He smiled at the thought of the scramble, the panic, that would ensue if the people had any idea why this innocent-looking white boat was cruising back and forth out here, less than five hundred yards from the beach. People loved to read about sharks, loved to see movies about sharks, loved to believe they understood sharks and wanted to protect them. But tell them there was a shark in the water anywhere within ten miles—especially a great white shark—and their love changed instantly to fear and loathing.

If they knew that he and Max and Tall Man were tracking a sixteen-foot white shark that likely weighed a ton or more, their affection would turn to blood lust. They'd holler for it to be killed. Then, of course, as soon as someone did kill it, they'd go right back to mouthing off about how they loved sharks and how all God's creatures ought to be protected.

"The shark's coming up," Max said, reading digital numbers on the screen.

Chase bent to the screen again, shading it. "Yeah, she's been cooling off at two hundred feet, but she's already at less than a hundred."

"Where'd she find two hundred feet between here and Block?" asked Tall Man.

"Must be a ditch out there. I tell you, Tall, she knows her territory. Anyway, she's coming up the slope." From a hook on the bulkhead Chase took a still camera with an 85-mm–200-mm zoom lens and hung it around his neck. He said to Max, "Let's go see if she'll pose for us." Then, to Tall Man, "Check the monitor now and then just to make sure she doesn't buzz off somewhere."

He went to the doorway and looked at the shore again. "I hope she doesn't come up between us and the beach. Mass hysteria, we do not need."

"You mean like Matawan Creek," Max said, "in 1916."

"Yeah, but they had reason to be hysterical. That shark killed three people."

"Four," Max said.

"Four. Sorry." Chase smiled and looked down—he could still look down, but barely; the boy was already five-ten—at the gangly replica of himself, but skinnier and better-looking, for he had his mother's sharp nose and narrow mouth.

Chase took a pair of binoculars from a shelf and handed them to Max. "Here, go see if you can find her."

Tall Man called to Chase, "Never argue with a kid about sharks. Kids know sharks. Sharks and dinosaurs."

It was true, Chase thought: kids were dinosaur freaks, and most kids were shark freaks. But he had never met a child who knew half as much about sharks as Max did, which pleased him and also saddened and pained him, for sharks had always been the main, if not the sole, bond between father and son. They hadn't lived together for the past eight years, had seen each other only occasionally, and (phone-company TV commercials to the contrary) weekly long-distance calls were no way to reach out and touch someone.

Chase and Max's mother had married too young and too hastily. She was an heiress to a timber fortune, he an impecunious Greenpeacer. Their naive premise was that her money and his idealism would interact synergistically, benefiting the planet and allowing them to live in Eden. They soon discovered, however, that while they shared common ideals, their means of attaining ends were less than compatible. Corinne's notion of being on the front lines of the environmental movement included giving tennis parties, swimming parties, cocktail parties and black-tie dinner-dances to benefit the movement; Simon's involved being away from home for weeks at a time, living in the stinking fo'c'sles of ratty ships and confronting ruthless foreigners on the high seas.

They tried to compromise: Simon learned to play tennis and to give speeches; she learned to scuba dive and to differentiate between the Odontoceti and the Mysticeti. But after four years of drifting apart, they agreed to disagree . . . permanently.

The only synergy that came from the relationship was Max—handsomer than either of them, smarter, more sensitive.

Corinne got custody of Max: she had money, a large and caring family, a home (several, in fact) and, by the time the divorce was final, a stable relationship with a neurosurgeon who had been the number-one singles tennis player in Northern California.

Simon was the only son of deceased parents, and he had no steady income, no fixed residence and fleeting relationships with several women whose prime assets were their looks and their sexual fervor.

Through her lawyer, Corinne had offered Chase a generous financial settlement—she was neither cruel nor vengeful, and she wanted her son's father to be able to afford a decent home for Max to visit—but in a fit of self-righteous nobility, Chase had refused.

Several times since, Chase had regretted what he now regarded as misplaced sexist lunacy. He could have put the money to good use. Especially now that the Institute—*his* institute—was teetering on the brink of insolvency. He had been tempted to reconsider, to call Corinne and offer to accept that last beneficence. But he couldn't bring himself to do it.

What mystified him, what he could not fathom, was the fact that somehow, over the years and the thousands of miles, his son had been able to see through the sheltering veil of private schools and country clubs and trust funds, and to maintain an image of his father as a figure of adventure . . . someone not only to long for, but to emulate.

· · ·

As Chase followed Max outside onto the open stern of the forty-eight-foot boat, he slid his sunglasses down from the top of his head. The day was bound to be a scorcher, 95-plus degrees even out here on the ocean, one of those days that used to be rare but in the past few years had become more and more common. Ten summers ago, there had been eight days when the temperature had reached 90 degrees in Waterboro; three years ago, thirty-nine days; this year, meteorologists were predicting fifty days over 90 and as many as ten over 100.

He used the zoom lens as a telescope and scanned the surface of the glassy sea. "See anything?" he asked Max.

"Not yet." Max rested his elbows on the bulwark, to steady the binoculars. "What would she look like?"

"If she came up to bask on a day like this, her dorsal fin would stand out like a sail."

Chase saw a tire floating, and a plastic milk jug, and one of the lethal plastic six-pack holders that strangled turtles and birds, and globules of oil that when they reached the beach and stuck to the soles of children's feet would be cursed as tar. At least he didn't see any body parts today, or any syringes. Last summer, a woman at the town beach had had to be sedated after her four-year-old presented her with a treasure he had found in the wavewash: a human finger. And a man had taken from his dog what appeared to be a rubber ball but turned out to be a perfect orb of sewage sludge.

He looked over the stern at the rubber-coated wire that held the tracking sensor, and checked the knot on the piece of twine that held the sensor at the prescribed depth. The coil of wire on the deck behind him was three hundred feet long, but because the bottom was shoaly and erratic, they had set the sensor at only fifty feet. The twine was fraying. He'd have to replace it tonight.

"You still see the shark?" he called forward to Tall Man.

There was a pause while Tall Man looked at the screen. "She's up to about fifty," he said. "Just hangin' out, looks to me. Signal's nice and strong, though."

Chase spoke to the shark in his mind, begging her to come up, to show herself, not only for him but for Max. Mostly for Max.

They had been tracking her for two days, recording data on her speed, direction, depth, body temperature—eager for any information about this rarest of the great ocean predators—without seeing anything of her but a white blip on a green screen. He wanted them to see her again so that Max could enjoy the perfection of her, the beauty of her, but also to make sure the shark was all right, had not developed an infection or an ulcer from the tagging dart that contained the electronic signaling device. It had been perfectly placed in the tough skin behind the dorsal fin, but these animals had become so scarce that he worried about even the remote possibility of causing her harm.

They had found her almost by accident, and just in time to save her from becoming a trophy on a barroom wall.

Chase maintained good relations with the local commercial fishermen, carefully staying out of the increasingly bitter controversy over limiting catches because of depleted stocks. Since he couldn't be everywhere at once, he needed the fishermen to be his eyes and ears on the ocean, to alert him to anomalies natural and man-made, like massive fish kills, sudden algae blooms and oil spills.

His assiduous neutrality had paid off on Thursday night, when a bluefisherman had phoned the Institute (he'd had sense enough not to use his radio, which could be monitored by every boat in three states). On his way home, he told Chase, he had seen a dead whale floating between Block

Island and Watch Hill. Sharks were already feeding on the carcass, but they were school sharks, mostly blues. The rare and solitary whites had not yet picked up the spoor.

But they would, those few that still patrolled the bight between Montauk and Point Judith. And soon.

The word would reach the charter-fishing boats, whose captains would call their favored customers and promise them, for fifteen hundred or two thousand dollars a day, a shot at one of the most sought-after trophies in the sea—the apex predator, the biggest carnivorous fish in the world, the man-eater: the great white shark. They would find the whale quickly, for its corpse would show up on radar, and they would circle it while their customers camcorded the awesome spectacle of the rolling eyeballs and the motile jaws tearing away fifty-pound chunks of whale. And then, drunk with the dream of selling the jaw for five thousand or ten thousand dollars and blinded to the fact that they could make more money if they left the shark alone and charged customers for the privilege of filming it, they would harpoon the animal to death . . . because, they would say to themselves, if we don't do it, someone else will.

They would call it sport. To Chase, it was no more sport than shooting a dog at its dinner.

He and scientists from Massachusetts to

Florida to California had been lobbying for years to have great white sharks officially declared endangered, as they had been in parts of Australia and South Africa. But white sharks were not mammals, were not cute, did not appear to smile at children, did not "sing" or make endearing clicking noises to one another or jump through hoops for paying customers. They were omnivorous fish that once in a while—but rarely, much more rarely than did bees or snakes or tigers or lightning—killed human beings.

Everyone agreed that white sharks were marvels of evolution that had survived almost unchanged for scores of millions of years; that they were biologically wonderful and medically fascinating; that they performed a critical function in maintaining the balance in the marine food chain. But in an age of tight budgets and conflicting priorities, there was little public pressure to protect an animal perceived as nothing more than a fish that ate people.

Before long, Chase was sure, perhaps before the turn of the millennium, they would all be gone. Children would see whiteshark heads mounted on walls, and filmed records of them on the Discovery Channel, but within a generation they wouldn't even be a memory; they would be no more real than the dinosaurs.

His first impulse after talking to the bluefisherman was to collect some explosives, find the whale and blow it to pieces. It was the best solution, the quickest and most efficient: the whale would disappear from the charter fishermen's radar, the sharks would disperse. But it was also the most dangerous, for destroying a whale carcass was a federal crime.

The Marine Mammal Protection Act was a masterwork of contradictions. No one—scientists, laymen, filmmakers or fishermen—was allowed to get near a whale, dead or alive. No matter that the entire save-the-whales movement (including the act itself) had been born of the excellent films made by dedicated professionals. No matter that a whale carcass could become an environmental catastrophe. If you messed with a whale, you were a criminal.

Chase's days as an environmental firebrand were over. Five years ago, he had made a decision to work within the system rather than from outside it. He had swallowed his anger and kissed some ass and wangled scholarships to graduate school, and had returned to Waterboro, with no specific idea about what he wanted to do. He could teach, or continue to study, but he was impatient to be free of the classroom and the laboratory: he longed to learn by *doing*. He could apply for a job at Woods Hole or Scripps or any of the other marine institutes around the country, but he was still a dissertation shy of his doctorate, and he had no confidence that anyone would hire him to be anything more than a drone.

The one certainty in Chase's life was that he would spend his life in, on, around and under the sea.

He had loved it from first memory, when his father had taken him aboard the *Miss Edna* on balmy days and let him savor the feel and the sounds and the smells of the sea. He had learned affection and respect, not only for the sea itself but for the creatures that lived in it and the men who harvested them.

He had become particularly (perversely, his father thought) fascinated by sharks. Sharks seemed to be everywhere in those days—basking on the surface in the sun, assaulting the nets balled full of thrashing fish, following the boat's bloody wake as fish were cleaned and their guts tossed overboard. At first, Simon had been enthralled mostly by their appearance of relentless menace, but then, as he read more and more about them, he came to see them as a wonderful representation of natural continuity: unchanged for millions of years, efficient, immune to almost all diseases that afflicted other animals. It was as if nature had created them and thought, Well done.

He still loved sharks, and though he no longer

feared them, now he feared *for* them. Around the world, they were being slaughtered recklessly, wastefully and ignorantly—some for their fins, which were sold for soup; some for their meat; some simply because they were perceived as a nuisance.

By coincidence, Chase had returned to Waterboro at precisely the time a small island between Block Island and Fishers Island had come on the market. The state of Connecticut had taken the island from a troubled bank and was auctioning it off to collect tax liens. The thirty-five-acre tract of scrub and ledge rock was too remote and too unattractive for commercial development and, because it had no access to municipal services, impractical for subdivision into private homesites.

Chase, however, saw tiny Osprey Island as the perfect spot for oceanographic research. Armed with the proceeds from the sale of his parents' house and fishing boat, he put a down payment on the island, financed the balance and established the Osprey Island Marine Institute.

He had no trouble finding projects worthy of study: dwindling fish stocks, vanishing marine species, pollution—all demanded attention. Other groups and institutes were doing similar work, of course, and Chase tried to complement their work with his, while always reserving time and what money he could muster for his specialty: sharks.

So now, much as he hated to admit it, at thirty-four and as director of the Institute, he was a card-carrying member of the Establishment. He was attaining a respectable reputation in the scientific community for his research on sharks; his papers on their immune systems had been accepted by leading journals and were received as interesting, if somewhat eccentric. And he himself was regarded as a scientist worth watching: a comer.

If he were to be caught blowing up a whale, however, he knew he would be instantly discredited, as well as fined and probably jailed.

And so he had opted for compromise. He had faxed the Environmental Protection Agency in Washington and the state Department of Environmental Protection in Hartford, requesting emergency permission not to destroy the whale but to move it before it could wash up on a public beach. He had no idea what direction the carcass was moving in, but he knew that the threat would be persuasive: no government—federal, state or local—wanted to be stuck with the cost, possibly as much as a hundred thousand dollars, of removing fifty tons of putrefying whale from a beach. He gave inaccurate coordinates for the whale's current position, placing it where he wanted to tow it, so that if he was denied permission he could claim that he hadn't moved it, and if permission was granted, he could tow it even farther away, into the deep ocean where no sportfisher-men would be likely to come upon it.

He hadn't waited for a reply from either agency. He and Tall Man had loaded grappling hooks and a barrel of rope into the Institute's boat and gone looking for the whale. They had found it right away, and, at around midnight, in the glow of the moon, they had sunk the hooks into the rotting meat and begun to tow the carcass out into the Atlantic beyond Block Island. The vile stench of decay followed them, and the horrid grunting sounds of sharks leaping out of the water to rip at the fatty flesh.

The whale was a young humpback, and at first light they saw what had killed it. Fishing nets floated like shrouds around its mouth and head. It had blundered into huge commercial nets, had ensnared itself further by thrashing in its struggle to escape and had strangled to death.

The white shark had arrived just after dawn. She was a big mature female, probably fifteen or twenty years old, of prime breeding age. And she was pregnant, which Chase had discovered when the shark rolled on her back as she plunged her massive head deep into the pink meat of the whale's flanks, exposing her swollen belly and genital slit.

No one knew for sure how long great whites

lived or when they first began to breed, but current theory favored a maximum age of eighty to a hundred years and a breeding cycle that began at about age ten and produced one or two pups every second year.

So, to kill her, to hang her head on the wall and sell her teeth for jewelry, would not be to kill a single great white shark. It would be to wipe out perhaps as many as twenty generations of sharks.

They had inserted the transmitter dart quickly and easily. The shark had never felt the barb, had not interrupted her feeding. They had watched her for a few minutes, and Chase had taken pictures. Then, as they prepared to leave, Tall Man had turned on the radio and heard charter fishermen talking back and forth about the whale. Clearly, the bluefisherman had gone to a bar and, feeling that he had done his duty by phoning the Institute first, had been unable to resist making points with his mates by talking about the whale.

Where had it gone? the fishermen would have wondered. Who took it? The goddamn government? Those bleeding hearts from the Institute? East. They had to have taken it east of Block.

The fishermen were coming, coming to slaughter the pregnant shark.

Chase and Tall Man had had no discussion. They had fetched some explosives from below—a brick of plastique left over from the building of the Institute's docks—and had carefully inserted charges into parts of the whale farthest from where the shark was feeding. They had detonated the charges one by one, blasting the whale carcass into pieces that immediately began to disperse and sink. The fishermen's radar target was gone; now they could never find the remains of the whale—or the shark.

The shark submerged, following pieces of blubber down into the safety of the deep.

If the EPA or the DEP wanted to try to make a case against them, Chase thought, let them. There had been no witnesses, the evidence would be flimsy and if any of the charter fishermen were smart enough to figure out what he'd done and why, and fool enough to lodge a complaint, they'd be hanging themselves by admitting they'd been intending to get closer to the dead whale than the law allowed.

Most important, the shark would still be alive.

They had lowered their tracking sensor and followed the white for a few more hours as she moved eastward into deeper water and then turned to the north.

Under normal circumstances, Chase would have pursued the shark without interruption, for to break away meant risking losing her: she could wander out of range, and they might not find her

again before the transmitter's batteries gave out—
two days, three at most.

But Max had been scheduled to arrive at the
Groton/New London airport that evening, flying in from Sun Valley via Salt Lake and Bos-
ton. For the first time ever, Max was going to
spend a solid month with his dad, and Chase
was damned if he'd let the boy be met by a taxi
driver from the nearby town of Stonington, and
then ferried, alone and in twilight, out to a rock
that would have looked to him about as appeal-
ing as Alcatraz.

So he and Tall Man had abandoned the shark,
praying that she wouldn't roam up to New
Hampshire or Maine or out to Nantucket, and
that with luck they could be back tracking the
animal within six hours. Chase had no idea how
close she was to giving birth, but the electronic
sensor would record the event if it occurred,
would transmit changes in body temperature and
chemistry. They might even see the birth if it happened near the surface. No one—no scientist or
sportsman—had ever witnessed the birth of a
great white shark.

Max had said he didn't need to unpack, and
they hustled out of the airport, into the truck,
onto the ferry, out to the island and onto the boat.
Red-eyed, exhausted, the boy had also been deliri-

ously excited at the thought of seeing a live white shark. When he called his mother from the cellular phone on the boat, the only adjective he could summon was "awesome."

Corinne had been less than thrilled, had asked to speak to Simon, had lectured him to be careful. Max had settled the matter. He had taken the phone back from Chase and had said, "Chill out, Mom, it's okay. Great whites don't want to hurt people."

"What do you mean?"

Max had laughed and said, "They just want to eat them." But when he had heard his mother gasp, he had added, "Just kidding, Mom . . . a little shark humor."

"Do you have your windbreaker?" Corinne had asked.

"We're fine, Mom, really . . . love ya." Then Max had hung up.

Within an hour, they had relocated the shark, which Chase regarded as a fortuitous confirmation of one of his pet theories.

He was particularly interested in—and in fact was considering writing his dissertation about—the question of territoriality in great white sharks. Researchers in South Australia, at places like Dangerous Reef and Coffin Bay, where the water temperature varied little from season to season, had concluded that the region's whites were definitely territorial. Their food source was stable—colonies of seals—and in the course of roughly a week each white would make a tour of its territory and return to begin again.

Here on the East Coast of the United States, where the water temperature varied by as much as thirty degrees from winter to summer, and food supplies appeared and disappeared unpredictably, territoriality would seem to be impractical. Though no one knew for certain, Chase had been gathering evidence suggesting that these whites might be migratory: they seemed to go south in the winter, reappear in the spring or early summer (traveling, some of them, as far north and east as the Canadian Maritimes), stay till late September or early October and then begin to move south again.

But what intrigued Chase most was that the records of years of tagging were beginning to show that some whites returned to the same area year after year and reestablished the same general territory during their stay in that area. If he could prove that there were patterns of repetition, he might be able to open up a new field of research into the navigational capacities and memory-engram imprinting in great white sharks.

That is, as long as there were any great white sharks left to study.

. . .

"She's goin' down again," Tall Man called from the cabin.

"I guess she's one fickle lady," Chase said, disappointed. He looked toward shore. Napatree Point was abeam, the town of Waterboro just beyond. "Where to now?"

"She's off to Montauk, looks like. But not with any great purpose. She's strolling."

Chase walked forward into the cabin, hung up the camera and wiped sweat from his eyebrows. "Want a sandwich?" he called to Max.

"Not one of those gross sardine-and-onion things."

"No, I saved you a peanut-butter-and-jelly."

"Crack me a beer," Tall Man said, looking at his watch. "This watch may say it's nine-fifteen, but it doesn't know diddly about what time it really is." They had been sleeping in erratic four-hour shifts for the past forty hours. "My guts tell me it's straight up on beer o'clock."

Chase took a step toward the ladder that led to the galley below, when suddenly the boat lurched, lurched again and lost forward motion. The bow seemed to heave up, the stern to drop.

"What the hell's that?" Chase said. "You hit something?"

"In a hundred feet of water?" Tall Man frowned at the Fathometer. "Not hardly." The engine seemed to be laboring.

They heard a sound, as of rubber stretching—a complaining screech—and then the television monitor and the signal receiver began to inch backward on their mounts. The connecting wire was stretched taut through the doorway.

"Reverse!" Chase shouted as he ran to the door.

Tall Man shifted into reverse; the connecting wire went slack and drooped to the deck.

Outside in the cockpit, Chase saw that the coil of rubber-coated wire was gone; three hundred feet had spooled overboard. "The twine must've broken," he said. "The sensor's hitched in something on the bottom."

Chase took the wire in his hand and began to pull, and Max coiled it on the deck behind him. When the wire tautened again, Chase jigged it, pulling it left and right, giving it slack then hauling it tight. There was no give; the sensor was caught fast.

"I can't figure out what it's hitched in," he said. "Nothing down there but sand."

"Maybe," Tall Man said. He put the engine in neutral, letting the boat drift, and joined Chase and Max in the stern. He took the wire from Chase and held it in his fingertips, as if trying to decipher a message from its vibrations. "That nor'easter last week . . . forty knots of breeze for a day and a half will kick up hell with the bottom.

Sand'll shift. It could be anything: a rock, a car somebody deep-sixed."

"It could be a shipwreck," Max said.

Chase shook his head. "Not around here. We've charted every wreck in the area." To Tall Man he said, "We got any tanks aboard?"

"Nope. I didn't plan on diving."

Chase went forward, into the cabin, and adjusted the scale on the Fathometer to its most sensitive reading. When he returned, he was holding a face mask and snorkel.

"Thirty meters," he said. "Ninety-five feet, give or take."

"You gonna dive for that sensor?" Tall Man asked, his voice rising. "*Free*-dive? Are you nuts?"

"It's worth a try. I've dived ninety feet before."

"Not without a tank, you haven't. Not since you were eighteen. Hell, Simon, you'll black out if you try *forty* feet."

"You want to try?"

"Not a chance. This country's already got enough dead redskins."

"Then we got a problem, 'cause I'm damned if I'm gonna lose three thousand bucks' worth of wire and three thousand more of transmitter."

"Buoy it," Tall Man said. "We'll get some tanks and come back for it later."

"By then we'll have lost the shark for good."

"Maybe . . . but we won't have lost you."

Chase hesitated, still tempted to try to free-dive for the sensor, or at least to go far enough down to be able to see what had snagged it. He was curious to know if he could still dive that deep. As youngsters, he and Tall had free-dived to bottoms invisible from the surface, had swum around the hulks of old fishing boats, had stolen lobsters from traps nestled in crevices in deep reefs. But Tall was right; he was no longer a teenager, an athlete who could party all night and swim all day. He might make it to the bottom, but he'd never make it back. Starved for oxygen, his brain would shut down and he would pass out—near the surface if he was lucky, far below if he was not.

"Talk to the man, son," Tall Man said to Max. "Tell him you didn't come all this way just to take your daddy home in a box."

Max started at Tall Man's bluntness, then put a hand on his father's arm and said, "C'mon, Dad. . . ."

Chase smiled. "Okay, we'll buoy it," he said.

"Can we get some tanks and come back and dive on it?" Max asked. "That'd be cool."

"You know how to dive?" Chase felt a pang, almost of pain, as if the fact that Max had learned to dive without him, somewhere else, from someone else, was a reprimand for his failures as a parent. "Where'd you learn?"

"At home, in the pool. Gramps got me some lessons."

"Oh," Chase said, feeling better. At least the boy hadn't really been diving; he'd been preparing for his visit. "We'll put you in the water, sure, but I think we'll start a little shallower."

Tall Man went to the cabin to disconnect the wire and waterproof the plug with O-ring grease and rubber tape. Chase lifted a hatch in the stern and found a yellow rubber buoy, eighteen inches in diameter, on which the initials "O.I." were emblazoned in red Day-Glo tape.

Walking aft, Tall Man coiled the wire around his shoulder and elbow. He had removed his sweat-soaked shirt, and the muscles in his enormous torso glistened as they moved beneath his cinnabar skin as if he had been oiled. He stood six feet six, weighed about two-twenty, and if he carried any fat, as his mother used to say as she pressed more food on him, it had to be between his ears.

"Whoa!" Max said as he looked at Tall Man. "Rambo meets the Terminator! You work out every day?"

"*Work out?*" Chase said, laughing. "His two exercises are eating and drinking; his diet's a hundred percent salt-fried grease. He's a cosmic injustice."

"I'm the Great Spirit's revenge," Tall Man said to Max. "He's gotta do something to make up for five hundred years of white man's oppression."

"Believe that," Chase said to Max, "and you might as well believe in the tooth fairy. His Great Spirit is Ronald McDonald."

"So?" Tall Man guffawed. "A man's gotta pray to somebody."

Max beamed, loving it. It was men's talk, grown-ups' talk, and they were including him, letting him be a part of it, letting him be grown-up.

He had heard of Tall Man all his life—his dad's best friend since childhood—and the huge Pequot Indian had become a mythic figure for the boy. He had almost been afraid to meet him, lest reality spoil the image. But the human being had turned out to be as grand as the myth.

Chase and Tall Man had separated several times: while Chase had gone to college, Tall Man had served in the Marines; while Chase had gone to graduate school, Tall Man had tried his hand as a high-steel worker in Albany.

But their lives had intersected again, when Chase had begun the Institute. He had known he would need an assistant proficient in the technical skills he himself lacked, and he had found Tall Man working as a diesel mechanic at a truck dealership. Tall Man didn't mind the work, he told

Chase, and twenty dollars an hour wasn't a bad wage, but he hated somebody telling him when to come to work and when to leave, and he didn't like being cooped up indoors. Though Chase could offer him no fixed salary and no guarantees, Tall Man had quit on the spot and joined the Institute.

His job description listed no specific duties, so he did whatever Chase wanted done and whatever else he saw that needed doing, from maintaining the boats to hydro-testing the scuba gear. He loved working with animals, and seemed to have an almost mystical gift for communicating with them, calming them, getting them to trust him. Seabirds with fishhooks embedded in their beaks would allow him to handle them; a dolphin whose tail had been snared and slashed by monofilament netting had approached Tall Man in the shallows, and had lain quietly while he removed the strands of plastic and injected the animal with antibiotics.

He had freedom and responsibility, and he responded well to both. He arrived early, left late, worked at his own pace and took great, if unspoken, pride in being a partner in keeping the Institute running.

· · ·

When the coil of wire was secured to the buoy, they tossed both overboard and watched for a few moments to make sure that the wire didn't foul and that the buoy would support its weight. The wire was heavy, but in water it was nearly neutral—one pound negative for every ten feet—and the buoy was designed to support a dead weight of more than two hundred pounds.

"No sweat," Tall Man said.

"If nobody steals it. . . ."

"Right. Why would anybody want three hundred feet of wire?"

"You know as well as I do. People are ripping carriage lamps off houses to get the brass; they're torching light poles down for the aluminum; they're stealing toilet fixtures for the copper. In this economy, specially thanks to the crowd your blood brothers have brought in with their casino up in Ledyard, a smart man walks down the street with his mouth closed so no one can steal his fillings."

"There he goes again," Tall Man said to Max, grinning, "the racist blaming the poor Indians for everything."

Chase laughed and walked forward to put the boat in gear.

10

"BIRDS," TALL Man called down from the flying bridge, pointing to the south.

Chase and Max were on the foredeck—Max out at the end of the six-foot wooden pulpit that extended beyond the bow, from which he had been looking down into the water in hopes of seeing a dolphin. Chase had told him that dolphins sometimes frolicked in the bow wave of the boat.

Chase shaded his eyes and looked to the south. A swarm of birds—gulls and terns—was wheeling over half an acre of water that seemed to be aboil with living things. The birds dove and splashed in a flurry of wings and rose again, their heads bobbing as they hurried to swallow a prize so they could dive for another. The southwest breeze carried the sound of frenzied screeching.

"What are they doing?" Max asked.

"Feeding," Chase said. "On fry . . . tiny fish. Something's attacking the fry from underneath, driving them to the surface." He looked up at Tall Man. "Let's go have a look."

Tall Man swung the boat to the south, leaving the distant gray hump of Block Island to the north and the closer, but smaller and lower, profile of Osprey Island to the east.

As the boat drew near the turmoil in the water, Tall Man said, "Bluefish."

"You're sure?" said Chase. He hoped Tall Man was right: a big school of hungry bluefish would be a good sign, a sign that the blues were making a recovery. Recently, their numbers had been dwindling—they were victims of overfishing and pollution from PCBs, pesticides and phosphates from agricultural runoff—and many of the survivors were manifesting tumors, ulcers and even bizarre genetic mutations. Some were being born with stomachs that ceased functioning after about a year, so the fish starved to death. The Institute and various environmental groups had helped clean up the rivers that fed the bays that led to the ocean, and the amount of pollutants had been reduced significantly though by no means completely.

If the bluefish were breeding successfully again . . . well, it was a tiny step, but it *was* a step forward, at least, and not back.

"Gotta be blues," Tall Man said. "What else kicks up a shower of blood like that?"

A bird veered away from the flock and soared over the boat, and Chase saw the telltale signs of bluefish carnage: the white feathers of the bird's belly were stained red from fish blood. The blues were running amok in a vast school of panicked bait, chopping and slashing with blind fury, dyeing the water crimson.

Tall Man throttled back, letting the boat drift in relative silence so as not to drive the school away. "Big bastards, too," he said. "Five-, six-pounders."

The bluefish rolled and leaped and lunged, their gunmetal bodies flashing in the sunlight, and the birds dove recklessly among them, plucking fry from the bloody water.

"Gross!" Max said, mesmerized. "Can we go have a look?"

"You're having a look."

"No, I mean, can we put on masks and go down there?"

"Are you crazy?" said Chase. "No way. Those fish would cut you to ribbons. You didn't want to bring me home in a box . . . how'd you like me to send you home to your mother in a doggie bag?"

"Bluefish attack people?"

"In a frenzy like this, they attack *any*thing. A few years ago, a lifeguard in Florida was sitting on a surfboard when a feeding school came by. He lost four toes. They've got little triangular teeth as sharp as razors, and when they're feeding—"

Tall Man interrupted, "—they're one mean-tempered son of a bitch."

"Cool," Max said.

As if on cue, a large gull swooped down, reached for a baitfish, missed, braked with its wings and landed on the water. It snatched up the fish and began its takeoff run, when suddenly a blue body rolled beside it. The gull stopped, jerked backward and shrieked—a bluefish had it by its legs. The bird flapped its wings futilely and arched its neck forward, trying to peck at the tormentor.

Another bluefish must have grabbed it then, for the bird lurched to the side, submerged and popped back to the surface. It shrieked again, and beat with its wings, but now other fish sensed savory new prey, and they flung themselves out of the water, onto the blood-soaked feathers.

The bird's body was pulled below the surface tail-first. A final tug snapped its head back, and the last they saw of it was the yellow beak pointing at the sky.

Chase looked at Max. The boy's eyes still stared at the spot on the water where the bird had been, and his color had faded to a greenish gray.

· · ·

They continued toward the island, Max and Chase on the foredeck, Tall Man driving from the flying bridge. Now and then, Chase would signal Tall Man to slow down, and he would take a net and dip it into the water and bring up something to show Max: a clump of seaweed in which tiny crustacea—shrimps and crabs—took shelter until they were mature enough to fend for themselves on the bottom; a fist-sized jellyfish with a translucent purple membrane on its topside that looked like a sail, and long dangling tentacles that, Chase explained, stung its prey to death—a Portuguese man-o'-war. Fascinated, Max touched one of the tentacles and recoiled with a yelp as it stung his fingertip.

"It's early for them to be around," Tall Man remarked. "The water must be warming up fast."

When they were half a mile from the island, Chase pointed to a small Institute buoy bobbing off the starboard bow. Tall Man took the boat out of gear, letting it coast up to the buoy, as Chase picked up the boat hook and held it over the side. Chase snagged the buoy and brought it aboard. It was attached to a length of rope.

"Pull," he said to Max.

Max grabbed the rope and began to haul it aboard. "What is it?" he asked.

"An experiment," Chase said, dropping the boat hook and helping Max pull on the rope. "A big problem around here is lost lobster pots. Boat propellers cut the buoys off, or storms carry them away or the ropes just rot and fall apart. Anyway, there are pots lost all over the bottom."

"So?"

"They're killers. All sorts of creatures, not just lobsters—fish, crabs, octopuses—go inside after the baits and can't get out. They die and become bait themselves, so more and more creatures come in and die. The pots keep killing for years and years."

The pot bumped against the side of the boat, and Chase leaned overboard and heaved it up onto the gunwale. It was a rectangular wire cage, reinforced with wooden slats. On one end was a wire funnel—the way in; on the other, a square door made of a flimsy mesh material and secured with twine.

"What Tall and I've been trying to do," Chase said, "is design a biodegradable door. Pots should be pulled at least once a week, preferably twice, so we've been looking for a cheap material for the door that'll degrade after about ten days. The lobsterman can change the door every week, but if the pot's lost, the critters can get free before they die."

Max bent close to the pot and peered inside. "It's empty," he said.

"We didn't put any bait in it," Chase explained.

"We're not trying to catch things, we're trying to save 'em." He tugged gently at the mesh in the door, and several strands broke. "This cotton blend may be the thing," he called up to Tall Man. "It's breaking down real well."

When Tall Man didn't reply, Chase looked up at the flying bridge and saw him bend down, his hand cupped over one ear, listening.

Suddenly Tall Man straightened up. "We got trouble, Simon," he said. "A couple of yahoos are yammering over channel sixteen that they've just hooked Jaws."

"Damn!" Chase said. "Can you tell where they are?"

"About three miles to the northeast, sounds like, just this side of Block."

"Let's go," Chase said. He shoved the lobster pot overboard and tossed the rope and buoy after it.

Tall Man put the boat in gear, pushed the throttle forward and, as the boat leaped ahead, turned it in a tight arc and headed toward Block Island.

Max held on to the railing and bent his knees as the bow of the boat thumped into the waves. "Do you think it's our shark?" he shouted to his father.

"I'd bet on it," Chase said. "She's the only one we've seen."

The boat rose up onto a plane and skimmed

over the surface. The hump of Block Island grew swiftly larger, and as they watched, a small white dot took shape on the surface of the sea and soon became the hull of a boat.

"What are you gonna do?" Max asked. "What *can* you do?"

"I'm not sure, Max," Chase said, staring grimly ahead. "But something."

· · ·

"They're two kids," Tall Man said, looking through a pair of binoculars. "Sixteen, eighteen, maybe . . . fishin' from a twenty-foot outboard. Stupid bastards. They better *hope* they don't land the shark; it'll turn that boat into splinters."

Tall Man throttled back as he approached the outboard, then took the boat out of gear and let it idle thirty or forty yards off the outboard's port side.

One boy sat in a fighting chair in the stern, the butt of his rod snugged into a socket between his legs. The rod was bent nearly to the breaking point, and the line led straight out behind the boat: the shark was near the surface, but still fifty yards or more away. The other boy stood forward, at the console, turning the wheel and using the gears to keep the stern of the outboard facing the shark.

"Can he really catch a shark that big?" Max asked. "On a fishing rod?"

"If he knows what he's doing," Chase said. "He's using a tuna rig, probably sixty- or eighty-pound test line with a steel leader."

"But you said the shark weighed a ton."

"He can still wear her out. Great whites aren't great fighters, they're not true game fish. They just pull and pull and finally give up."

As they watched, the boy with the rod tried to reel in some line, but the weight was too great, and the drum of the reel skidded beneath the spool of line. So the boy at the console put the outboard in reverse, backing down toward the shark, giving the angler slack to reel in.

As Chase had feared, the boys knew what they were doing.

"Get closer," he said to Tall Man. "I want to have a talk with them."

Tall Man maneuvered so that the stern of the boat was within ten yards of the side of the outboard. Chase walked aft and stood at the transom.

"What've you got there?" he asked.

"Jaws, man," the boy at the console said. "Biggest damn white shark you ever seen."

"What're you gonna do with it?"

"Catch it . . . sell the jaws."

"How're you gonna get it aboard that little boat?"

"Don't have to . . . gonna kill it, then tow it in."

"Kill it how? That's one big angry shark."

"With this." The boy reached under the console and brought out a shotgun. "All we have to do is get close enough to him for one clean shot."

Chase paused, considering, then said, "Did you know he's a she?"

"Huh?"

"That shark is a female, and she's pregnant. We've tagged her, we've been studying her. If you kill her, you're not just killing her, you're killing her and her children and her children's children."

"It's a fish," the boy said. "Why should I give a shit?"

"Because white sharks are very rare . . . endangered, even. I'll make you a deal. You cut that shark away—"

"Fuck you!" shouted the boy with the rod. "I been busting my hump—"

"—and I'll get your names in the paper for helping the Institute. You'll get a lot more mileage than if you just kill her."

"Not a chance." The boy with the rod yelled over his shoulder, "Come back some more, Jimmy. He's takin' line again."

The boy at the console put the outboard in reverse, and Chase saw the angle of the line increase as the boat neared the shark.

"Dad," Max said, "we've gotta *do* something."

"Yeah," Chase said, leaning on the bulwark as

he felt rage rise within him. The problem was, there was nothing he *could* do, not legally anyway, for the boys were breaking no law. And yet he knew that if he let this happen, he would never forgive himself. He turned away and went below.

When he returned, he was carrying a mask and a pair of flippers, and a pair of wire cutters was stuck in the belt of his shorts.

"Jesus, Simon . . ." Tall Man said from the flying bridge.

"Where is she, Tall?"

Tall Man pointed. "About twenty yards thataway, but you don't—"

"She's so worn out and confused, she won't pay any attention to me. Last thing she wants to do is eat anybody."

"You know that, do you?"

"Sure," Chase said, forcing a smile and pulling on his flippers. "At least, I *hope* that."

"Dad!" Max said, as Chase's intent suddenly dawned on him. "You can't—"

"Trust me, Max." Chase pulled the mask over his face and rolled backward off the bulwark.

The driver of the outboard saw the splash as Chase fell into the water, and he shouted, "Hey! What the hell's he up to?"

"What you shoulda done way back when," Tall Man said.

The boy picked up his shotgun and cocked it.

"You get him back, or—"

"Put that away, you little prick," said Tall Man, in a voice as flat and hard as slate, "or I'll come over there and make you eat it."

The boy looked up at the huge dark man towering over him on the flying bridge of the much larger boat, and he lowered the shotgun.

· · ·

Chase located the line feeding down from the outboard and followed it with his eyes until he saw the shark. He took three or four deep breaths on the surface, held the final one and thrust himself downward with his flippers.

The shark had stopped fighting, for in its initial thrashing it had rolled up into the steel leader and then into the line itself, and now it was circled with monofilament strands that pressed into its flesh. It lolled on its side, perhaps resting for a final, futile attempt to escape, perhaps already resigned to death.

Chase swam to it, staying away from the snarls of line until he was within arm's reach of the tail of the shark.

He had never before swum in the open with a great white shark. He had seen them from the safety of a cage, had touched their tails as they swept by the bars in pursuit of hanging baits, had marveled at their power, but he had never been alone in the sea with this ultimate predator.

He permitted himself a moment to run his hand down the steel-smooth skin of the back, then backward against the grain of the dermal denticles, which felt like rubbing sandpaper. He found his tagging dart and its tiny transmitter, still securely set in the skin behind the dorsal fin. Then he leaned over the shark; its eye gazed at him with neither fear nor hostility, but with a blank and fathomless neutrality.

There were six loops around the shark—one of steel, five of monofilament—starting just forward of the tail, ending just forward of the pectoral fins. Chase hovered above the shark, nearly lying upon its back, took the wire cutters from his belt and cut the loops one by one. As each muscle group in the torpedo-like body sensed freedom, it began to shudder and ripple. When the last loop was gone, the shark swung downward, suspended only by the wire in its mouth that led to the hook deep in its belly. Chase reached his hand into the mouth of the shark and snipped the wire.

The shark was free. It began to fall, upside down, and for a moment Chase feared that it had died, that the lack of forward motion had deprived it of oxygen and it had asphyxiated. But then the tail swept once from side to side, the shark rolled over and its mouth opened as water rushed over its gills. It turned in a circle, its eye fixed on Chase, and rose toward him.

It came slowly, relentlessly, unexcited, un-afraid, its mouth half open, its tail thrusting it forward.

Chase did not turn or flee or backpedal. He faced the shark and watched its eyes, knowing that the only warning he would have of an imminent attack would be the rotating of its eyeballs, an instinctive protection against the teeth or claws of its victim.

He heard his temples pounding and felt arrows of adrenaline shooting through his limbs.

The shark came on, face-to-face, until it was four feet from Chase, then suddenly rolled onto its side, presenting its snow-white belly distended with young, and angled downward, like a banking fighter plane, disappearing into the blue-green depths.

Chase watched until the shark was gone. Then he surfaced, snatched a few gasping breaths and made his way back to the boat. He pulled himself out of the water, and as he sat on the swimstep to remove his flippers, he noticed that the pulpit of the Institute boat was hovering over the hull of the outboard. He heard Tall Man say, "So, we got a deal, right? The story is, you hooked the shark, saw that it was tagged and reported it to us. We tell the papers what fine citizens you are."

The sullen boys stood in the stern of the out-board, and one of them said, "Yeah, okay. . . ."

Tall Man looked down, saw that Chase was aboard, then put the boat in reverse. "Thanks," he called to the boys.

Chase passed Max his flippers and climbed up through the door in the transom.

Max looked angry. "That was really dumb, Dad," he said. "You could've—"

"It was a calculated risk, Max," Chase said. "That's what dealing with wild animals is. I was pretty sure she wouldn't bite me; I made a judgment that the risk was worth taking, to save the life of that mama shark."

"But suppose you'd been wrong. Is a shark's life worth as much as yours?"

"That's not the point; the point is, I knew what I had to do. The Bible may say man has dominion over animals, but that doesn't mean we've got the right to wipe them off the face of the earth."

· · ·

Max was standing at the end of the pulpit, Chase behind him on the foredeck, as they passed through a stretch of deep water between the islands.

Suddenly Max shouted, "Dad!" and pointed down into the water.

A dolphin had appeared from nowhere and was riding the bow wave of the boat, coasting effortlessly on the bulb of water created by the boat's forward motion. They could see its shiny gray back, its pointed snout, the puckered blowhole in the top of its head. They could hear sounds—faint clicks and trills—coming from somewhere within the animal.

"He's talking!" Max said excitedly. "That's how they talk! I wonder what he's saying."

"Probably just jabbering . . . maybe calling his buddies over, maybe saying something like 'Whee!' "

For several moments, the dolphin's body barely moved; it let the momentum of the boat carry it along. Then, for some reason, it accelerated, thrusting its horizontal tail up and down, and pulled ahead of the boat. It slowed, waited for the boat to catch up and resumed its ride.

"Look at that tail," Chase said.

Max leaned over the pulpit. "What about it?"

"The left fluke. Look at the scars."

Max looked, and saw five deep white slashes, an inch or two apart, in the flesh of the tail fluke. "What did that?" he asked.

"This dolphin was attacked by something," Chase said. "I'd say he was lucky to get away."

"A shark?"

"No, not a shark, no shark did that. A shark bite would be semicircular."

"A killer whale?"

"No, you'd see punctures or drag marks from the conical teeth, not sharp slashes like those."

Chase frowned. "They look like claw marks, like a tiger's or a bear's."

"What lives in the ocean and has five claws?"

"Nothing," Chase said. "Nothing I've ever heard of."

11

THE DOCK had been built in a cove on the northwest corner of the island, and as the boat puttered up to it, Chase nudged Max and pointed overhead and smiled: a pair of ospreys were flying high over the water, searching for food for their young, which were sheltered safely on nesting poles that Chase had built.

"Once ospreys were almost wiped out," he told Max. "For some reason, their eggs had become so weak they were cracking before the chicks could hatch. A scientist got to wondering what was doing it, and he found out: DDT. The pesticide was leaching into the water and poisoning the food chain, and the fish the ospreys were eating were destroying their eggs. That discovery was the beginning of the Environmental Defense Fund. Once they got DDT banned, the ospreys started coming back. They're in pretty good shape now."

A one-winged blue heron stood sentinel over his tidal pool by the dock.

"Hey, Chief," Tall Man called to the bird, then he looked at Chase and said, "The Chief is pissed. His lunch is late."

"That's Chief Joseph," Chase explained to Max. "Some kids found him over at the borough beach. He had a broken wing; the vet they took him to said the wing was too badly smashed to fix, he wanted to put him to sleep, but I said no, just amputate the wing and let us have him. He's become a real prima donna. Twice a day he walks around in the shallows, the rest of the time he stands there and complains that we don't feed him enough."

"Why'd you name him Chief Joseph?" Max asked.

"Tall named him that, after the Nez Percé chief . . . you know, the Battle of Bear Paw Mountains. He said that with only one wing the heron reminded him of what Chief Joseph said after the battle: 'I will fight no more forever.' "

"Is the Chief friendly?"

"If you've got food he is. If you don't, he's a perfect pain in the ass."

Max grinned. "Maybe *I'll* find some special animal, something I can take care of and name."

"Sure," Chase said. "Maybe you will."

Tall Man guided the boat into its slip between

two smaller craft—a Whaler and a Mako—and Chase hopped onto the dock and retrieved the lines. He tossed the stern and spring lines to Tall Man and returned aboard to show Max how to cleat the bow line.

Then, while Tall Man went to find food for the heron, Chase and Max went on up the hill.

. . .

Osprey Island had been a private family compound for nearly a hundred years, but over four generations the family had outgrown the five houses that local zoning permitted. Periodically, family members had tried to buy one another out, but they had found themselves caught in a paradox.

Technically, because it consisted of thirty-five acres of waterfront property, the island was worth a fortune, and the state and township had taxed it accordingly. Over the past two decades, taxes had doubled, and doubled again, until finally the cost of running the enclave had approached a hundred and fifty thousand dollars a year. One by one, family members had discovered that for their allotted two weeks on the island every summer, they were paying more than the cost of renting a decent house on Nantucket or Martha's Vineyard for two months.

They had tried to sell the island, and discovered that, in fact, it wasn't worth very much at all because nobody—including the family members themselves—wanted to pay its assessed value.

And so, in a calculated act of revenge against the local "taxocrats," the family corporation, an entity that existed solely to run the island, had taken out as large a mortgage as the local bank would permit—half the assessed value—had split the proceeds among the twelve families within the family . . . and had then dissolved itself and abandoned the island, leaving its liens, its taxes and its upkeep in the hands of the bank.

Simon Chase had been welcomed by the bank and the town as the new owner. He had deep roots in the local community, and though as a nonprofit entity the Institute might not pay local taxes, some of Chase's projects might generate substantial revenue for the townspeople. For example, he might find a way to bring the shellfishing industry back. For years, the beds of clams, scallops and mussels around Waterboro had been so badly polluted that no one was permitted to dig, eat or sell any of the mollusks. Perhaps Chase could find a way to clean up the beds.

Local merchants knew, furthermore, that the Institute wouldn't be competition for any of them. And finally, Chase's grand plans for the island promised to bless the area with what it needed most: jobs.

Defense cutbacks had slashed jobs from the

largest employer in southeastern Connecticut, Electric Boat in Groton, and the ripple effect from EB and other damaged companies had decimated service industries. Restaurants and grocery stores, saloons and gift shops had shut their doors, to be replaced here and there by antique stores and art galleries. Waterboro was being gentrified and ossified, and it was hoped that the Institute would be able to restore life to the community. Hundreds of people would be employed to build it, wire it and plumb it, and when it was completed, dozens more would find full-time jobs there or in one of the many businesses that serviced it.

For a year, it had seemed that the dream might come true. Chase had taken a course in preparing grant applications, and he had received a hundred-thousand-dollar grant to buy boats and basic scientific equipment. He had also received preliminary approval for grants for projects involving endangered species, commercial fishing and medical research from the federal government, the state of Connecticut and several private foundations. One of the grants would have enabled him to study the curious fact that sharks, which had no bones, were immune to both cancer and arthritis and could exert phenomenal bite pressure—as much as twenty tons per square inch—with a jaw made entirely of cartilage. Another would have let him contribute to studies testing the remote possibility that powdered shark cartilage contained cancer-killing properties. Doctors working with a control group in Cuba had claimed a 40 percent reduction in tumors among patients who were given high doses of the cartilage.

And then, in late 1995, the bottom had fallen out of the economy. The national debt had grown to six trillion dollars; the President and the Congress, obsessed with reelection, had refused to make the hard decisions necessary to deal with the budget deficit. The Germans and the Japanese and the Arabs, who had supported the vaunted American way of life for more than a dozen years, looked across the water and, disgusted at long last, proclaimed the United States effectively extinct as a world power and pulled their money out.

Inflation had begun to soar; interest rates were reaching double digits; the stock market had dropped a thousand points and so far showed no signs that it had bottomed out; unemployment nationwide was 11 percent; one family in four now lived below the poverty line.

In the space of a single week, every one of Chase's grants had been refused. New construction was the last thing he had money for. He could barely pay his staff of three, could barely feed himself. Had he not been successful in obtaining tax-exempt status for the Institute, he would already have had to follow his predecessors and abandon the island.

And he might yet have to pack up and go, if his last roll of the dice came up craps.

Months ago, he had received a call from a Dr. Amanda Macy in California. He knew her by reputation, had read a story about her in some journal or other. She was doing pioneering research in the use of trained sea lions to videotape gray whales in the wild. Notoriously skittish, gray whales resisted being photographed by divers, and even when a diver succeeded in capturing a few images, there was no way to determine if the whales' behavior was natural or skewed in some way because of the presence of the diver. Macy's theory was that since sea lions often accompany whales in the wild, the whales would tolerate them without altering their behavior, so she had trained sea lions to carry video cameras as they swam with the whales. According to the report, she was already rewriting much of science's knowledge of gray whales.

Now she wanted to try the same technique with another species of whale, the Atlantic humpback. She had heard about the new institute and had read some of Chase's papers on sharks. She knew he had boats, guts and experience with large deep-water animals. She knew the humpbacks passed just to the east of the island every summer on their way north. Would he be willing, she wondered, to have her and her team of sea lions come to the island for three months, to take them to sea and help her with her research . . . for a fee of, say, ten thousand dollars a month?

Chase had agreed instantly, while trying to temper the excitement in his voice. This could be salvation, not only financially but intellectually as well—a terrific project, well funded, with a respected colleague.

The only problem was, Dr. Macy was due to arrive in a few days, Chase had spent a lot of money, money he didn't have, building facilities for her and her sea lions, and Dr. Macy's first check hadn't come yet. If she had changed her plans, if she had decided to cancel without having the courtesy to call him, if . . . well, he wouldn't think about it.

. . .

The Institute's nerve center was a twenty-two-room clapboard Victorian pile that had formerly been the main house for the island's clan. Though its structure hadn't changed, its function had: it was used for the Institute's housing, dining, administration and communications. It was ramshackle and inefficient, and Chase's original, grandiose plans had called for it to be razed and replaced at a cost of more than a million dollars.

By now, though, he was delighted that the house had remained untouched, for he had come to love it. His office was large, high-ceilinged and airy, with a working fireplace and French doors that gave him a view of Fishers Island and, on a clear day, Long Island.

When Chase and Max came into the office, Mrs. Bixler was polishing pewter and watching The Weather Channel.

"Morning, Mrs. B.," Chase said.

"Morning's long gone," Mrs. Bixler replied, "and you look like you've been on a three-day toot." She looked at Max. "Did you really take this boy sharking?"

"I did, and he did just fine . . . thanks to the sandwiches you sent along."

"You were lucky," Mrs. Bixler said, frowning and returning to her polishing. "You were lucky, pure and simple. Don't push your luck, I say."

Nominally, Mrs. Bixler was Chase's secretary; in fact, she was the Institute's majordomo and his self-appointed caretaker. A sixty-year-old widow whose children lived somewhere out West, she was a member of the island's founding family and had lived there year-round since the Korean War, shuttling back and forth to the mainland in her own boat, a 1951 wooden speedboat that she kept in her own cove.

Initially, when the family had left the island, she

had moved to a small house on the water near Mystic, but as soon as Chase had taken over—and had found himself calling her daily for advice and counsel about the island, its buildings, its septic systems, its generators, its wells—he had asked her to come back to the island and work for the Institute. She had, on her terms, which included the restoration of her four-room apartment off the kitchen of the main house.

The pewter collection, a museum-quality array of seventeenth- and early-eighteenth-century mugs, flagons, plates, candlesticks and flatware, was Mrs. Bixler's own and was probably worth several hundred thousand dollars. She could have sold it, stashed it in a vault somewhere or kept it in her rooms, but it had traditionally resided in the room that was now Chase's office, and that, she told Chase, was where it would continue to reside.

"Why are you watching that, ma'am?" Max asked, pointing at the television set mounted in a bookcase.

"Can't be too careful," Mrs. Bixler said. "That's one thing you can never be, too careful."

Mrs. Bixler was tuned to disaster. She had been three years old in 1938, when the colossal hurricane had devastated New England—she claimed to recall seeing houses fly off Napatree Point and float out to sea; she had lived on the island through half a dozen other hurricanes. After Hurricane Bob had knocked down a bunch of trees and blown out a bunch of windows and put a lobster boat high and dry on her lawn in 1991, she had taken out a loan to buy a satellite dish so she could keep The Weather Channel on at all hours of the day and night, and be ready for the next big blow.

"What's going on?" Chase said.

"Nothing much, not enough to wet a frog's socks. But there's a nasty-looking low-pressure convection cooking down east of Puerto Rico."

"I meant about business. Anything from the EPA or the DEP? Did we get an okay to move the whale?"

"Not a peep. I called 'em both, and I got a robot that told me to have a nice day."

Chase ruffled through a pile of letters on his desk. "Did we get the check from Dr. Macy?"

"Not yet. If I was you, I'd tell that woman you're gonna make two parkas and a pair of gloves out of her seals if she doesn't pay up." Mrs. Bixler paused. "One thing, though. I was over to town collecting the mail; Andy Santos told me Finnegan's fixing to make a run at your tax status."

"Damn!" Chase said. "He won't give up, will he?"

"Not till he's got you turn-tail and running

. . . or till you roll over and sell out to him."

"I'll blow the island off its pins first."

Mrs. Bixler smiled. "That's what I told Andy."

Brendan Finnegan was a land speculator whose acumen was very sharp . . . and usually about a year too late. He had made a fortune in the seventies, lost it in the early eighties, made it back in the late eighties and been hammered by the most recent turnaround. Currently, his empire was teetering on the lip of bankruptcy, and he was in desperate need of a big score.

A month after Chase had closed his deal for Osprey Island, Finnegan had received a feeler from a third-rank Saudi prince who was worried about the explosive resurgence of Moslem fundamentalism and was seeking a safe haven for several million dollars' worth of sterling and deutsche marks. Distrustful of markets and banks, he wanted to own hard assets, and he believed that despite America's troubles, waterfront property on the U.S. East Coast was among the world's hardest assets. Its value might stall, might retreat, but would never collapse . . . not with 70 percent of the population living within fifty miles of the coasts, and more fleeing the middle of the country every day. There were houses for sale by the score between North Carolina and New Hampshire, but no islands, and the prince was a dedicated paranoid who needed the security of a self-contained redoubt.

Finnegan saw the prince as his big score, if only he could find an island to sell him. He didn't just want a broker's commission; he wanted the seller's profit too. Thus, he'd have to own the island.

Chase's financial problems were no secret. The price he had paid for the island was public record, and his difficulties meeting day-to-day expenses were common knowledge.

Finnegan had first offered Chase the same amount Chase had paid for the island. Ignoring Chase's insistence that he didn't want to sell, Finnegan had upped his ante in increments of 10 percent. His latest offer had been for 180 percent of Chase's purchase price, or nearly two thirds of the assessed value of the island.

Chase knew the game Finnegan was playing, and he wasn't trying to hold the man up. As he told Finnegan while they were still on relatively amicable terms, he had finally found something he loved, something he wanted to preserve and pursue, and he intended to keep it.

Finnegan had stopped being friendly. He had begun to file nuisance complaints—with the zoning board, the planning board, the Coast Guard and the EPA. None of the complaints had been sustained, but each had had to be answered, if not by Chase himself then by his two-hundred-dollar-an-hour lawyer.

"What grounds has he thought up this time?" Chase asked Mrs. Bixler.

"Says you're not doing any real science out here, says your experiments haven't produced anything concrete yet, so why should the taxpayers support you."

"The argument's got a certain appeal." Chase paused. "Dr. Macy's arriving just in time . . . the cavalry to the rescue."

"Long as she pays the bills."

Max had appeared to be ignoring the conversation, watching the hypnotic drone of the weather reports. But now he said suddenly, "Can't you afford all this? Are you gonna lose the island?"

"No," Chase said, forcing a smile. "Now let's go get us some scuba tanks and have a lesson before we go back and dive up that sensor."

"Not likely," said Mrs. Bixler. "Compressor's down."

"For God's sake . . . what now?" Chase said, seeing Max's shoulders slump in disappointment.

"Gene said it's probably the solenoid. But then, Gene thinks all the world's problems can be traced to solenoids. If I were you, I'd have Tall look at it."

"Okay," Chase said. He felt panicky; now there

were problems with the compressor. What would break down next? What he wanted to do more than anything was take a nap.

But Max was here, and Chase was determined that Max was going to have the time of his life. He smiled and said, "We'll go talk to Tall, help him feed Chief Joseph. Then we'll go check the tank racks. Maybe there're still a couple of full tanks."

· · ·

Tall Man was already in the equipment shed, working on the diesel compressor, whose problem was not the solenoid but clogged injectors. He'd have it running by late this afternoon, he said; there would be full tanks by tomorrow morning.

Chase didn't know how Max would react— with sullenness, perhaps, or resignation—but the one attitude he would have bet against was enthusiasm. So he was surprised and pleased when Max said, "That's the great thing about being here for a month; there's always tomorrow." He gestured. "C'mon, Dad, gimme a tour of the rest of the place."

There were three other buildings on the island. All had been homes, all had been scheduled for demolition and all had instead been jury-rigged as laboratories, storage facilities and, in one case, a makeshift infirmary.

The living room of the smallest house had been stripped of furniture and carpeting, its floor had been tiled, its Sheetrock walls plastered over. In the center of the room, bolted to the floor, lit by large ceiling-mounted fluorescent tubes, was a cylinder twelve feet long and six feet high, with a round hatch on one end and a small porthole in the middle. Plastic tubing and coated wires ran from the cylinder to a control panel on one wall.

"That's our decompression chamber," Chase said. "We call it Dr. Frankenstein."

"What's it for?"

"Well, let's see how much you learned from your diving lessons. What are the three main dangers in diving? Aside from stupidity and panic, which are the two most important and the ones they don't tell you about."

"That's easy. Embolism first—that's from holding your breath on the way up. The bends. And . . . I forget the other one."

"Some people call it the rapture," Chase said. "The rapture of the deep." He led Max to a small refrigerator, from which he took two cans of Coke. He passed one to Max and said, "You ever been drunk?"

Max flushed. "Me?"

"Never mind, that wasn't a question you have to answer. What I'm getting at is, the thing they call the rapture is like getting drunk underwater. Its real name is nitrogen narcosis. When you breathe compressed air in deep water, there's a high ratio of nitrogen in what you take into your body, and nitrogen can become poison, pretty much like alcohol. It affects people at different depths, in different ways. Some people never get it, some people get it once and never again, some people get it so often they're almost used to it. And some people die from it."

"Why?"

"Because getting drunk underwater is . . . well . . . a real bummer. The worst thing is, a lot of times you don't know what's happening. It's a mellow, dreamy kind of drunk. You forget where you are; you don't care; that deep reef down there at two hundred feet is so pretty you think you'll go have a look for a while, and if you think to check your depth gauge or your air gauge, you find you can't read them, the numbers are all blurry, but you don't give a damn so you go anyway.

"They've done tests on divers and found that, as a rule, at a hundred and fifty feet a twenty-five-year-old male in peak physical condition can't perform simple tasks he wasn't prepared to do."

"Like what?"

"One of those puzzles you did when you were little, where you put the round thing in the round hole and the square thing in the square hole. He can't do that, he can't figure it out. He's lost all power of innovation. He can't change his dive plan. If he has an emergency, if he runs out of air or his mouthpiece pulls away from his regulator, he survives by instinct and reflexes conditioned by experience and training. Or he doesn't survive."

"Emergencies kill them?"

"Not always. Sometimes they kill themselves. You'd think it was suicide if you didn't know better."

"How?"

Chase took a breath and looked off into the middle distance, remembering. "Ten years ago, I was a safety diver for a guy who wanted to film black coral on the Little Cayman wall. Deep stuff, two hundred feet, two-fifty, about the limit of safe compressed-air scuba diving."

"People breathe other things?" Max asked.

"Yeah, if you have to work deeper than that, you use mixed gases. Helium-and-oxygen is one. Anyway, we took all sorts of precautions: put a weighted line down to two-fifty, posted a diver every fifty feet with a spare tank so the cameraman would have someone watching over him all the time and plenty of air for decompression on the way up. I was the guy at a hundred, and there was a guy below me at one-fifty. The cameraman was wearing twin eighties pumped to thirty-five hundred psi—big tanks, so no way he'd run out of air. He said he'd never been narced before, so nobody gave it a thought.

"We got positioned, and the cameraman jumped in and started down. He went by me and gave me a wave, same for the next guy, then he grabbed the line at two hundred and stopped to adjust his camera and turn on his lights. The water was clear as gin, so I could see everything. He looked fine, in control, his bubbles coming up nice and regularly, which meant his respiration was good, no anxiety, no panic, nothing.

"A big grouper came out of his hole in the wall and hung there looking at the cameraman, who cranked off some film of him. Then the grouper got bored and began to mosey down the wall.

"Well, all of a sudden the cameraman looks up at the guy below me, waves, takes off his mask— his *mask,* for God's sake!—tosses it away and starts chasing the grouper down the wall.

"I started after him, so did the guy below me, and we were *humming,* but there was no way. We quit at two-fifty, and all we could see were the camera lights going down and down into that blackness, till they looked like little pinpoints."

"How deep was it there?"

"Two miles. I imagine he's still down there."

"Two miles!" Max said. "Did you feel it . . . the rapture?"

"Mostly I was in shock. But there was one second when I felt a kind of weird envy of what the man must be seeing way down there in the abyss.

As soon as I felt it I knew what it was, and it frightened me, so I grabbed the other diver and dragged both of us up to where we felt normal again."

"What about the bends? Have you ever had that?"

"No, thank God, and I hope I never do." Chase gestured around the room. "Sitting right here," he said, "we have fourteen and a half pounds of air pressure on every inch of our bodies. Okay? Fourteen-point-five psi. Every thirty-three feet you go down diving, you pick up another atmosphere, as they call it; the air in your tank is compressed another fourteen-point-five psi. So at thirty-three feet, you've got twenty-nine psi; at sixty-six feet, forty-three and a half; and so on. You with me?"

"Sure," Max said.

"Now, remember what I said about the deeper you go the more nitrogen you breathe? Well, here it is again—nitrogen's a bad actor. If you stay down too long and come up without giving it a chance to vent out of your system—it's what's called decompression, you just hang in the water and breathe it off—a bubble of nitrogen can lodge in an elbow or a knee or your spinal cord or your brain. That's the bends. It can cripple you or kill you or give you what you think is bursitis for the rest of your life." Chase pointed at the steel cylinder. "That's why we have the decompression chamber, in case somebody gets the bends. The chances of it happening around here are pretty slim, considering how little deep diving we do, but when the Navy offered us this surplus chamber, I snapped it up."

"What does it do?"

"If a person gets bent, you put him inside and pump the chamber full of air and pressurize it to the equivalent of the depth the dive tables say he should be at to begin safe decompression—a hundred feet, two hundred, whatever. We can pressurize the chamber to the equivalent of a thousand feet. Pressure puts the nitrogen back into solution in the person's bloodstream, so the bubbles disappear and he feels normal again. Usually. But it depends on how long ago he was bent and how much damage was already done.

"Then comes the tricky part. You reduce the pressure in the chamber very gradually, which is like bringing the person up from depth very slowly, almost inch by inch, so the nitrogen has a chance to flush itself from his tissue. Sometimes it takes as long as a whole day."

"What happens if he comes up too fast?"

"You mean *really* too fast? He'll die."

They tossed their soda cans into a trash basket, and went outside.

On the southeast corner of the island, an enormous circle of concrete, fifty feet in diameter, had been poured into forms set in craters blasted into the ledge rock. The circle had been filled with water, and the natural boulders had been left within it to make platforms and caverns.

"It looks like the sea lion house at the zoo," Max said.

"Good for you . . . that's what it is. I had it custom-built for Dr. Macy's sea lions."

"Do you think I'll be able to play with them?"

"I don't see why not." Chase looked at his watch. "But right now, I've got to go make a couple of calls. Want to come?"

"Can I go ask Tall Man for a fish, maybe try to feed Chief Joseph?"

"Sure." Chase started away, then stopped. "But, hey, Max, remember . . . this is an island . . . water, water everywhere."

Max grimaced. "Dad . . ."

"I know, I know, I'm sorry," Chase said. Then he smiled. "But you've got to remember, I'm pretty new at this fathering business."

• • •

Chase sat at his desk and stared at the fax copy of the bank-transfer slip. Dr. Macy's money would be good funds in the Institute's account at the borough bank tomorrow morning. He could pay Mrs. Bixler, he could pay Tall Man and the care-taker, Gene, he could clear his tabs with the fuel dock and the grocery store. He could even pay his insurance premium on time, avoiding a late charge for the first time in months.

He should probably frame the fax and hang it on the wall, the way some people framed the first dollar their business took in, because this ten thousand was a real lifesaver, the first step on the Institute's road to solvency. If he could keep Dr. Macy and her sea lions here for the full three months—and why shouldn't he? The weather would be good, and the whales should be passing back and forth till the end of September—he'd take in thirty thousand dollars, enough to keep him afloat till the end of the year. Maybe by then grant money would have loosened up for the bite-dynamics project; maybe he'd be able to wangle some charters from cable TV companies doing shows on sharks or whales; maybe . . . maybe what? . . . maybe he'd win the lottery.

Yes, he'd copy the fax and frame the copy. He'd enjoy looking back at it later on, when times were better.

He wondered if Dr. Macy had any idea how critical her ten thousand was to him. And what did ten grand mean to her? Nothing, probably. The state university system in California sucked up hundreds of millions in grants every year. Ten thousand was probably petty cash to her.

He wondered what Macy herself would be like. All natural, he'd bet, fiber-loaded, fully organic, no preservatives, one of those women who smelled of lamb fat because their sweaters were knit from raw New Zealand wool, who wore little round eyeglasses and had dirt between their toes from walking around in orthopedic sandals and refused to eat anything that had ever lived.

He knew them well, from his days in Greenpeace, and found most of them to be either insufferably smug and self-righteous or ditsily, dangerously naive.

Anyway, he didn't care if Dr. Macy was the spawn of Tiny Tim and Leona Helmsley. Her money was good, and so was her project. The Institute's public relations—an element of his job that Chase loathed and wasn't adept at exploiting—could benefit from an association with her. Good video images of humpback whales, especially if they were breakthrough images of the kind Dr. Macy had supposedly gotten of the California grays, would be tangible evidence of serious scientific work. There would be stories in newspapers and on television. Brendan Finnegan would have to eat his words and find someone else to harass.

12

MAX'S FOOT slipped on the slick boulder, and before he could catch himself he skidded down its face and found himself standing in water up to his ankles. He called himself a few names, then sloshed through the shallow water till he came to a place where the rocks were smaller. He climbed them and continued his circuit of the island, stepping carefully from rock to rock, aware now of the truth of what Tall Man had told him: low tide makes for slippery rocks.

Tall Man had given him two fish to feed to the heron. He had approached the bird gingerly, for it was big, its beak was long and sharp and its dark eyes followed him as if he were prey.

Max had dropped the first fish, fearing for his fingers, and the heron had snatched it from the water, craned its neck and swallowed it whole. The heron had seen the second fish, and had taken a step toward Max. Max had forced himself to stand his ground, dangling the fish from his fingertips, and the heron had plucked it from him with surgical precision, its beak missing Max by millimeters. Then Max had tried to touch the heron, but it had turned away and marched back to the center of its tidal pool.

Max had nothing special to do, his father and Tall Man were both busy, so he had decided to go exploring. At low tide, Tall Man had said, you could walk all the way around the island on the rocks, and he had already made it nearly halfway around, had reached the far southern end of the island, before skidding off the slimy boulder and soaking his sneakers.

He came to a small pool—a big puddle, really—where the tide had receded from a basin in a boulder, and he knelt down and bent close to the water. He saw tiny crabs scuttling among the stones, and periwinkles clinging motionless to the bottom, as if patiently awaiting the next high tide. He watched the crabs for a moment, wondering what they were doing that made them look so busy—feeding? fighting? fleeing?—then stood up and continued on.

The larger rocks were spattered with guano and littered with clam shells and crab shells dropped from the air by gulls, which would then swoop down and peck the succulent meat from the shattered shells. The smaller rocks closer to the water were coated with algae and weeds, and in niches between them Max saw matchbooks, plastic six-pack holders and aluminum pop-tops from soda cans. He picked up those he could reach and stuffed them into his pockets.

He came to a spot where the rocks looked too slimy and their faces too slippery for him to climb over them safely, and so he walked up the hillside and crossed twenty or thirty yards of high grass toward the biggest boulder he had ever seen: at least twelve or fifteen feet high, probably twenty feet long, a remnant of the retreat of the glaciers at the end of the last ice age. He circled the boulder, looking up at it with awe, then began to search for a way down the hill to the rocks.

He walked between two bushes, tested his footing and started down.

Something caught his eye, something in the water, not far out, no more than ten yards away. He looked, but saw nothing, and he tried to articulate for himself what it was he had seen: movement, a change in the shape of the water, as if something big was swimming just beneath the surface. He kept looking, hoping to see the dorsal fin of a dolphin or the shimmering shower caused by a school of feeding fish.

Nothing. He kept going, walking slowly, stepping carefully among the wet rocks.

He heard a sound behind him: a splash, but a strange kind of splash, a plopping splash, as if an animal had risen out of the water and submerged again. He turned and looked, and this time he did see something—a ring of ripples spreading from a spot just offshore. There was a vague hump in the surface of the water, but as he watched, he saw it disappear.

He wondered if there were sea turtles around here. Or seals. Whatever it was out there, he wanted to see it.

But again, there was nothing. He walked another few yards and looked up to gauge the terrain ahead. The rocks on this side of the island seemed to be smaller, more cluttered with debris. There were pot buoys and big chunks of plastic and . . .

What was that? Ten or fifteen yards away, something was caught in the rocks, half in the water, half out. An animal of some kind. A dead animal.

He walked closer and saw that it was a deer, or the remains of a deer, for the corpse had been savaged, its flesh torn and stripped. There was no sickly smell of rot, no gathering of flies, which told Max that the deer had not been dead for long; this was a fresh kill. He couldn't imagine what had done this to so large an animal. Hunters? He looked for bullet wounds in the body, but saw none.

He was about to turn away, when he saw something in the head of the deer, something strange. He stepped forward, bent down, reached out. His foot slipped; he flung out his arms and tried to straighten up to regain his balance, but overcorrected and fell backward into the water.

The water wasn't deep, only three or four feet, and Max quickly found footing on the loose gravel. He stood up.

Suddenly he sensed something behind him— movement, a change in pressure, as if a mass of water was being shoved at him. He turned and saw the same vague hump in the surface. This time it was moving toward him.

He splashed the water to try to frighten it away, but it kept coming.

A surge of panic washed over Max; he turned back toward shore, leaned into the hip-deep water and paddled with his hands. He gained a yard, two yards, and now he was scrambling up a slope on his hands and knees, scattering rocks and gravel behind him. He pushed with his feet and reached for a handhold. His hand found the head of the deer, and he pulled. Something sharp dug into his palm, cutting it, but he held on and kept pulling.

He reached the dry rocks, lurched to his feet and ran. He didn't stop until he got to the top of the hill. Gasping ragged breaths that were more like sobs, he looked down at the water. The hump had vanished, and rings of ripples were fading from the glassy surface.

Trembling from cold and fear, Max ran toward the house. He had covered half the distance before he felt a stinging in his palm. He looked at his hand and saw, protruding from the fleshy bulb beneath his thumb, the thing that had cut him.

· · ·

Chase looked up from his desk and saw Max standing in the doorway, soaked from the shoulders down; a puddle was forming on the floor around his sodden sneakers. He was shivering. His face was gray, his lips nearly blue. He looked terrified.

"Max!" Chase jumped up from his desk, knocking his chair back against the wall, and crossed the room. "Are you okay?"

Max nodded.

Chase knelt down and began to unlace Max's sneakers. "What happened? You fall off the rocks?"

"A deer," Max said.

"A deer? What deer?"

Max tried to speak, but stammered as a spasm

wracked his chest and shoulders and made his teeth clatter.

"Hey," Chase said. "It's okay." He removed Max's sneakers, socks, jeans and underwear, balled them up and threw them out the front door onto the lawn. He took two bath towels from a linen closet in the hall, dried Max off with one and wrapped him in the other. Then he led him to the sofa in his office and sat him down.

"Deer swim over here," he said. "Usually from Block Island but sometimes all the way from town. I don't know why they bother, there's nothing here for them they can't find somewhere else. They're a nuisance: they eat everything Mrs. Bixler plants, and they're loaded with ticks, Lyme ticks. They—"

Chase stopped, for he saw that Max was shaking his head. "What?"

"It was dead," Max said.

"What? In the water? It drowned. Yeah, they—"

"Something killed it . . . tried to eat it . . . *did* eat it, a lot of it." Max spoke haltingly, for he was still shivering. "I was on the rocks by the point . . . near that giant boulder Mrs. Bixler said her family always called Papa Rock . . . saw something in the water, caught in the rocks . . . saw its head and part of the rest of it. . . . I got closer . . .

saw there was nothing left behind about here. . . ." Max touched his rib cage. "I thought maybe blue-fish had got it . . . like they did to that bird."

"It's possible, if it was bleeding. One of them might take a bite out of it, and then the others see how easy it is and get in a frenzy and—"

"No." Again Max shook his head. "I thought maybe a shark, but when I got real close I saw . . . the deer had no eyes. Everything around the eyes was all torn. A shark wouldn't do that . . . couldn't."

"No. So you were right the first time . . . blue-fish, probably."

Max ignored him. "I saw something sticking out of its cheek . . . something shiny. . . . I tried to reach for it but couldn't, so I took a step and slipped . . . fell in."

"What was it?"

Max opened his right hand. The wound in his palm was small and shallow, and already the bleeding had stopped. He passed the shiny thing to his father.

"Looks like a shark tooth," Chase said as he took the thing and turned out of the shadow cast by his own torso.

"That's what I thought, too."

But then, as Chase moved to the light on his desk and examined the thing in his hand, he started, and felt his pulse leap.

It did look like a shark tooth, a great white shark's tooth, perhaps fossilized, for it was a dingy gray color. It was a triangle, about half an inch on a side, and two of its three sides had finely serrated edges that, when Chase ran his thumb along them, shredded his skin as swiftly as a scalpel. The third side was slightly thicker and had a flat base, and on each end of the base was a tiny barbed hook. The two hooks faced each other. One had been broken off just above the barb.

Chase took a ruler from his desk and measured the triangle. It was not half an inch on a side but five eighths—exactly five eighths. The thing was a magnificently machined, perfectly precise equilateral triangle.

Chase rubbed it between his thumb and index finger. The gray patina felt like slime, and as he rubbed it, it transferred to his skin.

Now the tooth, or whatever it was, shone like polished silver.

Chase looked at Max. "Is this a joke?" he said. "Tell me you're jerking my chain."

"A joke?" Max shivered and gestured at the goose bumps on his arms and legs, and at the wound in his hand. "Some joke."

"Well, then . . . what kind of animal is there that's got stainless steel teeth?"

13

IT WAS two-fifteen when Buck and Brian Bellamy pushed off from the dock, nearly two hours later than Buck had wanted to leave, and Buck was furious. He had told Brian to fill the two scuba tanks, but his brother had been so wrapped up in helping his girlfriend put together her costume for Waterboro's parade for the Blessing of the Fleet that he hadn't gotten around to it. He had told Brian to be sure the boat was full of gas, but Brian had forgotten, so they'd had to wait for forty minutes in line at the fuel dock while some richbitch put two thousand bucks' worth of diesel into a Hatteras so big that it blocked off all the pumps on the dock.

But Buck held his tongue. It wouldn't do any good to give Brian a chewing-out; Brian was immune to reprimands. After his time in the Army, those two years down in Texas near the border with Mexico, with all that cheap pot and tequila and God knows what else, Brian was pretty much immune to life. Nothing got to him; he was perpetually mellow. The last time Buck had hollered at him, for forgetting all the bait on a fishing trip, Brian had just said, "Aw, piss on it," and had jumped overboard and started swimming. They had been twelve miles offshore.

Buck, though, wasn't mellow; he was damn well excited, this could be the biggest day of his life. So instead of saying anything snappy to Brian he just asked him nicely to please sit on the padded box amidships so it wouldn't bounce around, and then he rammed his throttle forward. There were sailboats thick as flies everywhere in the harbor, and dinghies threading their way among them—people who'd come all the way from down-east Maine and the Jersey shore to watch all the half-assed Blessing folderol—but Buck didn't give a damn. If there was a marine cop around, let him try to catch them. There wasn't much afloat that could catch the *Zippo*. Buck had taken a stock Mako hull and modified the bejesus out of it, then added a turbocharged power plant that could generate four hundred and fifty horses and make the hull get up and *go*.

He cleared Waterboro Point going about thirty, pulled back so as not to jar his precious box while he crossed the wakes of the big boats going in and out of the Watch Hill channel, then hammered the throttle again and kicked in the turbo, heading for Napatree with his speedometer quivering around sixty.

If everything went well with the tests today and the meeting tomorrow, by midweek he could be adding a whole bunch of zeros to his prospects, and he'd be able to tell the folks at Waterboro Lumber to find some other sap to peddle plywood and paint to yuppies. If Brian wanted to come along on the gravy train, he'd let him—all corporations had dim-witted brothers on the payroll—though if he had to put money on it, he'd bet that Brian would choose to stay out there making change at the gas station on the turnpike.

There was no swell rolling in, so Buck kept speed up as he swung around Napatree and headed southeast, aiming for the space between the two humps that were Block Island and Osprey.

"Where we goin'?" Brian shouted over the shriek of the engine.

"To the *Helen J.*"

"Long ways."

"Got a better idea?"

"Nope," Brian said, leaning toward the cooler. "Think I'll have me a foamie."

"Later, Brian. We got head work to do."

"Well, hell, Bucky . . ." Brian sat back.

Brian was right, the wreck of the old schooner *Helen J* was a long way away, but it was the only wreck around decent enough for videotaping. It was shallow, so the light would be good, and it was relatively intact, so it looked good. Buck needed a nice set for the demo movie he was going to make to show the honchos from Oregon. Sure, he could run the tests in a swimming pool somewhere, but it wouldn't look like much, certainly not enough to impress hi-techies with fat checkbooks. Presentation was everything, details counted, and if Buck Bellamy was anything, he was a details man.

"Look there," Brian said, pointing off to starboard.

Buck looked, and saw a big yellow buoy with lettering on it. "So? A buoy."

"Never seen a buoy like that. Wonder what's under it."

"Got no time to look, Brian. We lost a lot of time."

"Could be a boat," Brian said thoughtfully. "Storm last week, maybe somebody lost a boat, buoyed it for the barge to find . . . could make pretty pictures."

"Fat chance," Buck said, but as he passed the buoy, he thought: Why not have a look? Give it five minutes, and if it is a boat, a newly sunk boat, those five minutes could save me two hours. He throttled back and swung the boat in a tight circle. "Good idea," he said. "You're thinking, Brian."

Brian beamed. "I can, Bucky, when I put my mind to it." He leaned over the bow and grabbed the buoy and brought it aboard, straining at the weight of the coil of wire.

"Power wire," said Buck.

"What's the 'O.I.' mean?"

"Who cares? There's *some* thing down there. Put a tank on and have a look while I set up the gear."

"Right, I'll have a look."

"But just a look, Brian. Down and up, that's it. I don't want you sucking up a bottle of air dicking around on some lobster trap."

Brian nodded. "A bounce dive. I like bounce dives."

"And you're good at 'em, too," Buck said. Maybe compliments would accomplish what reprimands couldn't.

"Damn right." Brian put the tank harness on over his T-shirt and buckled the belt to which he always kept ten pounds of lead weights attached. He picked up a sheath knife and began to strap it to his calf.

"Think some monster's gonna eat you?" Buck said, smiling.

"You never know, Bucky, and that's a fact." Brian slipped a pair of flippers on, spat in his face mask and rinsed it overboard. Then he sat on the side of the boat, fit the mask over his face, put his mouthpiece in and flung himself backward into the water.

Buck watched until Brian had cleared his mask and, with a burst of bubbles, begun to recede downward into the gray-green gloom. Then he opened the padded box nestled before the console.

There were two full-face masks in Styrofoam beds inside the box. Each resembled half of the helmet of a space suit, and contained an air-regulator apparatus, a microphone and an earphone. On the back of each mask, secured by straps, was a small rubber-covered box about the size of a cigarette pack. It was this box that represented Buck's future.

What Buck had invented was an inexpensive, compact, self-contained underwater communications system. His was not the first device to allow divers to talk to one another underwater—he had no illusions about that—but all the existing systems had two major drawbacks: conversations had to be relayed through a receiver-transmitter on a boat or platform on the surface, and they cost several thousand dollars, which limited their use to commercial or scientific professionals. With Buck's system, two or three (or five or ten) divers could talk directly to one another, just like on a telephone conference call, and the devices could be manufactured for less than two hundred dollars apiece. The average sport diver spent well over a thousand dollars on equipment, so a couple of hundred more—especially for something exotic, glamorous and potentially lifesaving— amounted to nickels.

Buck had run the numbers so many times that by now they were burned into his memory: there were said to be about four million divers in the U.S. alone; if his system was mass-produced, its unit cost could be halved; add another fifty bucks for distribution and advertising. If he went with an aggressive company that marked each unit up 200 percent, and if they sold units to a quarter of the divers in the U.S., and if he took a 10 percent gross royalty, he could be looking at thirty million dollars.

And all thanks to a chance discovery . . . no, that wasn't true, he didn't believe in chance, not after ten years of tinkering with video and sound systems in his father's garage. Anyway, it was all thanks to discovering a new combination of wires and transistors and relays.

Now all he had to do was make a decent three-minute video for the guys who were flying in from Oregon, with high-fidelity sound of him and Brian talking crystal-clear across fifty or a hundred feet of open water. And if the guys still weren't convinced, why, he'd bring them out here and let them try it themselves. That was another beautiful thing: the system was so simple it could be used by anybody. Even his brother.

"Bucky!" Brian burst from the water and grabbed the low bulwark on the stern of the boat. "There's a coffin down there!"

It took a moment for Brian's words to sink in. Then Buck said, "Bullshit, Brian . . . come on . . ."

"I swear! Either that or a treasure chest. You gotta come see it."

"Brian . . . we been diving out here a thousand times. There's fishing boats, car wrecks, a tow barge, a bunch of barrels and the *Helen J.* There's no fuckin' coffin! There's no treasure chest. Besides, you wouldn't know a treasure chest if it up and—"

"There is now, Bucky. A big one, too . . . looks like it could be made of *bronze.*"

Brian was slow, but he didn't have much of an imagination, he didn't make up things. If there was a big chest down there, with something in it . . .

"I wonder . . ." Buck said, ". . . that storm . . ."

"That's what I was thinkin'. Probably churned it up."

Buck reached over and helped Brian aboard. "Let's go for it," he said.

He rigged the masks and connected Brian's wires for him and reminded him of the procedures for clearing the faceplate. Then he mounted the video camera in its housing, attached a bracket that held two 250-watt lamps—for insurance if the water was dark, for fill light if it wasn't—and plugged the connector from the housing into his own mask. He ran a few seconds of tape of himself and Brian in the boat, then watched the playback through the viewfinder to make sure everything was working. The picture was sharp, the sound perfect.

They sat on either side of the boat and, on cue, flopped overboard.

Buck went down first, kicking as hard as he could and guiding himself with his free hand on the wire. The water was murky, and there was a moment when he found himself suspended in a green haze, unable to see either the surface or the bottom. He gripped the wire and stopped.

"Did you check the depth?" Buck's words reverberated hollowly in his mask.

"I didn't go all the way down," Brian said from a few feet up the wire. "I just went till I got a good look."

Buck heard each of Brian's words as clearly as if he were standing beside his brother on the surface. "Isn't the sound in this thing fabulous?" he said.

"You're at fifty now," said Brian. "Drop down another ten, twenty feet."

Buck exhaled and thrust downward with his legs, pushing the video camera in front of him.

What he saw first looked like a yellow-green blur in a pea-green murk; then, as he drew nearer, it took shape: a perfect rectangle, at least eight feet long, maybe ten, and about four feet wide and four feet thick. When he was ten feet above it, Buck framed it in his viewfinder, turned on his lights and swam in a slow circle around it, taping as he went.

He heard Brian say, "Must be somethin' good if they bothered to buoy it."

"They didn't buoy it, they snagged it. Look there: that's some kinda sensor head caught underneath, between the thing and that rock." Buck swam closer. "I don't even think they know what they got."

"Then it could be *really* good."

"It could . . . or it could be fuck-all . . . just some bronze somebody chucked overboard."

"Why'd anybody do that? You can sell bronze for good money."

" 'Cause people are assholes," Buck said. "Anyway, we won't know till we open it."

"You're gonna *open* it?"

"Think of the tape, Brian. Even if the guys from Oregon jerk us around, think of the tape we'll get. First guys to open a long-lost bronze box. I tell you, we can sell it to *Eyewitness News* for . . . who knows how much?"

"But suppose there's a body in it. That wouldn't be—"

"There's no body, unless it's King Kong himself. Look at the size of the damn thing. It must've fallen off a ship, probably something valuable, too, if they took the trouble to case it in bronze." Buck turned off the camera and let himself drift down to the sand bottom. He steadied himself, adjusted the lamps, the focus of the lens. "Okay, Brian, swim down to it and sit on it so I can take your picture, show how big it is."

"I don't know . . ." Brian hesitated, kicking slowly to maintain a position six or eight feet above the box.

"C'mon, Brian . . . don't you want to be famous?"

14

IN THE sealed box the ambient pressure was constant, but in the electromagnetic field nearby, there was a change. It sensed this. There was life nearby, life of size and substance.

And then a sound—though it did not recognize sound as sound but only as a minuscule compression of the tympanic membranes on either side of its head.

Then the sound stopped.

It was ravenous with hunger. When all the nourishment it had derived from the meal it had had in the alien and threatening surroundings above had been used up, it had left its box and hunted.

It had found that there was no food here. It had emerged and sought to feed on some of the countless tiny animals to which it had become accustomed, but had found nothing. Confused, it had swum up and down the water column, seeking life—any life—that would give it sustenance.

It had seen living things, but they had been too swift, too wary, too elusive. It had struck one or two, but been unable to catch them.

Increasingly desperate, driven by signals that it knew only as need, it had swum farther afield.

It had found food—some, not much, barely enough to maintain life.

There had been a small thing that had suddenly appeared above, thrashing in panic, and it had grabbed the thing and taken it down and consumed it, collecting indigestibles—fur and gristle—in the side of its mouth, like a cud, and then spitting them out.

There had been a larger thing, almost as large as itself, also above, not at home here, and it had seized it from below and dragged it down and tried to consume it. But it had been too big to consume at once, and the uneaten part had drifted away. It had followed the body until a wave had carried it out of the water, out of range.

Then another living thing, slow and clumsy, had fallen into the water, almost within its grasp, but had escaped.

Its programming told it that it must hunt soon, and successfully, or surely it would cease to exist.

It knew there was a living thing nearby now.

It would eat it.

15

"STRADDLE THE box," Buck said, "like a horse."

"I can't, it's too wide."

"Then sit sidesaddle. Pose for me. Pretend you're in *Playgirl.*"

Tentatively, awkwardly, Brian swung his legs over the side of the box. To steady himself against the current, with one hand he gripped the heavy black wire that led up to the surface.

He's spooked, Buck thought as he watched Brian through the viewfinder. In another minute, he's gonna bolt for the boat. To distract him, Buck asked, "How's your air?"

Brian reached for his gauge, raised it to his mask. "Fifteen hundred. How long we been down?"

"We got another ten, fifteen minutes anyway."

Brian leaned over the edge of the box and ran

his hand along the lip of the lid. "How you gonna open the thing?" he said. "Don't look to be a latch anywheres."

"If we have to, we'll go up and get a pry bar."

"S'pose it's alive in there . . . a specimen, like."

Buck laughed. "That box coulda been here years. What the hell could be alive?" He finished shooting, turned off the camera and let it hang from the thong around his wrist. "Now, let's see if we can crack that sucker open."

Brian slid down off the box, and as he landed, his flippers disturbed the fine sand, kicking up a cloud of milky silt. He saw something fly upward in the cloud, then settle again a few feet away. "What's that?" he said.

"What'd you see?" asked Buck, and he kicked slowly over toward Brian.

Brian dropped to his knees and ran his fingers along the surface of the sand until they touched something solid. He picked it up and looked at it. "A bone," he said.

"What kinda bone?"

Brian held it up. It was about five inches long, and curved. "Looks like a rib bone. I dunno what from."

"Size of it, I'd say a dog."

"What's a dog bone doing down here?"

"Beats me," said Buck. "See if there's any more."

He dropped down beside Brian, and together they began to dig.

· · ·

It sensed faint sounds from the sand nearby.

Prey.

It felt for the release button. It pressed the button. Slowly the lid began to rise.

· · ·

"Look here," Buck was saying. "A jawbone. It's a dog for sure, and something ate it." He held up the jaw and pointed to slashes in the bone. "Tooth marks."

Buck saw something dark in the ashy silt, and he reached for it. It was round and blackish and hard, roughly the size of a plum. He ran his finger over its surface, first one way then the other. "I'll be damned, Brian . . . it's a fur ball . . . like what a cat pukes up."

Buck rose to his feet and took a step backward. He raised the camera and switched it on. "Two shots, Brian, then we're gone," he said. "Hold up a couple bones and the fur ball. You can go back up to the boat if you want, while I open the box."

· · ·

It swam out of the box and landed on the sand. Because its body contained no air spaces, it was not weightless in water, it was negatively buoyant: it would sink. But because, like all of its kind, its chemical composition was more than 90 percent water, it was only a few pounds negative. It could hover with almost no effort, and—thanks to the webbing on its extremities—it could swim very fast, it could actually fly through the water.

Now it propelled itself off the bottom and veered toward one end of the box.

. . .

Buck had composed a perfect shot. Brian filled the frame, on his knees, holding two bones in one hand and the fur ball in the other, all nicely contrasted against the white sand. Buck pushed the "record" button.

"Good job, Brian," he said. "Now smile, like you're selling something in a commercial." He saw Brian try to smile, then look up at the camera.

Suddenly Brian's eyes opened wide, and he dropped everything and shouted something.

"Brian!" Buck said. "Goddamnit!"

. . .

There were two things, not one. They were big and slow and very close.

It pushed off the bottom and lunged forward, thrusting porpoise-like with its posterior webs. It covered the short span of open water in less than a second.

From somewhere in its numbed brain came a recollection of these beings, a familiarity, and with the recollection came a sense of purpose: its mission was to kill these things.

As hungry as it was, as satisfied as it would have been with eating only one of them, it was programmed to kill both.

It seized the first, and buried its claws in soft flesh.

· · ·

Brian reeled backward on the sand and watched, paralyzed, as a cloud of blood—dark green at this depth—exploded from Buck's carotid artery. Buck's legs jerked, throwing up a cloud of silt, and his hands flew upward.

Brian couldn't see what had Buck, but it was big, and whitish, and it had come from somewhere near the bronze box.

Through the murk he saw silver flashes tearing again and again at Buck's throat, until his head was connected by nothing but bones and sinew.

Brian scuttled backward, and then he realized that safety lay not horizontally but vertically; he pushed off the bottom and kicked upward, reaching frantically for the rubber-coated black wire that led up to the buoy on the surface. He found it and began to pull himself upward.

But the wire had bowed in the running tide, and Brian's weight merely consumed the slack in the bow: instead of pulling himself up, he was pulling the wire down. Relieved of tension from above, the sensor that had snagged beneath the box slid free and bounced along the sand. Now the boat above was drifting free, carrying the sensor, and Brian, with it.

Brian looked down and saw Buck's body sag to the sand, still spilling blood.

Then the thing turned toward him.

It had eyes, chalky white, hueless eyes.

It pushed off the sand like a rocket. It seemed to be flying up at him.

Still kicking, still pulling with one hand, Brian reached for the knife strapped to his calf. His fingers scrabbled at the rubber safety ring that held the knife in its sheath. It stretched, snapped back, stretched again and flopped away. Brian yanked the knife from its sheath.

The thing continued to soar upward, kicking like a dolphin, making no sound, blowing no bubbles. Its claws reached for Brian—ten of them, each curved like a little scythe.

Brian glanced up; the surface wasn't far, he could see the sun. Rays of brilliance slashed downward through the green water.

Then he looked down, and the thing was upon him. Its mouth opened, and a flash of sunlight struck row upon row of triangular teeth and made them glitter like silver stars.

Into his mask Brian screamed, "No!" But there was no one to hear him.

Claws dug into his ankle, puncturing the flesh and dragging him down.

He raised the knife and swung it blindly. Something grabbed his wrist, and steel slivers cut through the veins and tendons. The knife fell away.

He released the wire and flailed with his other hand, but it, too, was grabbed, and his arms were forced wide and his head thrust backward.

He tried to scream, but as he opened his mouth, something thudded against his mask, stunning him.

And then he felt the teeth at his throat.

His last sight was of a cloud of his own blood billowing up against the rays of yellow sun, a mist of orange.

· · ·

It sensed that the thing was dead. It held on with claws and teeth, and spiraled downward with its prey in a slow ballet of death.

Once on the bottom, it carried the prey over to where the other one lay on the sand, rolling back and forth in the current. And then it began to feed.

· · ·

On the surface, the small boat was caught in the flooding tide. It moved quickly, spinning erratically in lazy circles because of the drag caused by the heavy rubber-coated wire dangling off the bow.

It grounded briefly on a shallow reef, but the surge from a distant ship lifted it gently up and over the reef and sent it on toward shore.

16

CHASE AIMED the bow of the Whaler toward an empty slip in one of the floating docks in front of the tiny yacht club on the western edge of the borough. He wasn't a member of the club—he didn't play tennis, race sailboats or wear pastel slacks emblazoned with ducks—but he had known most of the members for decades, liked many of them, and they never begrudged him the loan of one of their coveted slips.

The water was glass calm in this hour after dawn, as if the day's breeze hadn't decided which direction to blow. Seabirds hadn't yet begun to feed, so beds of fry made barely a ripple as they scurried aimlessly between anchored yachts.

Chase pulled the gearshift lever back into neutral, then turned the key that killed the engine, letting the boat nose silently into the slip. He saw Max standing in the bow, ready to fend off the dock, and told himself: keep your mouth shut, don't warn him again to be careful that his fingers don't get squashed between the boat and the dock, don't tell him again to watch his balance so he doesn't fall overboard.

Max bent his knees and braced himself and fended off perfectly, hopped up onto the dock with the painter in one hand and cleated it off like an expert.

Chase didn't say anything as his son cleated the stern line, didn't congratulate Max or even nod in acknowledgment of a job well done. But he did congratulate himself as he noticed Max's little smile of pride, for he realized that he was learning something nearly as difficult as how to be a parent—when and how to *stop* being a parent.

He passed Max his knapsack and climbed up onto the dock, and they walked together toward the parking lot.

A single gull cawed in the distance, and somewhere in the borough a dog barked. Otherwise, the loudest sound they heard was the soft hiss of their feet on the dewy grass.

Then, carried across the treetops, came the muted bong of a church bell ringing six times.

"Six o'clock," Max said, and he looked around as if in discovery. "I've never been up at six before. Ever. I mean, since before I can remember."

"At this time of day, everything's new and clean," said Chase. "It's the time for belief in second chances."

"I should've come with you before." Max started to say something more, hesitated, then took a breath and said, "You're worried about money, aren't you . . . about maybe losing the island?"

"Not at six o'clock in the morning, I'm not." Chase smiled. "It's impossible to worry about money at six o'clock in the morning."

They reached the parking lot, and Chase leaned against the wall of the clubhouse and stretched his calves and thighs while Max unzipped his knapsack and spread his gear on the pavement.

For the first days Max had been with him, Chase had gone running alone, waking, automatically as always, at five or five-thirty and circling the island six times, a course of two miles, more or less. He had showered, shaved, dressed and eaten, and was at his desk or in one of the labs by the time Max got up at eight or nine, grumpy and uncommunicative until infused by Mrs. Bixler with glucose and protein.

Last night, for no apparent reason, Max had asked if he could go with his father in the morning.

"Sure," Chase had said. "Why?"

"I don't want to miss anything."

"What's to miss? You huff and you puff."

"And you feel great, right?"

"On good days, yeah. You pump the beta-endorphins, and you feel great."

"So," Max had said, "I want to go with you."

Chase hadn't pressed the boy because suddenly, blessedly, he had understood what Max was really saying—that he had a month to be with his father and, though he probably didn't know he was looking for them, to uncover things, find answers, solve riddles about himself. Thirty days to make up for eight years. Like an archaeologist digging for clues to a lost people, Max was determined to scrape away the overgrowth of years and find out who he was and where he had come from.

The only problem was, Max didn't actually want to run, he wanted to Rollerblade, because his hockey coach had said it was the best way for him to improve his skating so he'd have a chance to make the varsity hockey team this coming winter. That meant going into town, for there was no paved surface on Osprey Island and thus no place on which to Rollerblade for more than five feet.

Chase had debated pressing Max to run with him on the island, arguing that to waste gasoline in search of pavement rather than to run on nature's own grass and rocks was a kind of corruption. But as he had formed the words in his mind, he realized that he was sounding like a pious pain in the ass.

So they had taken the Whaler and left the island at sunrise and gone into Waterboro.

As they had planed across the flat water, Chase had felt a niggling sensation that something was awry . . . missing or out of place or just . . . wrong. He didn't know what it was, but it was there, somewhere in his mind.

His buoy. That was it. The one he and Tall Man had dropped the other day to mark the sensor head. They had meant to come back and dive the sensor up, but the compressor needed a part from New London, and so they didn't have air. They had gotten busy with other things; after all, the sensor wasn't about to go anywhere.

But where was the buoy? He should have seen it as they approached Napatree Point, but he hadn't, and now they were past Napatree, and as he looked eastward he was blinded by rays of the rising sun.

He dismissed it; the buoy was surely there, they'd find it on the way back.

· · ·

Chase finished stretching and pretended to be busy, double-knotting his running shoes and doing knee bends, as he glanced at Max putting on his elaborate outfit: knee pads, elbow pads, helmet and, finally, a pair of black high-top lace-up shoes soled with yellow rubber wheels. The boy looked like a B-movie robot.

All Chase said was "That's safe, is it?"

"Sure."

"So how come all the pads?"

"Well . . . it can be kinda hard to stop."

"So you're like a runaway train." Chase grinned. "Okay, killer, let's go for it."

"Where to?"

"You haven't seen the borough yet." Chase pointed. "We'll make a circuit: down Beach Street to the point, then back up Oak Street and down here. That's a mile plus. If you're still feeling your oats, we can shoot out to Route One and back."

"Okay." Max stood up on the grass, as shaky as a newborn calf, and hobbled onto the pavement. The first foot to hit the hard ground skidded forward, and he staggered, windmilled with his arms, tottered, splayed and recovered. He smiled sheepishly and said, "Little rusty."

"That's a *sport*?" Chase shouted in mock alarm. "Jeez, maybe after breakfast we can have a friendly game of Russian roulette."

"Just watch," Max said, and he leaned forward, pushed off with one foot, took a couple of long, striding steps, spread his arms and, as Chase watched in surprise, described a graceful circle around the parking lot. Then he pumped a fist in triumph and skated off toward the road that led into town.

Chase wanted to shout out warnings about traffic, pedestrians—about all the perils of growing up too fast—but he didn't. He took a few deep breaths and started to run.

As he crested the gentle hill that led into the borough, he smelled the aroma of cinnamon buns and frying bacon from the two restaurants on Beach Street that catered to the locals who worked early shifts at Electric Boat.

There was no traffic this early, so he ran down the middle of Beach Street, waving to Sally, who was stacking vegetables in front of the Borough Market, to Lester, who was unloading cases of beer from his truck at the back of his liquor store, and to Earl, who had been purveying newspapers, magazines, cigarettes, gum and paperbacks from the same storefront since long before Chase was born.

Everybody waved back, everybody had a word for him and Chase suddenly regretted that he didn't come into town more often. This was home, home was people and he wondered if his passion for his island was becoming unhealthy, turning him into a recluse.

He ran past Veterans Square and the old bank building that still displayed the tattered flag that had flown on the point when the British, in a fit of malicious whimsy, had shelled Waterboro during the War of 1812.

Chase met Max at the end of the point, where they spent a moment appreciating the sunrise. Then they turned back and, with Max zigzagging like a minesweeper in front of his father, threaded their way through the little side streets until they emerged onto Oak Street, with its stately captains' houses from the glory days of whaling.

Oak Street was wide, straight, open and empty. "I'm gonna pump," Max said. "See you back at the club."

"Go for it. Just be—"

But Max was gone, churning with his legs, sweeping with his arms, head down, back bent, his rubber wheels humming on the macadam.

Chase sprinted after him, more for the exercise than from any real hope of being able to keep up with him, but after two blocks he was winded, and he slowed to his normal rhythmic lope.

Max pulled away, a block ahead, then two, then became only a dark blur speeding down the shaded street.

Chase saw the girl first, saw her step out of the door of the house and turn back to pull the door closed and cross the sidewalk—looking not at the street but down into her tote bag—and step into the street.

He shouted, but his words were whipped away in the wind.

Max probably never saw her, for his head was down; he certainly never heard her, for the padding in his helmet pressed tightly against his ears.

Chase saw the girl's head suddenly snap up, the tote bag fall from her arms, and her hands rise toward her face.

Max must have sensed her then, somehow felt her presence, for he jerked upright and tried to veer to the right. One foot must have hit the other, or crossed over it, for his feet came to a sudden stop and his upper body catapulted forward. One of his wheeling arms struck the girl and spun her into a parked car. She bounced off the car and fell to the street in a billow of blue cotton skirt.

Chase saw Max fly for a moment in gangly slow motion and fall like a shotgunned bird, striking the ground first with his knees, then with his elbows, then with his head. He somersaulted once, and lay still.

Chase accelerated to a sprint, his mind cursing and praying while his body gasped for oxygen.

He saw the girl grasp the bumper of a car and pull herself to her feet. She walked over to Max and knelt down and touched his face. Max sat up, they looked at each other and Max said something; the girl shook her head.

Chase saw the girl turn her head his way, see

him and suddenly jump to her feet, grab her tote bag and, with a last look at Max, disappear down an alley between two houses.

By the time Chase reached Max, the girl was gone.

Max was on his hands and knees. He reached a hand up, and Chase took it and pulled him to his feet, keeping an arm around his waist to steady him. "Are you okay?"

"Sure." Max smiled wanly. "That's why the pads." He gestured at his knees, and Chase saw that the fabric covering the pads was tattered.

"What about the girl?"

"She's fine . . . just shaken up."

"She said that?"

"Not . . . not exactly." Max frowned, as if unsure what the girl had said.

"So how do you know she's fine?"

"I don't know . . . I just know."

"Max . . ." Chase felt himself growing angry, and he fought to keep his mouth from surrendering to his temper. "Look, you *creamed* that kid. Maybe she's hurt and doesn't know it. Maybe she's looking for a doctor right now."

"She's not," Max said flatly.

"Why'd she run off?"

"I don't know."

"What did she say?"

"Nothing."

"What d'you mean, nothing? She has to have said *some*thing . . . like, 'It's okay' or 'How are you?' or 'Why don't you look where you're going?' "

"No," Max said, "she never said a word. She came over, and I said, 'I'm really sorry, are you okay?' and all she did was touch my face and smile. But it was like she *was* talking, like inside my head I could hear the words."

"What words?"

"I'm not sure, maybe they weren't even real words but more a kind of feeling . . . sort of a 'Don't worry' and 'I'm glad you're not hurt' kind of thing." Max paused. "Then she saw you and took off."

"Christ, we don't even know who she is. I didn't notice what house she came out of." Chase glanced down the alley as if expecting to see the girl, but the alley was empty. Then he turned back to Max. "Well," he said, pointing at Max's blades, "you want to take those things off and we'll walk back to the club?"

"No, I'm fine, let's keep going. It's this helmet, that's the problem. I never heard her."

"Stick close to me, then, I'll be your eyes and ears."

"Right," Max said. "I'll circle you like you're a defenseman."

Chase smiled. "Great, maybe we can share a

room in the intensive-care unit." He started off at a jog.

When they reached the end of the street, Chase had to make a choice: they could proceed ahead and return to the club and get in the boat and go back to the island, or they could take more time, get more exercise, by winding through the small back streets on the east side of the borough.

Jogging in place, he looked at Max, who was happily skating backward and pretending to cradle a puck with an imaginary hockey stick, and decided that the boy was indeed unhurt and could use the workout. So he turned right off Oak Street and ran down toward the big red-brick building that had once been the borough school and was now a complex of apartments.

The street dead-ended in a chest-high stone wall beside the building. Normally, Chase would have turned several yards before the end of the cul-de-sac, but in the bay beyond he saw a flock of terns feeding, and the sunlight on their white bodies and on the water that splashed as they dove looked like a spray of diamonds. He kept going toward the wall, pointing out the terns to Max, who sped by him and circled to a stop.

They watched the terns for a moment, turned to go, and as Chase's eyes left the water, he saw something in the rocks at the water's edge. He paused.

"What?" Max said.

"I'm not sure." Chase looked again, scanning the narrow expanse of pebbles and boulders. Max leaned on the wall beside him. "Where are you looking?"

"By that mess of weed," Chase said, pointing.

A wave lifted the clump of weed and moved it a couple of feet closer to shore.

"Dad!" Max shouted. "It's a hand!"

17

ITS FINGERS were locked in a claw, as if whoever it was had been trying to climb something or grab something or fight off something at the moment he or she had died.

"Stay here," Chase said, and he hauled himself up onto the wall, swung his legs over and dropped down onto the pebbly strand.

"But Dad . . ." Max was already unlacing his Rollerblades.

"Stay *here!*" Walking toward the clump of weed, Chase tried to recall if he'd heard of anyone reported missing. Then he wondered how long it took a drowned body to rise to the surface again. It happened, he knew that: after a while the gases in a body built up, and as they expanded, the corpse would float.

The clump of weed was huge, extending far out into the water. Chase didn't want to touch the hand—what if that was all there was to it, or what if there was more but it was so rotten that it fell apart?—so he used his running shoe to nudge aside the rubbery strands of weed.

He saw a head then, and what was left of a face, and bile rushed up the back of his throat and poured into his mouth. He dropped to his knees, coughing and spitting.

The skin was whitish gray; the eyes were gone, and the earlobes and the lips. There was more of the body snarled in the weed—no blood left in it, just shredded white flesh interlaced with strands of neoprene wet suit.

"Call the police," he said to Max. "Go down to Beach Street, the news office, and ask Earl to call the police."

"Who . . . who is it?"

"I don't know."

"What happened?"

"Just *go!*" Chase said, and almost immediately he heard the rattle of Max's wheels on the pavement.

When he thought he could look again without retching, Chase crawled closer. The face was unrecognizable, but there was something familiar about the hand.

The watch. The watch on the wrist of the hand with the rigored claws was one of those diver's watches that did everything but rinse your socks—told the time in every zone on the planet, had windows for bottom time, lap time and phases of the moon. It was the watch of a gimmick freak, and he'd seen it before. But where?

It came to him: Waterboro Lumber, holding out a can of WD-40. He had remarked on the watch, and the owner had insisted on explaining every function and had told him how to order one.

Buck Bellamy, that's who it was. Could this be what was left of Buck Bellamy? But why? Buck was an expert boatman, a certified scuba diver, and in high school he'd been a competitive swimmer.

He had been diving, the wet suit was evidence of that. What could have killed him? Maybe he'd gotten bad air—people sometimes were careless about where they filled their tanks, and died of carbon monoxide poisoning. Maybe he'd had a heart attack or a stroke, or been chopped up by a boat propeller, or . . . Christ knew what.

Chase peeled more of the weed away, and he saw the other arm. All the flesh between elbow and shoulder was gone, and there were deep gashes in the bone of the upper arm, as if a big fish or a small shark had grabbed the arm and shaken it back and forth and gnawed on it like a dog with a bone too big to crush.

Around the wrist was a thong, and attached to

the thong was a steel housing containing a video camera.

. . .

"*You* tell *me,* Simon," said Police Chief Roland Gibson. "You're the shark expert. What kind of shark'd do a job like that?"

"None," Chase said. "None I know of. Not around here."

They were sitting in Gibson's office in the station house on Route 1. Polaroid pictures of Buck Bellamy's remains were spread out on Gibson's desk, and Buck's video camera was plugged into a television set in a bookcase.

A police car had arrived within five minutes, an ambulance a few minutes later, and by the time the body had been photographed and bagged and taken away to the medical examiner in New London, a small crowd had gathered by the stone wall.

At Gibson's request, Chase and Max had been brought to the station house, and their statements had been taken. Now Max sat in the lobby while Chase and Gibson talked.

"Nice, Simon," Gibson said. "First you tell me it looks like a shark attack, then you tell me there are no sharks around here that attack people."

"I didn't say a shark *attacked* him, Rollie, I said it looks like a shark might've bitten him . . . after Buck was already dead."

"What makes you think so?"

"Shark attacks are rare anywhere, and un-heard-of around here. A man's got a better chance of being killed by a feral cat or a farmer's pig than by a shark. For one thing, there are damn few dangerous sharks in these waters. Sand sharks are bottom feeders; they'd never go after a swim-mer, let alone a diver, but they might nibble on a dead body on the bottom. Makos are scarce, they're loners, and they live in deep water and follow schools of pelagics—tuna and jacks. The odds are a million to one against a mako wander-ing into shallow water, especially murky shallow water like around here. A blue shark's a possibil-ity; a blue might make a run at a person if he was bleeding, and if a bunch of them went after some-one, they'd rip him to pieces. But we'd see the evidence—the bite marks are obvious."

"What about white sharks? They're around, you've told me so yourself."

"Sometimes," Chase said, unwilling to tell Gib-son about the big white he and Tall Man had tagged only last week. The last thing he wanted was a mass vendetta against white sharks by an armada of bloodthirsty macho loons. "But rarely . . . almost never. And, hell, if a great white shark had wanted to eat Buck, it would've eaten him. Period. If it had made a run at him by mistake, maybe thinking he was a seal—divers in wet suits on the surface look like seals to a shark—Buck would've probably been sheared in half. We might find the other half, we might not, but if we did, the bite marks would be definitive: big, nasty half-moons. We sure wouldn't find him with his throat torn out and meat bitten off him here and there like he'd been served up at a banquet."

Gibson paused. "I guess we have to wait for what the M.E. says. Maybe like you say, Buck just died. People do."

There was a rap on the door, and a patrolman stepped into the room. "They found Buck's brother, Chief," he said. He hesitated, then added, "Over on Seagull Point."

"What's the matter? You look awful."

"He's dead, too. Half et. Just like the other one. Like Buck. Only difference, this one, Brian, had a knife scabbard strapped to his leg."

"Just the scabbard?" Gibson said. "No knife?"

"Nope, the knife was gone. The scabbard had one of them rubber safety rings, too, so the knife didn't just fall out."

"Which means Brian *had* it out, in his hand." Gibson looked at Chase. "So much for natural causes, wouldn't you say?" He nodded to the patrolman. "Okay, Tommy."

"There's Nate Green out here wants to see you."

"Shit, I knew the fucking press would get onto

this." Gibson sighed. "You might's well send him in, else he'll have it all over Connecticut that Hannibal Lecter's out there eating people." When the patrolman had left, Gibson said to Chase, "At least it's Nate and not some hotshot looking for a Pulitzer prize. I can keep Nate on the leash with an exclusive or two and a couple scotches."

Nate Green, a reporter for the Waterboro *Chronicle,* was a thirty-year veteran who had once wanted to work for a big-city daily but had finally reconciled his modest talent with a comfortable life by the seashore.

Green came into the room and closed the door behind him. He was in his mid-fifties: soft and overweight, drinker's veins crisscrossing his nose and cheeks like a road map.

"I hear we got some excitement," he said as he smiled at Gibson and shook hands with Chase and sat down in the empty chair facing the desk.

"Maybe," said Gibson. "Do me a favor, Nate. Let's not go jumping to any conclusions."

"I hear Buck had a video camera on him."

Gibson hesitated, then said, "Yeah, but it flooded, the tape got wet. Maybe one of my geniuses did it when they unloaded it, I don't know. Anyway, there's not much on it."

"Mind if I look?"

"Only 'cause I trust you." Gibson gestured to Chase, who got up and turned on the television set and pressed the "play" button on the video camera. "But keep all this to yourself. We don't know exactly what happened here."

"You know me, Rollie," said Green.

A blurred image of Brian Bellamy came on the screen, the tape flickering and jumping as if the signal wouldn't lock in. He seemed to be holding something up to the camera. They heard Buck's voice telling Brian to smile. Then Brian's face changed. His eyes popped wide and his mouth opened and he dropped whatever he was holding and shouted something incoherent.

"Looks like he's seen something," said Green.

"Yeah," Chase said, "but what?"

They heard Buck say, "Brian! Goddamnit!"

"Listen to that," said Gibson. "Buck's cussing him, like maybe Brian started screwing around . . . or went apeshit."

Suddenly the camera zoomed in on the sand bottom, and the screen went dark. There were sounds of shouts and screams, and the camera jolted up again, whirling around in a cloud of fuzz. The water seemed to take on a greenish tone.

"What's that?" Green asked.

"Could be blood," Chase said, "depending on how deep they were. Below thirty-three feet, blood looks green."

The camera fell to the bottom again, more lazily, as if it had been dropped, and all that filled the screen was water.

There was one last word, a voice yelling, "No!"

Green said, "Who was that?"

Chase said, "We don't know."

"Run it again for me, Simon," Gibson said.

Chase rewound the tape and played the scene again. When it was over, Gibson said, "Looks to mc like maybe Brian killed Buck."

"Then what killed Brian?" asked Chase.

"Could be they killed each other."

Green shook his head. "Doesn't make any sense. They were as close as brothers can be. Brian worshiped Buck. Why would he kill him?"

"Drugs," Gibson said. "Brian had a history. Could be he had a relapse and wigged out."

"No, Brian was scared to death of drugs. He went to every N.A. meeting he could find, and if there wasn't one, he'd go to A.A. or Al-Anon . . . even church if he had to. I remember one day I was getting gas, he told me he'd already killed so many brain cells, he was taking care of the ones he had left. A beer now and then was all he ever allowed himself. The Bellamy boys kill each other? No, Rollie, it makes no sense at all."

"You got any better ideas?" Gibson leaned back in his chair and stared at the ceiling.

"Just a mystery, I guess," Green said. "Mysterious death always makes good copy."

"Scares the shit outta people, too," Gibson said.

After a long moment, Gibson made a show of looking at his watch, and stood up. "Speaking of killing brain cells . . . it's only nine-thirty in the morning, and already it's been one long sumbitch of a day." He took a key from his pocket and opened the bottom drawer of a file cabinet, pulled out a bottle of scotch and a stack of paper cups and returned to his desk. He poured two inches of whisky into a cup, passed it to Green, poured another and offered it to Chase, who shook his head. Then he took a sip himself and again leaned back in his chair. "You got people coming in for the Blessing of the Fleet, Nate?"

"My sister and her kids. They'll probably find some excuse to hang around for a week." Green sipped his drink. "Jesus."

Chase didn't know why Gibson had suddenly started talking about the Blessing, but he didn't want to hear about it. He wanted to find Max and return to the island and get to work. He leaned forward as if to rise, started to say something, but Gibson cut him off.

"They say this'll be the biggest Blessing ever, folks coming in from everywhere, specially now the casino gives 'em something to do if it rains and at night."

"So they say," said Green.

"Could give us a real shot in the arm."

"Uh-huh."

Now Chase realized what Gibson was doing, and he knew he'd have to sit there and listen.

"Now, Nate," Gibson said, "I know you have to fill all those column inches, so whyn't you let Simon and me give you a hand with the logic?"

"Okay."

"First off, there's no way this was a shark attack. Simon as much as gave me a deposition about that. Right, Simon?"

"More or less," said Chase. "I said—"

"And the tape," Gibson said to Green. "Remember, you're the only one's seen it, that's an exclusive, and you'd have to agree it sure looks like Brian just suddenly went ape."

"Or saw something that made him go ape."

"Saw what? The Ghost of Christmas Past?" Gibson barked out a laugh.

"Well, that's the question."

"Here's my point: nothin' down there *to* see. The only conclusion a reasonable man can reach is that Brian had an acid flashback or something and went after Buck and got himself killed, too, in the process."

"Where's all the blood come from?"

"Brian's knife."

"Brian had a knife?"

"Sure," Gibson said. "Didn't I tell you that? Strapped to his leg. But when they found him, the knife was gone. There's another exclusive for you."

Green set his cup on the desk and turned to look at Chase. "What do you think, Simon?"

"I don't know what to think," said Chase. "But it all seems a little—"

"You got a better explanation?" Gibson snapped at him.

"No," Chase said, for he didn't. All he would swear to, if it ever came to that, was that neither man had been killed by a shark . . . at least not by any shark he had ever heard of.

"There you have it then, Nate," said Gibson. "You're too good a reporter to go off half-cocked with a lot of dingbat speculation."

Green paused, then said, "You'll let me know what the M.E. says?"

"Soon as he certifies the cause of death." Gibson splashed more whisky into Green's cup. "But I'll bet a dollar to a dime it'll be death caused by a sharp instrument. Seems to me one lesson to pass along to your readers is, drug addicts and maniacs shouldn't go diving."

The patrolman rapped on the door again, opened it and said to Chase, "There was a call for you."

"I'll take it outside," Chase said, standing up.

"No, she's gone," said the patrolman. "It was Mrs. Bixler. She said to tell you the Little Mermaid's arrived."

"Good. Thanks, Tommy." Chase said to Gibson, "Three months' reprieve from debtor's prison . . . I hope." He turned to go.

"Simon . . ." Gibson said, stopping him. "We're all agreed here, right? I mean, in case one of those half-ass TV reporters calls you and wants to make a big deal out of this."

"Sure, Rollie."

"Good." Gibson smiled. "Your institute's getting a real good reputation. You wouldn't want to muddy it up by poking around in police business."

Chase left the room with an uneasy feeling; by the time he reached the lobby, he was sure he had just been threatened.

The patrolman was waiting in the lobby with Max, ready to drive them back to their boat.

"There was one of your buoys about a hundred yards from where they found Brian," the patrolman said. "Length of rubber wire, some electronic thing on the end. I told 'em to leave it there, you could pick it up on your way home."

"Thanks," Chase said. "It must have sprung loose from whatever it got snagged in."

When they were in the car, Max leaned forward from the backseat and said to Chase, "I found her."

"Who?"

"The girl. The one I almost hit."

"What d'you mean, you found her?"

"In the newspaper back there, while I was waiting. There was a picture, some prize she won. And I knew there had to be a reason why she didn't hear me coming. She's deaf."

"Who is she?"

"Her name's Elizabeth."

18

CHASE SLOWED the Whaler as he approached the tip of the low spit of land called Seagull Point, and turned toward shore so he could cruise close to the beach. Brian's body had been found about halfway down the peninsula; Chase's wire should be just this side of the spot, or just beyond.

Max stood in the bow, steadying himself with a rope attached to a cleat. "What'll it look like?" he asked.

"Against that white sand," Chase said, "it should stand out like three hundred feet of black snake."

Seagull Point had once been private property, then a state beach; now it was a bird sanctuary. Gulls bred there, and terns, and though people sometimes beached their boats to swim or picnic, anyone who ventured inland beyond the dunes risked scalp lacerations from being dive-bombed by birds protecting their nests.

Chase could hear the birds screeching at one another, and saw them circling over their nests, but he noticed that there were none diving or floating on the water. He wondered why. Usually, on a day this calm, dozens of birds would be sitting on the surface, waiting for a signal from sentinels overhead that schools of baitfish were on the move.

"Look!" Max said, pointing off the starboard bow.

Chase turned, following Max's gesture, took the boat out of gear and let it coast. He saw something white on the surface; it slipped along the side of the Whaler until Chase reached over the side and stopped it.

It was a dead seagull, floating belly-up. At first Chase thought it was whole, but then he picked it up by one leg and saw that the bird's head was gone.

"Jeez!" Max said, startled.

Chase examined the stump of the bird's neck. He looked for tooth marks, slash marks, anything that might tell him what had decapitated the gull, but there was nothing. As far as he could see, the bird's head had simply been torn from its body.

"There's another one!" Max said.

Chase dropped the dead gull into the bottom of

the boat and put the motor in gear.

The second gull was floating upright, its head lolling forward. It almost looked asleep, but it lay too low in the water, and it bobbed unsteadily. Chase picked it up by its neck, turned it over. Its legs had been ripped off, and there was a ragged wound in its belly.

"What the hell . . ." Chase said.

"Bluefish?" asked Max.

"No, I think bluefish would've finished the job, eaten the whole bird."

"What, then? What did it?"

Chase shook his head. "I don't get it. I don't get *any* of this."

Max stood on tiptoe in the bow, bracing himself with the rope, and looked toward the beach. "There's our wire," he said. "And more birds. Lots more. In the waves."

Chase aimed the boat at the shore and gunned the motor. When he reached shallow water, he turned off the outboard, raised it and locked it in place so the propeller wouldn't catch in the sand. The boat had enough momentum to coast through the wavewash and nudge its bow onto dry sand.

It was like traveling through a slaughterhouse. Dead birds were scattered everywhere in the wavewash—some decapitated, some eviscerated, some with their throats cut. Chase picked up one or two, glanced at their wounds and dropped them back into the water.

"It almost looks like something kids would do," Chase said.

"What do you mean, kids?" said Max.

"Sickos . . . you know . . . vandals. Practically nothing in the ocean kills for the sake of killing. Animals kill for two reasons: to eat and to defend themselves."

Max hopped off the bow; Chase followed and pulled the Whaler farther up onto the sand. They walked up the beach to the black wire, which the policemen had coiled and tied.

They dragged the wire back to the boat, loaded it aboard and pushed off from shore. When Chase judged that the water was deep enough, he lowered the motor and started it. As the propeller roiled the water, another dead bird surfaced and bumped against the side of the boat. Chase lifted it from the water. It was a young tern; its wings had been torn from its body.

"Whatever did this," Chase said, setting the bird gently back into the water, "did it just to do it. Almost for the thrill of it."

He aimed the boat eastward, toward the island.

• • •

When they were halfway home, slicing through long, easy swells, they saw a big, slow, broad-beamed boat heading toward them. The boat had a tiny deckhouse forward and a huge open stern with a davit on each side. As they passed port-to-port, the captain of the big boat tooted his horn, leaned out of the deckhouse door and waved. Chase waved back.

"Who's that?" asked Max.

"Lou Sims. He hauls freight. I guess he just dropped off Dr. Macy and her sea lions . . . must've picked them up at the New London docks."

In the wake of the freight boat was another boat, still a quarter of a mile away but coming fast. It was a sleek white sportfisherman, with a flying bridge and outriggers. As it drew near, it slowed, and a man on the flying bridge signaled to Chase that he wanted to talk.

Chase took the motor out of gear and let the Whaler drift. "Hold on tight," he said to Max. "That thing pushes a mountain of water around it."

As the fishing boat stopped, its deep hull wallowed, and waves surged out from its sides. Chase braced himself as the waves tossed the Whaler from side to side; he saw Max stagger, then half fall, half sit onto the forward thwart.

"Been lookin' for you, Simon," said the man on the bridge. "We were trolling off Watch Hill; I seen a dead dolphin, for crissakes, hitched up in the rocks."

"A dolphin," Chase said. "You're sure it wasn't a shark? It was a dolphin . . . a porpoise?"

"You think I don't know a dolphin from a shark? It was a porpoise. Just like Flipper, only younger, a baby. I couldn't get too close, but the thing looked all cut to ribbons, like something had had at it. I thought you might want to have a look."

"I appreciate it, Tony," said Chase. "I will, right now. Where was it exactly?"

"Just this side of the lighthouse. What the hell lives around here that can catch and kill a porpoise?"

"Beats me." Chase picked up one of the dead birds. "Maybe the same thing that's cutting the heads off seagulls." And maybe, Chase thought to himself, the same thing that killed two divers.

"Well, anyway . . . give me a call when you figure it out."

"I will."

"Is that your boy?"

"Yep," Chase said. "Max . . . Captain Madeiras."

Max waved, and Madeiras said, "Come work for me some summer. You can earn your lunch-pail degree."

"Thank you," Max said, "but I don't have much exper—"

"Don't worry, you couldn't do any worse than

that worthless Bobby down there." Madeiras laughed and gestured at the stern of his boat. Then he shoved his throttles forward, and as the boat leaped ahead, its two propellers scooped a deep cavity into the water.

A teenaged boy stood in the stern, looking unwell and unhappy.

19

BOBBY TOBIN decided that the chances were excellent that sometime in the next five minutes he would throw up. With every breath the stink of blood and guts and diesel exhaust got to him, and he had to swallow constantly to keep bile from oozing into his mouth. Every time the boat yawed in the following sea he felt his stomach drop into his feet and then rush up as if it would burst from the top of his head.

Though he knew it would make him feel better, he didn't want to throw up—wouldn't throw up, refused absolutely to throw up—for Captain Madeiras would never let him forget it. Every customer that came aboard would be regaled with the story of Bobby sprawled on the bulwark heaving his breakfast overboard; lessons would be drawn about landlubbers, teenagers, summer people, Protestants and kids who had life too easy.

Bobby rose off his knees and, careful not to touch his shirt or any part of the gleaming white fiberglass with his bloody hands, leaned over the side and drew several deep breaths of clean air, air that didn't smell of diesel oil and dead fish. He could see Osprey Island behind them, and beyond it Napatree Point, and, far in the distance, the water tower in Watcrboro.

"Hey, asshole," Madeiras called down from the flying bridge, "nobody told you to take a break. Swab that shit off the deck before it dries."

"Yes, sir," Bobby said, and he sucked in a last breath and turned to face the carnage on the after-deck. He had already cleaned ten big bluefish—scaled and gutted them and wrapped each carcass in newspaper—and another twenty waited in the fish box on thc starboard side.

What did two fishermen want with thirty fish? They wouldn't eat more than one or two, there was no market for the rest—bluefish were so plentiful this summer that the fish stores could make money only if they were given the fish for free—and chances were they wouldn't even be able to dole them out to friends.

Trophies, that's all they were, badges of manhood.

A dozen gulls hovered over the boat's wake, cawing impatiently as if hurrying Bobby along.

He picked up the dip bucket by the six-foot length of rope tied to its handle, walked to the open transom in the stern, got a firm grip with his free hand, leaned over the transom and tossed the bucket into the water. It hit, bounced, tipped and suddenly filled, and the weight jerked at Bobby, almost pulling him overboard. He hauled back on the rope and brought the bucket aboard. He sloshed the water on the deck and scrubbed with a brush at the patches of drying blood and scales, shoving them overboard through the transom and the scuppers.

The gulls wheeled over the new blood in the water and squawked when they spied no bits of meat.

Bobby put the bucket aside, dropped to his knees, took the filleting knife from the scabbard on his belt and reached into the box for another bluefish. He slashed its gills to start the blood draining, then slit its belly from throat to tail, reached inside the body cavity and pulled the guts out and tossed them overboard through the transom.

The gulls dove frantically, two of them snatching at the same piece of viscera, and they rose from the water, flapping their wings and screaming as they tugged at the rubbery guts.

Bobby flipped the fish onto its side and began to scale it with the blade of his knife, cursing himself and his father and Madeiras and fate.

God, how he wished he'd gone to summer school instead of taking this job. His father had given him the option, go to summer school or get a paying job. In this economy, jobs were as scarce as teeth in a goose; college graduates were bagging groceries, business school students were tending bar. He'd been turned down everywhere from the Mystic Seaport Museum to the Waterboro marina, and he'd been about to start calling around to summer schools when all of a sudden his father had called in an IOU from the Madeirases.

Manuel, the family's gardener, who had no medical insurance and whose hip-replacement surgery had been paid for by Mr. Tobin, let slip one day that his brother Tony's mate had just come down with hepatitis. Without asking Bobby, Mr. Tobin had called Tony and gotten him the job.

True enough, Bobby had gone along with it. The job had sounded great: mate on a sportfishing boat. Five bucks an hour, plus tips, maybe as much as a hundred bucks a day on good days. Outdoor work. Learn how a professional fishes.

The work was long—seven days a week, weather permitting—but he had every night off, and there were bound to be at least ten days of rain and wind that would keep the boat ashore.

But there were a few things that nobody had told Bobby. First of all, motorboats, especially thirty-eight-footers like the *Sea Hunter,* weren't like sailboats. They didn't ride the wind and cut the waves and stay relatively stable; they bounced and pitched and rolled, soaking you and bruising you and making you sick all day long.

Second, the word *mate* really meant waiter, busboy, garbageman, slopsman, fish-gutter, ass-kisser and drudge. If a customer lost a fish, it was the mate's fault: he hadn't set the hook properly or hadn't grabbed the leader at the right time. If a customer puked, the mate cleaned it up. Worst of all and most common, if a customer clogged the head, ignoring the prominent sign over the flushing mechanism and tossing into the bowl a tampon, a cigarette filter or a condom (it had happened), it was the mate's job to unclog it and clean it out.

Finally, nobody had told Bobby that Tony Madeiras was a sadistic bully, one of those people who inflate themselves by belittling others. He was also an alcoholic, and though he claimed he never drank on the job, "the job" seemed to be ending earlier and earlier every day. A month ago, he wouldn't touch a drop till the boat was tied to the dock; now he was drinking from a flask stowed on the flying bridge as soon as he started in from the fishing grounds.

Most of the customers didn't know or didn't care—like today's two, firemen from New London, who had started on beer at seven in the morning and segued into Bloody Marys at nine.

Bobby cared, though, because he took the brunt of Madeiras's seesawing moods, which could swing from obscene vitriol to lachrymose affection but which tended to linger more on the former than the latter.

He could quit, of course, but he wouldn't because he knew what would happen. He would tell his side of the story to his father, who would pretend to believe him but really wouldn't. His father would call Madeiras and be told (in the polite code that adults used) that Bobby was a whining, spineless, lazy crybaby. His father would never actually *say* that he believed Madeiras, but there would be allusions to disappointment and regret that would go on for at least a year.

Quitting would be too expensive. Better to stick it out for another six weeks.

Bobby was gutting another fish when the glass door to the air-conditioned cabin slid open and a voice said, "Hey, kid, we're outta ice."

"Yes, sir," Bobby said, and he dipped the bucket overboard again and washed his hands and went inside. His hands still stank of fish, but these two would never notice.

· · ·

It swam back and forth in the froth just below the surface, frenzied by a strong, pervasive scent of prey, and confused at finding nothing of substance. There had been a few bits of food, and it had closed on them, only to have them plucked from its grasp by things from above.

Tantalized, it swam onward, absorbing the oily, blood-laced water through its fluttering gills.

· · ·

"Fillet the last couple and put 'em in Baggies for me," Madeiras ordered. "I'll take 'em home to the missus."

"Yes, sir," Bobby said.

There were three fish left in the box, the first three of the day, and the biggest—eight-pounders at least, maybe ten. He grabbed the biggest by the tail and slapped it on the deck. It had been caught hours ago, and its body had already rigored stiff. Its glassy eyes stared in blank menace, and its mouth was frozen open, revealing a row of perfect tiny triangles.

"I'm glad you don't grow to a hundred pounds," Bobby said to the fish as he felt for its backbone and slipped the knife in beside and drew it backward.

He didn't scale this fish or gut it. Instead, with swift slashes of the knife he removed all the meat from one side of the fish, cutting along the backbone, around the tail, up the belly and across the gills. Then he turned the fish over and repeated the procedure on the other side. He shoved the carcass overboard—head, tail, bones, guts and all.

He watched the gulls swarm on the carcass as it bobbed in the wake of the boat. One gull tried to lift it by the head, but it was too heavy, and the bird couldn't get airborne. Another grabbed the tail, and for a moment it seemed that the two birds might cooperate in carrying the carcass away to a safe feeding place. But then a third bird struck the carcass, and it fell away and splashed into the water.

The birds swooped down upon it again. Before they could reach it there was a sudden flurry in the water, a flash of something shiny; when the flurry subsided, the carcass was gone.

· · ·

Its long, curved steel claws tore the dead thing to pieces. It sucked the viscera from the body cavity, and the eyes from the head. Its teeth crushed the bones of the jaw; it ate the tongue. It consumed everything, as it drifted to the bottom.

The large thing from which the food had come

moved away and became a fading pulse on the creature's tympanic membranes.

It wanted more. Not purely from hunger, for it had fed on many things recently—had fed until it regurgitated and then fed some more—but from programmed reflex. Prey was irresistible; killing and eating were its only functions. Though its body was fully fueled, its gastric juices continued to be stimulated.

It pushed off the bottom, its webbed feet thrusting up and down synchronously, its talons gleaming. It flew through the water toward the pulsing sound.

· · ·

Bobby finished filleting the last two fish, tossed the carcasses overboard and wrapped the fillets. He dipped the bucket and washed his hands, and was about to swab the deck, when he heard the engine subside and felt the boat slow, stop and wallow broadside to the little waves.

"Birds up ahead," Madeiras called down. "Looks like a school of blues kickin' shit out of a bed of fry. Ask them two if they want to toss a couple casts."

"Yes, sir," Bobby said. He opened the door to the cabin and felt a rush of icy air. The men had been playing gin rummy on the couch. One had fallen asleep, and the other was fumbling with the cards. An empty vodka bottle was upended in the wastebasket.

Let them say no, Bobby prayed. He didn't want to rig any more lines, clean any more fish. Besides, now that these anglers were plastered, they'd be bound to make mistakes, and he'd be bound to be blamed for them.

"Captain wants to know if you'd like to cast some," Bobby said.

The man looked at Bobby and frowned as if he didn't recognize him. "For what?" he said.

"Bluefish."

The man thought for a moment, then shook his friend's knee, but his friend didn't waken.

"Fuck it," he said.

"Yes, sir." Bobby shut the door and called up to Madeiras, "They said no thanks."

"They'll be sorry," said Madeiras, looking through binoculars at the diving terns. "Those could be real monsters."

Bobby sloshed the bucket of water on the deck, tossed the bucket behind him and scrubbed the blood and scales into the scuppers.

A few spots of dried blood remained, and Bobby picked up the bucket, wrapped the rope around his hand and walked aft.

"Hey, asshole," Madeiras said, "you missed some."

"Yes, sir," Bobby replied tightly. "That's why I'm getting more water."

Madeiras returned to his binoculars. "Soon's you're finished, fetch me my spinning rod. I think I'll try a couple casts from up here."

Go ahead, Bobby thought angrily. Maybe you're so wasted you'll trip and fall overboard and the bluefish'll tear you apart.

The exhaust from the idling engine billowed over the stern, stinging Bobby's eyes and clouding his vision. The gulls hovered high overhead, away from the noxious fumes.

There was no wake now, the boat wasn't moving, so Bobby didn't grip the transom as he flung the bucket. The bucket hit the water on its bottom and bobbed upright; Bobby jiggled the rope, trying to tip it over so it would fill.

· · ·

It approached a dozen feet below the surface. The large thing had stopped moving.

It hovered; its receptors sought signs of prey, but found nothing.

It rose a few feet, and through the still water it could see a refracted image of something moving.

There was a disturbance on the surface, a little sound and a few ripples; it saw something floating.

Prey.

It thrust itself upward, grasping with its claws. Its mouth was agape, its lower jaw rolled forward and a row of triangular teeth sprang erect, into bite position.

. . .

The bucket filled, Bobby pulled on the rope, but even without the drag of motion, the bucket was heavy—two gallons of water weighed sixteen pounds. Bobby pulled the rope hand-over-hand.

Suddenly the rope went taut, as if the bucket had snagged on something. Then it jerked away from him, as if a huge fish had grabbed hold of it.

Bobby lost his balance, turned to grab at the transom, but he was too far away, his fingers found only air and he tumbled overboard. As he hit the water, he thought, I hope it wasn't a big bluefish that grabbed the bucket.

. . .

It spiraled downward, clutching its prey in its claws, gnawing with its teeth at the soft white flesh. It sucked and drank and chewed and swallowed.

By the time it reached the bottom, it could eat no more, so it squatted on the sand and, with claws and teeth, tore the prey to pieces. One tooth caught in a mass of gristle and broke off. Another tooth, from the row behind it, rolled forward and took its place.

. . .

Tony Madeiras hung the binoculars on their hook, put the boat in gear and pushed the throttle forward. The engine growled, the bow rose and the stern settled.

"Where the hell's my rod?" he shouted without looking down. There was no response.

PART FOUR

▲ ▲ ▲ ▲ ▲ ▲ ▲

PREDATORS

20

WHEN CHASE nosed the Whaler into its slip, just after noon, he saw Mrs. Bixler walking down the path to the dock. She was carrying an ancient wicker picnic hamper, and Chase knew what was in it: a sandwich, a thermos of iced tea, a spool of fishing line and some bacon rind or beef fat or stale bread. Mrs. Bixler loved to spend her lunch hour hand-lining off the dock for little fish to feed to the heron. The heron saw her coming and took a couple of spindly steps toward the dock.

As soon as he had turned off the motor, Chase heard barking from the inlet beyond the hill.

"It sounds like Dr. Macy and her sea lions made it safe and sound," he said to Mrs. Bixler.

"Yep, her and her whole menagerie."

"Are those the sea lions barking?" Max asked excitedly. "Can I go see them?"

"Sure," Chase said. "But mind your manners,

introduce yourself. We've never met Dr. Macy."

Max nodded, hopped out of the Whaler and ran up the path.

Mrs. Bixler glanced down into the boat. "Somebody been on a killing spree?" she said, gesturing at the dead animals: two gulls and a juvenile bottlenose dolphin.

"Or some*thing*." Chase picked up the little dolphin. It was less than three feet long; its slick skin, which in life had been a lustrous steel gray, was now dull and flat, like charcoal ash. There were deep slash marks on its back; its belly had been torn open. "I brought it back for Dr. Macy to have a look at. She knows more about mammals than I do."

"What can she tell you that anyone can't? Something slaughtered it."

"Yeah, but what?" Chase returned the dolphin to the bottom of the boat. "I'll pack it in ice till we can do a proper autopsy." He stepped out of the boat, tied it fore and aft and climbed the steps to the dock. "Did you get Macy settled in?" he asked.

"I showed her around; Tall stowed her stuff."

"What's she like?"

Mrs. Bixler shrugged. "Seems to be full of enthusiasm, dresses like she's going on safari. But at least she doesn't parade her degrees like most of them do."

Chase started up the hill, and when he reached the crest, he heard Max's voice—screaming, he thought at first, but then he realized that what he was hearing wasn't screams but laughter.

He looked down and saw Max splashing in the shoulder-deep water in the tank Chase had had built for the sea lions. Four dark shapes zoomed around him, streaking by him underwater, paddling behind him on the surface, deftly avoiding him as he lunged at them.

A woman stood on the lip of the tank, gesturing to the sea lions and laughing with Max.

Because neither she nor Max had noticed him, Chase was able to study her as he walked down the hill.

Tall and sturdily built, Amanda Macy looked like either a model for the Lands' End catalog or the ambassador from the court of L.L. Bean. She was wearing Top-Sider moccasins, knee-length hiking shorts, a khaki shirt with epaulets, a Croakie to secure the sunglasses that hung around her neck, and a stainless-steel diver's watch. Her legs were tan and muscular, her hair sun-bleached and short.

She looked younger than he had imagined, though why he had assumed she would be his age or older he didn't know. He tried to see her face, but her back was to him. Suddenly an alarm sounded in his head, an alarm he had not anticipated. Oh Lord, he thought as he drew near, don't let her have a pretty face.

Some men were fixated on women's breasts, some on their buttocks or their hands or legs or feet. Chase had always been a sucker for a pretty face. All his life he had fallen for faces, irrationally—and fully knowing it was irrational—ignoring the neuroses, personality disorders, stupidity, greed and vanity that often lay beneath the skin of those faces.

He would have to work with this woman for three months. The last thing he needed was the added complication of being smitten.

Then Max saw Chase and shouted, "Dad!" and waved, and Dr. Macy turned around.

Chase blew out a breath of relief. Her face was nice, and well proportioned, handsome, even, but not a heart-stopper. He held out his hand and said, "Simon Chase."

"Amanda Macy," she said, taking his hand with a firm, confident grip, and smiling with lips that wore no lipstick.

"I see Max wasn't exactly shy."

"Oh, he was very polite," Amanda said. "It was me that cut off the small talk. I told him that if he wanted to get to know the sea lions, the best way was to jump right into the water with them. He's a natural in the water, by the way, and seems more gifted with animals than a lot of kids. They took to him right away."

"Dad!" Max shouted. "Watch!"

Chase looked into the tank. Two of the sea lions were facing Max, their heads out of water. Max splashed one of them, and suddenly both sea lions exploded in a blur of flippers, splashing Max like playground bullies. He shrieked with laughter and ducked underwater, and the sea lions dashed after him, brushing him with their silky bodies, spinning him in circles.

"Amazing," Amanda said. "They usually take a long time to trust someone. They must sense a benevolence, a kind of innocence, in children . . . or in *this* child, anyway."

"They never bite?"

Amanda laughed. "That's a parent asking, right, not a scientist?"

"Right," Chase said.

"The only reasons an intelligent mammal like this will bite anything or anybody are food, fear and aggression. These four are all females, so there's no problem with sexual aggression. They're well fed. And they don't have anything to fear." She paused. "They're not at all like sharks."

Chase's eyes followed Max as he frolicked with the sea lions. "So I see," he said.

"To me, these animals are a lot closer to people than to sharks. They need attention and affection, from each other and from me. They like to have their teeth brushed and their coats stroked. I've raised them since they were pups."

Max popped to the surface, laughing, and Chase waved him to the side of the tank. "Come on out of there," he said. "You're turning blue."

"But Dad . . ."

Amanda said, "The sea lions need a rest, Max, same as you. You've given them quite a workout."

Max hauled himself out of the tank, and Chase rubbed his shoulders and back. "You feel like a Popsicle," he said.

Max pointed at the sea lions, which, as soon as he had left the tank, had scrambled up onto the rocks and were sunning themselves.

"They're called Harpo, Chico, Groucho and Zeppo," Max said. "I don't know which is which, but Dr. Macy told me that when I get to know them better, I can pick one to be my special friend."

Chase felt Max shivering under his hands, and he said, "Go take a shower and put on some warm clothes."

Max started away, then turned back and said to Amanda, "Later can I play with them some more?"

"Sure," Amanda said with a little laugh, "but only when I'm here with them. You have to learn the signals, just like they did."

Chase had constructed a shed against the rocks behind the tank, and Amanda ducked inside and came back with a bucket of fish. "Lunchtime, ladies!" she called as she approached the edge of the tank. The sea lions slid off the rocks and into the water and, barking impatiently, swam over to her, lined up in a row and waited.

She fed them each a fish, then another and another, and when they had all had their allotted five, she rubbed each on the head and behind the ears.

She replaced the bucket in the shed, then said to Chase, "This is a wonderful place. Were you brought up around here?"

"Not on the island . . . in Waterboro."

"Where did you go to school?"

"All over the place," Chase replied, thinking, Here it comes. Briefly, he debated planting a lie, but because in his experience lies tended to grow until they became unsustainable, he told the truth. "The last place was URI—Rhode Island."

"They're really good in oceanography. Is your degree specifically in sharks, or all the elasmobranches?"

"No." Chase paused, then said, "It's in process."

She started. "You mean you don't have your degree? You're director of an institute and you don't have a doctorate?"

"That's right . . . Doctor," Chase said. "Can you live with that?" Before the words were out of his mouth, he felt like an ass.

Amanda blushed. "Of course . . . I didn't . . . I mean . . . I'm sorry. . . . It's just . . ." She threw her head back and laughed.

For a moment, Chase thought she was laughing at him, and he tried to think of a snappy put-down. Before anything came to him, however, something in her expression told him she was laughing not at him but at herself.

"It's great!" she said. "I love it!"

"What?"

"I spend four years in college, two years getting my master's, five years getting my doctorate. I'm *somebody*! My Ph.D. is my armor. I could be a jerk, a turkey, a fool, but I've got a Ph.D. It's the official label of my exalted status." She laughed again. "And then I meet someone who doesn't have his doctorate, can't be anywhere near as exalted as I am, but he's done more than I've ever done, set up an entire institute of his own. And what's my first reaction? 'Impossible!' I love it!"

They started up the hill together. "Let me take the topic from the top," Amanda said. "If you ever do a dissertation, what'll it be on?"

"Territoriality in white sharks," Chase said. "Which reminds me: there's been a white around here in the last week or two. We were tracking it for data till we lost our sensor. A couple of divers were killed, but I don't *think* the white's connected to it. Still, it's out there."

"You think you could find the shark again?"

"I'm going to try, but . . ." Chase stopped. "You mean you *want* to find it? A great white shark? What about your—"

"My sea lions are savvy about white sharks," Amanda said. "There are whites all over California, they know how to stay away from them. Sure, I'd love to find it. I've always wanted to do a study of the interaction between marine predators: mammals that prey on mammals, mammals that prey on fish, fish that prey on mammals."

"I thought you worked exclusively on whales."

"So far, yes, but the images the sea lions are bringing back on videotape are so extraordinary, the behavior they're recording is so remarkable, that I don't see why we can't expand our research."

"I don't get it," Chase said. "What can a sea lion with a video camera on its back see that a scientist in a boat, or even in a submersible, can't?"

"Nature," said Amanda. "Nature in action. Whales, sharks, other animals, most everything will stay away from a boat or a submersible because it's alien to them, and possibly threatening. It's a big, strange, noisy intruder, and if it does get close to them, the animals' behavior will be anything but natural. On the other hand, they're completely accustomed to having sea lions swim around them, so they go on about their business—feeding, mating, whatever, and we get it all on tape. Besides, a submersible's slow and clumsy, and it costs a fortune. A sea lion can keep up with a whale, and they're cheap—they work for a few pounds of mullet."

"How do they know to do what you want them to do?"

"Conditioning, plus native intelligence. When it comes to smarts, sea lions are in the league with dolphins and killer whales. We built a full-size model of a gray whale and fit it over an electric-powered submersible, to use to train them. From a boat, I give them a series of hand signals: swim alongside it, swim beneath it, circle around it. It doesn't take long to teach them things; they want to learn."

Chase thought for a moment, then said, "Do you think you could teach them to take pictures of something they're *not* accustomed to, something that maybe isn't natural, behavior they've never seen?"

"Like what?"

"I wish I knew," Chase said. "But things aren't right in the ocean around here. Either something new is in the area, or something's gone berserk." He told Amanda about the random slaughter of birds and animals, and about the mystery surrounding the deaths of the Bellamys.

"I can try," said Amanda, "once I get the sea lions used to the water around here, and to the humpbacks. My first priority, though, has to be to find the whales. I've chartered a spotter plane, starting this afternoon."

"A *plane*?" Chase whistled. "That's some kind of grant you got yourself. For that kind of dough, I'd strap on wings and fly myself."

"The grant? The grant's a joke, seventy-five hundred a year for three years. It keeps me in fish, but that's about it." She hesitated, looking embarrassed, then continued. "Basically, I'm my own angel."

"How do you manage that?" Chase asked.

"How do you think? The luck of the gene pool. My great-great-grandfather was one of the whaling Macys—sometimes I think my career is penance for what he did—and he saw the collapse coming in whale oil and put all his money in petroleum. We've been loaded ever since." She smiled. "Can you live with that?"

"Hell," Chase said, laughing. "I did." He told her about his marriage to Corinne. "If I'd had any brains, I'd've taken her up on her offer and let her finance the Institute. But no, I was too proud."

"Never mind. You got something even better out of the marriage."

"What's that?"

"Max."

"Oh," he said. "Yeah. I'm just now learning more about that."

They had reached the small house on the top of the hill, in which Chase had prepared living quarters for Amanda: a bedroom, a kitchen and, because the living room had been taken up by the decompression chamber, another bedroom furnished as a sitting room.

"Are you hungry?" Chase said. "We've got sandwich fixings in the big house."

"Later," Amanda said. "First, I want to show you the present I brought you."

"Present? You didn't have to—"

"My parents always told me never to go for a visit without a house present." Grinning, she took his arm and led him beyond the house, where the land sloped down to a cove in which the bottom had been dredged to permit the approach of deep-draft boats. "There," she said, pointing at the cove. "I wanted to wrap it, but . . ."

Chase looked and, when suddenly he realized what he was seeing, stopped walking. "My God..." he said.

On a slab of ledge rock at the edge of the cove sat something Chase had longed for ever since he had begun his graduate work: an anti-shark cage. It was a rectangular box, roughly seven feet high, five feet wide and eight feet long, made of aluminum bars and steel mesh. There were entrance hatches on the top and one end, and foot-square openings—camera ports—on each side. Two flotation tanks had been welded to the top of the cage, and even from this distance Chase could see gleaming brass fittings that told him the tanks contained their own air supplies, which meant that the cage could hover well beneath the surface.

Cages were a prime research tool for shark scientists, for they permitted safe underwater access to the animals in the open ocean. Most sharks couldn't bite through the aluminum bars, and those that probably could, like big tiger sharks or great whites, didn't. They might bite *at* the bars—testing them, determining if they were edible—but none had ever bitten through them.

From the moment he had opened the Institute, Chase had tried to acquire a cage—a discarded cage, a used cage, *any* cage—so he could perform experiments in deep water. He had found, however, that used cages were never available: there was so much demand for shark films from cable-television companies that rental houses snapped up every cage they could find and charged usurious rates for them. Derelict cages were derelict for a reason: they were battered and broken beyond repair.

And the price for a new cage, a good cage, started at around twenty thousand dollars.

This cage looked brand-new and very good indeed. "It's beautiful," Chase said, starting down toward the cove. "But how did you—"

"It was part of my divorce settlement," Amanda said. "My ex-husband had it built three years ago; he was going to be a macho shark photographer, but he discovered a lot of competition, and switched to sea otters." She paused, then added with a wry smile, "He couldn't make a go at that either, so he decided to concentrate on bimbos. He got the Toyota; I got the shark cage. I figured you could use it."

"I sure can. I've been hoping to—"

"I know, I read your paper on bite dynamics and arthritis research. From the cage, you should be able to do some productive work with your gnathodynamometer."

"You pronounced it!" Chase said with a laugh. *Gnathodynamometer* was a ten-dollar word for a simple concept, a method of testing the bite pressure exerted by a shark's jaws. "I've never met anybody else who could pronounce it."

"No sweat," Amanda said. "Just don't ask me to spell it."

When they reached the cage, Chase ran his hand over the aluminum bars and examined welds and fittings. "It's perfect," he said, smiling. "I can't wait."

"Why wait? What's wrong with today?"

"Today?" Reflexively, Chase looked at his watch.

"There are still seven or eight more hours of daylight," Amanda said. "How far offshore do you have to go to raise sharks?"

"Not very, not for blue sharks. An hour, maybe less."

"The sooner I put the sea lions in the water," Amanda said, "the better. They can swim with blue sharks; they *like* to. They love to tease them. Have you got bait . . . and chum to bring the sharks in?"

"Uh-huh." Then Chase remembered, and he said, "But what I don't have is air. The compressor's—"

"It's fixed," said Amanda. "I asked Tall Man. He's pumping tanks now. I tell you, he's jazzed at the thought of the trip."

Chase was impressed. More than impressed. Awed. He looked at her, and saw her smiling at him, a smile not of triumph or condescension, but of confidence. He shook his head and said, "I guess I really do have to get my degree."

"What? Why?"

" 'Cause you were right the first time." He grinned. "Lady, you *are* somebody. You are *something*!"

21

THE INSTITUTE boat sat low in the water, for it had been filled with fuel and fresh water and loaded to the bulwarks with scientific, photographic and diving gear. In addition to the two-hundred-pound cage, which Chase and Tall Man had swung aboard into the stern with a block-and-tackle rig hung from a davit on the starboard side, there were four camera cases; a videotape recorder; eight scuba tanks; fifty pounds of mullet for the sea lions; three ten-gallon cans of chum—minced mackerel and tuna—to create a smelly slick that would ride the tide and lure sharks from miles around; two twenty-pound boxes of frozen baitfish, now thawing in the sun; three dive bags packed with wet suits, masks and flippers; and, finally, a cooler full of sandwiches and sodas prepared by Mrs. Bixler.

Amanda had led the sea lions down the path to

the dock, and they had willingly waddled aboard the boat. Now they huddled together in the stern, their heads bobbing and whiskers twitching with excitement. Amanda stroked them and cooed to them.

Max knelt beside her. "Are they okay?" he asked.

"Oh, sure," Amanda said. "They know the boat means work, and they can't wait. They love to work; they get bored very easily."

Max reached out a hand, and one of the sea lions bent its head toward him to have its ears scratched. "Which one is this?" he said.

"Harpo."

"I think she likes me."

Amanda smiled. "I know she does."

On the flying bridge, Chase put the boat in reverse. Tall Man stood on the pulpit and used the boat hook to fend the bow away from the rocks. When the boat had cleared the cove and Chase had turned toward deep water, Tall Man came aft and went into the cabin.

He returned a moment later and said to Amanda, "Your spotter pilot just radioed, said to tell you he'll be up in the air and looking for whales in an hour or so. I said we'd monitor channel twenty-seven." Then he looked up at the flying bridge. "There's a bulletin on sixteen," he said to

Chase. "We're supposed to keep an eye out for a kid in the water."

"Who?" Chase asked.

"Bobby Tobin, the mate on Tony Madeiras's boat. They say he fell overboard. Tony swears he did a bunch of three-sixties, looking for him, but never saw a thing."

Amanda said, "Falling overboard seems to be epidemic around here."

"Why?" said Tall Man. "Who else?"

"Before I left California, I got a call from my cousin. A week or ten days ago, her boyfriend disappeared from a research ship just inside Block Island. He was a photographer for the *Geographic*. They never found him."

The boat was still moving slowly, the engine rumbling softly, so even from ten yards away, up on the flying bridge, Chase had heard what Amanda said. He called down to Tall Man, "See if you can find a life preserver for Max."

"Dad . . ." said Max. "C'mon . . . I'm not gonna fall overboard."

"I know," Chase said. "And I bet Bobby Tobin never thought he would, either."

. . .

As they passed to the south of Block Island, Amanda gave Max a few mullets to feed to the sea lions; she climbed the ladder to the flying bridge and stood beside Chase. Rounding a point of land, they could see a couple of dozen people on a sheltered beach. Children wearing inflatable water wings played in the wavewash; two adults wearing pastel bathing caps swam back and forth twenty yards beyond the surf line, and a teenager lolled on a surfboard.

"Every time I see people swimming offshore," Chase said, "I think how lucky it is that they can't see themselves from a couple of hundred feet in the air."

"Why?"

" 'Cause if they saw what swims within ten or fifteen feet of them every few minutes, they'd never set foot in the water again."

"Are there that many sharks?"

"No, not anymore, not the way there used to be. But it doesn't take many to start a panic. It only takes one."

A hundred yards off the beach, a lobsterman was pulling his pots. He cruised up to a buoy, grabbed it with a boat hook and hauled it aboard, fed its rope through a block and tackle suspended from a steel A-frame, wrapped the rope around a winch and brought the wood-and-wire lobster pot up onto his bulwarks.

Chase waved to him, and the lobsterman looked up, began to wave, then noticed the "O.I." stenciled on the side of the big white boat. He aborted his wave, and instead banged one fist into the crook of the other arm and shot Chase the finger.

"How charming," said Amanda.

Chase laughed. "That's Rusty Puckett," he said. "He doesn't like me very much."

"So I see."

"Lobstermen are a strange breed. A lot of them believe the sea is their private preserve, that they've got some God-given right to put traps wherever they want, whenever they want, to catch however much they want, and the rest of the world be damned. Lord help anyone who messes with their traps: they'll sink one another, shoot one another."

"And you messed with his traps?"

"Sort of. Before I owned the island, he used to use it as a camp, a storehouse, a trash dump. He set his pots everywhere, not just in the shallows but in the channel and by the dock. I couldn't get in or out, and kept fouling my propeller in his lines. I asked him to move them, he told me to piss off. I went to the Coast Guard, but they didn't want to get mixed up in it. So one day, Tall Man and I pulled all his pots, emptied them and gave the lobsters to the old folks' home, then reset his pots out here. It took him about two weeks to find them.

"He knows we did it, but he can't prove it, and

when he accused us, Tall just said it was a warning from the Great Spirit. Rusty's stupid, but he's not suicidal, he wasn't about to go up against Tall, a giant who feels the same way Rusty does about the law.

"So he left his pots out here, partly 'cause he's too lazy to move them, but partly 'cause the fishing's better out here anyway."

"He should be happy, then."

"You'd think. But Rusty harbors grudges. And he doesn't like it out here. Nothing ever happens, there's no excitement, nobody to get upset with or take a shot at."

They traveled on in silence for a few minutes, then Chase turned and looked aft. Block Island had receded behind them into a shapeless gray mass. He throttled back and took the boat out of gear. "We're here," he said.

"We're where?" Amanda looked around. "I don't see a thing, not a bird, not a fish, nothing but empty ocean."

"Yeah," Chase said, "but I can feel 'em, I can smell 'em, I can practically taste 'em." He grinned. "Can't you?"

"What?"

"Sharks."

22

RUSTY PUCKETT watched the boat speed away to the east, its white hull seeming to be absorbed by the ocean swells until, at last, all he could see were occasional flashes as the steel superstructure on thc flying bridge caught the sun.

Son of a bitch, he thought, I hope you sink, I hope you hit something and go down like a stone. Or maybe catch fire first, then sink. Yeah, fire's good, something nice and nasty about a fire.

Maybe he should go over to the island some night and set fire to something. Teach them a lesson about messing with him. 'Course, they'd likely know he did it, then that fuckin' King Kong of an Indian would be all over him like drool on a baby. He should probably think about it for a while.

He opened the door in the trap balanced on the bulwarks and looked inside. Two lobsters were in the far corner, their antennae waving back and forth. One was a good size, a couple of pounds at least, and Puckett reached in and grabbed it behind the head, avoiding the claws, and pulled it out and dropped it into the box on the deck.

The other was much smaller, probably a "short," a youngster that should be thrown back and allowed to grow for another year or two.

Puckett considered measuring the carapace to confirm that the lobster was a short, but then he thought: Hell, if I don't take it, someone else will. So he pulled the lobster from the trap and, with a single swift twisting motion, tore its tail off and dropped the head, legs and claws—still writhing—overboard, and watched them sink out of sight.

He set the tail on his cutting board. He'd shell it later and sell it for lobster salad. Nobody'd ever be the wiser.

He rebaited the trap, tied the door closed, shoved the trap off the bulwarks and let the rope slide through his hands till it went slack, which told him that the trap was on the bottom. Then he chucked the buoy overboard, put the boat in gear and motored slowly along the line to the next one.

Ten down, ten to go. He already had eighteen "bugs" in the box, he'd likely have thirty or more by the time he was through . . . not bad for a morning's work.

Puckett reached his next buoy, put the boat in neutral, leaned over the side, snagged the buoy and brought it aboard. He fed the rope through the block, wrapped it around the winch and turned the winch on, keeping a hand on the rope to guide it around the drum.

He heard a scream from the shore, and he looked and saw a tall blond girl being chased along the hard-packed sand by what had to be her boyfriend. She was wearing one of those bikini bathing suits that weren't so much a bathing suit as a come-on—what did they call them? Butt floss—and her hooters bounced up and down like two melons.

Nice, he thought. He wouldn't mind having some of that.

The girl suddenly stopped running and turned and kicked sand and water at the boy, and he shouted something and charged at her, but she veered away from him and dove into the water and started swimming.

Come on out here, honeybun, Puckett thought, I'll show you how it's done.

The girl treaded water beyond the wave line, taunting the boy until he dove in and swam to her. Together they breaststroked down the beach, moving swiftly with the tide.

The trap bumped against the bottom of the boat. Puckett shut off the winch and pushed the rope as far out over the side as he could, guiding the trap out from under the boat and up to the surface.

Something was wrong: the trap was hanging at a weird angle, as if one end were much heavier than the other. He leaned on the bulwark and grabbed the trap with both hands and heaved it aboard.

One end of the trap was gone. Splinters of wooden slats hung from pieces of shredded wire.

He looked inside. At first, the trap looked empty—no bait, no lobsters, nothing. Then, as he looked closer, he saw bits of shell and two lobster legs caught in the wire mesh.

What the hell? he thought. A poacher wouldn't do this, he'd do it the easy way: pull the trap, open the door, take the lobsters and toss the trap back. A shark? No, a shark would've beat the trap to pieces, maybe crushed parts of it as he ran away with it.

Puckett unshackled the rope from the shattered trap, pushed the trap overboard and walked aft to fetch a spare. He always carried four spares, because you never knew: traps got stolen, had their ropes cut by propellers, drifted away in storms. He rigged the spare, baited it and shoved it over.

The next trap he hauled was the same, only worse. Two sides were bashed in, and the door was ripped off, gone. Half a dozen lobster anten-nae were scattered around the bottom of the trap, which meant that there had been at least three lobsters in there. Something had torn them to pieces.

But what?

No octopus would do that to a trap. There were no giant eels around here, no squid big and mean enough.

How about a gigantic lobster? They were canni-bals, and a huge enough one might crush a trap.

Gimme a break, he told himself, that lobster'd have to be the size of a goddamn Buick.

Whatever did this was big and strong and either angry or crazy, and it had some kind of tools to work with.

A man. It had to be a man, but what man would want to . . .

Chase. Simon Chase.

Sure, it made sense. Why else would Chase have waved when he went by? They weren't exactly bosom buddies. He was sticking it to old Rusty, not content with running him off the island where he'd been lobstering the better part of twenty years, not content with pushing him all the way to hell-and-gone out here, now he wanted to drive Puckett out of business altogether.

Yeah, that wave was the key, the giveaway.

Okay, Mr. Simon *fucking* Chase from your Osprey *fucking* Island *fucking* Institute . . . you want a war, you *got* a war.

Conjuring up a suitable revenge, Puckett replaced the trap and gunned the engine, racing down the line to the next buoy. Chances were, Chase had wrecked all the rest of the traps, but he'd have to pull them all to find out.

Anger returned like an incoming tide as Puckett realized that he had only two more spares, which meant that he'd have to go all the way back to town, collect some more and come all the way out here again.

Anger distracted him as he reached for the next buoy. It should have been floating with the tide, its rope angling downward, but it wasn't; it was bobbing, as if something was tugging on it.

Puckett didn't notice. He hooked the buoy and brought it aboard and wrapped the rope and started the winch.

Immediately, the winch whined, the boat heeled over and the rope began to skid against the drum.

Now what? Puckett thought. The damn thing must've got itself hitched in the rocks.

No, that wasn't it, couldn't be, because now the rope was grabbing, the winch was bringing it in . . . slowly, as if it had a huge weight on it; but it was coming.

Weed. It probably had a hundred pounds of kelp wrapped around it.

He grabbed a six-foot gaff hook and leaned overboard, prepared to tear the kelp away before bringing the trap aboard.

Suddenly the boat popped upright and the rope came faster.

Maybe the kelp fell off. Maybe . . .

The trap came into view, a dark shape against the green mist.

There was something beside it, caught in it . . . no, pushing it . . . it was whitish, and . . .

Jesus Christ, Puckett thought, it's a body.

But, no, it wasn't a body, and it was swimming, and fast. Its mouth was open, as were its eyes. It had hands—or claws—and they were reaching up at him.

One of the hands grabbed the gaff hook

Puckett screamed, and tried to pull the gaff hook away, but it was yanked from his hand, and he stumbled backward, still screaming. His shoulder hit the throttle and knocked it forward, into gear, and he fell on it, and the weight of his body pressed it all the way down.

The engine shrieked and the stern sagged as the propeller cavitated and then bit into the water. The boat leaped ahead. The rope whipped off the winch, its coils fell into the water and the buoy caromed off the A-frame and disappeared.

Puckett didn't move until he heard himself screaming. Then he rolled off the throttle and straightened out the wheel.

He kept the boat at full speed, looking aft as if expecting whatever it was to come over the stern and into the cockpit.

When he had traveled perhaps five hundred yards, he throttled back and steered the boat into a wide circle around the buoy. Keeping the engine revs at fifteen hundred, which gave him a constant speed of twelve to fifteen knots, he approached to within a hundred yards of the buoy, and he stared at it. It was floating now, not bobbing, yielding to the pull of the tide.

Puckett's mind was a jumble; thoughts and images and questions ricocheted aimlessly like a ball in a pinball machine.

After a few moments, he felt a chill, then a rush of nausea.

He pushed the throttle forward and headed for home.

· · ·

From the spot on the beach where they had emerged from the water, the couple watched the boat roar away in a cloud of exhaust.

"I wonder what's the matter with him," the girl said.

"Maybe fouled his prop," said the boy. "I've

done that. You want to get home before the shear pin breaks." He looked up and down the beach. "Hey, guess what, we're alone."

"So?"

"So what do you say we go skinny-dipping?"

"You just want to cop a feel," the girl said, smiling.

"I do not."

"Yes, you do. Admit it."

The boy hesitated, then grinned and said, "Okay, I admit it."

The girl reached behind her and pulled a string, and her bra fell away. "See?" she said. "Honesty's the best policy." She pulled a knot at her hip, and the bottom of her suit dropped to the sand. She turned and bounded over the little waves and dove into the water, while the boy struggled to step out of his trunks.

· · ·

It swam aimlessly over the sand, searching for signs of life.

Though it had no understanding of time, no knowledge that cycles of light and darkness signaled the passage of time, it sensed that the intervals between the maddening urges to kill were growing shorter.

Responding to increased activity, its metabolism, which for years had functioned at a level barely adequate to sustain primitive life, was speeding up, restoring sentience to its brain and burning calories faster and faster.

It heard little movements somewhere ahead, beyond its range of vision, and it followed the sounds until it came upon another of the strange wood-and-wire boxes. There were two small living things inside; it destroyed the box and ate them.

It started down the sand slope into deeper water, when suddenly it sensed motion above. It stopped moving, willed its gills to cease their rhythmic pulsing; it focused the sensitive receptors in the sides of its skull on the source of the pressure changes in the water.

It could not isolate the location, but it did perceive a direction, and so—opening its cavernous mouth, letting its teeth spring forward, flexing its claws—it flew silently toward the prey.

· · ·

The boy caught up with the girl and, from behind, reached around her and cupped her breasts with his hands.

She shrieked and spun to face him, and raised a hand to slap him. He grabbed her hand and put it around his neck, and leaned forward and kissed her.

Clinging to each other, they sank until their heads dipped underwater, then they parted and surfaced.

"How deep is it here?" she asked, gasping for breath.

"I don't know, fifty feet, maybe more."

"It's creepy, not being able to see the bottom."

"You think something's gonna eat you?" The boy laughed.

"I want to go in."

"Okay."

"Just to where we can touch."

"So let's go." The boy took a couple of strokes toward shore. Then he started, and said, "What was that?"

"What was what?"

"Something underneath us. Didn't you feel it?"

"Shut up," the girl said. "You're not funny."

"I'm serious. Like a little pressure wave. It's gone now."

"I hate you, Jeffrey . . . you're not *funny*."

"I tell you . . ." the boy began, but the girl had already passed him and was churning the water, swimming toward shore.

. . .

It could see them now, far above, two living things—large, weak, awkward.

It swooped upward.

Suddenly it felt itself struck from above, bumped, but not damaged. Disoriented, it whirled around, looking for the thing that had struck it.

At the limit of its vision was something huge, bigger than itself, of a dull color almost indistinguishable from the surrounding water, with fins on its back and its sides. A crescent tail propelled it in a slow circle. Its mouth was ajar; its blank eye stared.

A word for this thing occurred to the creature, a word from the dim past. The word was *Hai*— shark—and with the recognition came a perception of danger. The creature turned with the shark, prepared to defend itself.

The shark flicked its tail and charged head-on, opening its mouth.

The creature dodged, backing up and swerving to the side, and the shark sped by. Immediately it turned and rushed again, and the creature ducked beneath it, reaching up with its claws. The claws found flesh, and slashed it, but the flesh was hard and thick. No blood flowed.

This time the shark did not turn, but kept going, roiling the water with its tail and vanishing into the gray-green mist.

The creature let itself slip to the bottom. It oriented itself, then searched the surface for the two large living things.

They were gone. The water was undisturbed by sounds or pressure variations.

The creature turned toward deep water, to hunt again.

. . .

Ashore, the girl wrapped herself in her towel, gathered up her bathing suit and stalked away, leaving the boy to search for his trunks in the dune grass where she had thrown them.

23

THE BOAT was anchored in two hundred feet of water; the cage floated twenty feet behind it, tethered by a rope cleated on the stern. For an hour, Chase and Tall Man had been ladling chum overboard, and the still air in the cockpit reeked of blood and fish oil. A slick fanned out behind the boat, carried by the tide, its rainbow flatness easily discernible against the calm water.

Two scuba tanks had been rigged with harnesses and regulators, and they lay on the deck beside flippers and masks. Amanda and Chase had pulled wet suits on up to their waists, letting the tops hang down. Sweat glistened on their arms and shoulders; Amanda's back was turning pink with sunburn.

She walked forward, dipped a bucket in the clean water, returned and gently doused the sea lions, which lay together in a heap, sleeping. "I'm going to have to put the girls in the water pretty soon," she said. "They can't take this heat."

"The radio said it might reach a hundred today," Tall Man said, wiping his face, "and I'll bet—"

"Shark!" Max suddenly shouted from the flying bridge. "I see one!"

They looked aft. Fifty yards away, a triangular dorsal fin sliced through the slick; a tail fin followed it, thrashing back and forth.

"It's a blue," said Chase. "I knew we'd raise them."

"How can you tell from this far away?" Amanda asked.

"Short, stubby dorsal . . . sharp caudal fin . . . dark blue."

"How big?"

"Gauging the distance between the dorsal and the tail . . . I'd say ten, eleven feet." He looked up at Max. "Good for you. Keep a sharp eye, there'll be others."

"There!" Max said, pointing. "Behind the . . . no, two! There're two more!"

As if sensing the excitement in Max's voice, the sea lions stirred and rose up on their flippers, sniffing the air.

"Let's get ready," Chase said to Amanda, and he dropped the ladle into the chum bucket.

By the time Chase and Amanda had pulled up

their wet suits, put on their tanks and rinsed their masks, six blue sharks were crisscrossing the chum slick, moving closer to the cage with each pass.

"Toss 'em a fish or two now and then," Chase said to Tall Man, "just to keep 'em interested." He opened a hatch between his feet, reached down and pulled out two pieces of white plastic, each about the size of a shirt cardboard, sewn together face-to-face. A piece of rope was braided into one corner.

"What's that?" Amanda said. "A plastic sandwich?"

"Exactly." Chase smiled. "But we world-class scientists, we call it a gnathodynamometer."

"You're kidding."

"Nope. Simple but effective. This is sensitized laboratory plastic. And inside here," Chase said, prying the pieces apart, "is a ripe mackerel. Once Tall gets the sharks feeding, I'll hold my sandwich out through one of the camera ports; a shark'll sniff the mackerel and bite down on the plastic. I'll let him gnaw the hell out of it, then take it away from him. When I get the plastic back to the lab, I'll use a micrometer to see how deep he bit, and a set of tables will tell me how much pressure he exerted."

"Amazing," Amanda said. "The whole thing must have cost about three dollars."

"Ten dollars, actually. But add the cost of the cage, the boat, the fuel and the crew, and now you're talking about a hundred thousand." Chase paused, watching the sharks circling close to the cage, then said, "Are you sure you want to put those sea lions in the water?"

"You watch," she said with a smile. "They'll make fools out of your sharks." She opened the door in the transom, stepped down onto the swimstep, pulled a bucket of fish to her and called each sea lion by name. One by one, they waddled over to her, received a fish and, when she swung her arm and thrust her hand toward the water, flopped down onto the swimstep and into the sea.

Chase watched their brown bodies flash between the gunmetal backs of the sharks, then dart away into the blue water.

"Ready?" Amanda said. She reached inside the door for her video camera.

Chase didn't answer. He kept watching the water, even after the sea lions were out of sight. He was excited, as he had expected to be; what he hadn't expected was the vague unease that shadowed his excitement—not fear, nothing specific, but rather a sense of foreboding.

"Don't worry about my sea lions," Amanda said. "They'll be fine."

"I'm not," Chase said. "I'm not worried about blue sharks, either. I just can't help wondering what the hell else is out there."

"Forget it, Simon," said Tall Man. He took the rope tied to the cage and pulled on it, drawing the cage up to the stern of the boat. "Nothing's gonna mess with that cage."

Chase said, "You're right." He dropped down onto the swimstep, leaned to the cage and opened the hatch in the top. A blue shark nudged the cage, then whirled away.

As Chase straightened up, put on his mask and put in his mouthpiece, he heard Max call, "Dad . . ."

He looked up to the flying bridge. The boy looked small and far away.

"Be careful," Max said.

Chase shot Max a thumbs-up sign, pulled down his mask, held the plastic sandwich to his chest and stepped through the hatch into the cold, dark water.

Amanda followed immediately. When Tall Man saw that she was safely inside the cage and had pulled the hatch closed, he let go of the tether; the cage drifted back till the rope went taut. He made sure the knot of the cleat was secure, then tossed a few mackerel overboard and resumed chumming.

· · ·

It took a moment for the bubbles to dissipate and the water to clear. Chase glanced at Amanda, saw her adjusting her video camera and gazed out into the surrounding blue.

A mackerel plopped into the water overhead and sank in front of the cage, yawing like a leaf. A sea lion swooped around the side of the cage, snatched the fish in its teeth and hovered for a beat, as if posing for Amanda's camera. Then it bit down on the mackerel, blood puffed from the sides of its mouth and, chewing, it swam away.

Chase looked for the sharks. He saw three, fifty or sixty feet away, at the limit of his vision: dark shapes cruising unhurriedly back and forth. It won't take long, he thought, they're just being cautious; in a minute they'll get used to us, and they'll come in to feed.

Three more mackerel fell before the cage, one on each side, one in front. A sea lion grabbed one; the other two continued to fall.

Two of the three sharks swung around and swam at the cage, their movements no longer slow and sinuous but quick and jerky; now they were not cruising, they were hunting.

A mackerel was directly in front of Chase, no more than three feet away. Like a fighter plane locked on to a target, one of the sharks closed in on the mackerel. Its mouth opened; it rolled on its side; the nictitating membrane that protected its eye slid downward. . . .

Suddenly the shark halted; its body arched. It

turned in a tight circle and fled into the gloom. The mackerel continued to fall, untouched.

Chase looked at Amanda and spread his hands: what was *that* all about? He knew that while blue sharks rarely attacked human beings, they were not afraid of humans; and yet it certainly seemed to Chase that the shark had suddenly panicked when it had seen him and Amanda. She shrugged and shook her head.

Chase pushed the plastic sandwich out through the camera port, squeezed it to force fish juices into the water and waved it tantalizingly.

A sea lion approached and sniffed it, but Amanda signaled for it to move away, and it obeyed.

Between the bars at the bottom of the cage, Chase saw a shark rising from below. It had caught the scent, was seeking its source. He held the plastic as far as possible from the cage, letting it dangle from the rope. The shark rose, and turned, homing.

Come on, baby, Chase murmured in his mind, come on.

The shark opened its mouth, showing rows of small white triangles. It was five feet from the bait, then three. . . .

Chase gripped the rope as tight as he could, knowing he'd have to fight to keep the shark from tearing the entire rig from him. As the shark rolled on its side, he could see its eye.

The shark froze, as if it had struck a wall. Its mouth closed, and with two thrusts of its powerful tail it disappeared into the deep.

Chase turned to Amanda and gestured upward with both thumbs. He kicked off the bottom of the cage, pushed the hatch open and hauled himself out of the water till his elbows rested on the top of the cage. He removed his mouthpiece and raised his mask.

"What's spooking them?" Tall Man asked. He had seen it all from the surface.

"Damned if I know."

Amanda squeezed up through the hatch and joined Chase in the opening.

"I've never seen that in my life," said Chase. "Blue sharks are not afraid of people."

"These sure are," Amanda said. "Did you see the scars on that last one?"

"No, where?"

"All down one flank. Not mating scars, either, I've seen mating scars. These weren't random, they were five big slashes, all pretty much parallel. And fresh."

"Five?" Chase said. "You're sure?"

"Positive. Why?"

"About a week ago, we saw a big dolphin with five deep cuts on its tail."

"From what?"

"That's the question." Chase looked up at Tall Man. "What d'you think?"

"Give it one more shot," Tall Man said. He emptied a bucket of chum into the water, and followed it with a dozen mackerel. "If that don't bring 'em around, nothing will."

They waited for a moment, letting the blood and guts disperse in the water, then dropped back into the cage.

Clouds of red billowed in the water; bodies of fish floated down like debris. Through the haze Chase saw two sharks, twenty or thirty feet away, but by the time he had reached up and secured the hatch above them, they were gone. He checked his watch, then gripped the bars and gazed out through the camera port. After five minutes, the blood had disappeared, the fish had sunk to the bottom. The only life Chase saw was the sea lions, which passed by the cage in ones and twos, playing.

He signaled for Amanda to go up.

• • •

When they had boarded the boat and shucked their tanks, Chase said to Amanda, "It doesn't make sense; something's wrong. It's almost as if they're passing the word: 'Stay away, humans are bad news.' But that can't be . . . unless there's some electromagnetic anomaly in the water that they're all sensing at once, and it's somehow connected to humans."

"You'd think my sea lions would pick it up first," Amanda said. "I don't mean to insult your sharks, but my ladies are a little higher on the chain of brains."

"Could be," Tall Man said, "but your sea lions haven't been around here when the bad stuff's been happening. They haven't had a lesson to learn yet."

Chase said, "Do you want to call them back, bring them aboard?"

"I can, if we're moving on," Amanda said. "Otherwise, they'll come back when they're ready."

"I thought we might try another spot, just for the—"

"Dad . . ." Max said from his perch on the flying bridge. "Can I go into the cage?"

"You mean with a tank on? I don't—"

"There're no sharks around."

"Yeah, but I don't think two hundred feet of water with a five-mile chum slick running is exactly the time to start—"

"Please? . . . Hey, I'd be in a cage. With you." Max smiled, teasing his father as he pleaded. "What're you worried about . . . that we'll get struck by lightning?"

Chase looked to Tall Man for support, then to Amanda, but neither would come to his rescue. Parenting time, he thought; these decisions always seem to come when you least expect them. At last, he said, "Okay."

Max didn't have a wet suit, so Amanda lent him hers. It was too big for him, probably wouldn't keep him warm, but it would prevent him from cutting or bruising himself on the cage. Chase rigged a tank for him and, when they were both dressed and ready, ran through the diving drill with him.

"The *most* important thing," Chase said finally, "is not ever to—"

"I know: hold my breath. But we won't be down too deep."

"We won't be deep at all, the cage'll be right on the surface, but you'll still be four or five feet below the surface. You can get an embolism in two feet." Chase paused. "Set?"

"Set."

"I'll go first; Tall'll tell you when to come; Amanda'll give you a hand." Chase glanced prayerfully at the sky, then stepped through the hatch into the cage.

A moment later, Max slipped through the hatch, landing on his feet. He cleared his mask and purged his regulator.

Chase saw that the boy was slightly under-weighted—the buoyancy of the wet suit tended to lift him off the bottom of the cage—so he gestured for Max to grip the bars. Max nodded and obeyed, and together they looked out at the empty sea.

They saw no sharks, no sea lions, nothing at all. Then Max dropped to his knees, looked down, tugged at Chase's leg and pointed. Far below them, barely visible, was a single small shark. A sea lion swooped around it, hassling it. Max pressed his face to the bottom of the cage, trying to see better.

The animals were just beyond the range of clear vision. If only they'd come up, Chase thought, even ten feet, Max could get a good look. Then he remembered the flotation tanks, and realized that if the animals wouldn't come up to him, he could take the cage down closer to them. He bent down and checked the air gauge attached to Max's regu-lator: two thousand pounds. Plenty. Then he reached up and opened the flood valves on both flotation tanks.

The cage began to sink. It jerked for a moment, then fell smoothly as Tall Man paid out slack from the rope on the boat. When the depth gauge on one of the tanks told Chase that the top of the cage was fifteen feet below the surface, he shut the flood valves and opened two other valves, squirting air into the tanks until the cage achieved neutral buoyancy.

The shark and the sea lion were clearly visible now, two dark bodies against a canvas of blue. A few bubbles floated up as the sea lion let air leak from its mouth.

Then, abruptly, the sea lion broke away from the shark and shot upward. At first, Chase thought the animal had tired of the game, or needed to breathe, but there was something about its movements, an urgency, that told him he was wrong. The sea lion sped past the cage and rushed toward the boat. As Chase's eyes followed it upward, he saw the other sea lions—two together, one alone—swimming at the boat with the same frenzied speed.

For God's sake, Chase thought, *now* what?

· · ·

"I guess they've had enough," Tall Man said as he watched the sea lions struggle onto the swimstep. They were barking, shoving one another, desperate to get aboard.

"No," Amanda said, alarmed. "Something's frightened them. Something's out there."

"Like what?" Tall Man looked overboard. He could barely see the cage, for as it had sunk it had drifted into the shade of the boat. Holding the rope, he walked from one side of the boat to the other, then returned to the stern. "Nothing," he said. "I can't see anything out there."

"It's there, though," Amanda said. "Something . . . somewhere."

"Then whatever it is has gotta be deep. Either that, or . . . shit!"

"What?"

"Under the boat." He pulled on the rope.

· · ·

The cage shuddered as the rope tugged it. Chase reached to turn the air valves.

A shadow passed overhead, so huge that it cast the entire cage in darkness. Chase started, and looked up. A flash of sunlight blinded him for a moment, disorienting him; by the time his eyes had adjusted, he was unsure of the direction the shadow had been traveling. He turned.

Ten feet away, emerging from the shade of the boat, swimming at the cage with a mighty gracefulness that Chase had once admired but now found horrid, was the great white shark. It did not slow or hesitate. Its eyes rolled backward in their sockets; its mouth opened; its gums rotated forward; serrated white triangles stood erect. It bit down on the cage.

Reflexively, Chase ducked and flung himself on top of Max. The boy turned his head, his eyes widened in shock.

There was a sound of teeth scraping on metal,

then a crunching sound of metal collapsing, then a sudden hiss of air and an explosion of bubbles.

The cage yawed crazily, swinging under the boat and slamming against the keel, and Chase knew instantly what had happened: the shark had destroyed one of the flotation tanks.

. . .

"Goddamn you!" Tall Man shouted. The sinews in his arms and shoulders stood out like wires as he strained at the rope. He had seen the shark only a second before it had struck, charging out from beneath the boat like a gray torpedo.

Amanda reached over, grabbed the rope and helped him pull. "I thought sharks never—"

"Yeah," Tall Man said. "But guess what: this one did."

"Why?"

"Christ knows."

They could hear the cage thumping against the keel, could feel the impact through their feet.

"Can you put the rope on the winch?" Amanda asked.

"I don't dare. The bastard weighs better'n a ton; the weight could tear the rope away from the cage."

"What do we *do*? We have to—"

"If he comes out from under the boat, I'll shoot the son of a bitch," Tall Man said. "Till then, let's just pray he goes away."

· · ·

Chase and Max huddled in the far corner of the cage, holding each other, holding the bars, as the cage swung wildly beneath the boat.

The shark had locked its jaws, and it twisted and thrashed its massive body as if trying to beat the cage to pieces.

Chase saw bubbles flowing from Max's regulator in a continuous stream. The boy was hyperventilating. He made Max look at him, pointed to his own regulator, then to Max's, and gestured for Max to slow his breathing. Terrified, Max nodded.

Suddenly the shark released the cage, and the cage swung downward, hanging askew. Chase saw the shark's wide white belly slipping slowly before his eyes as the animal let itself fall. There were five parallel slash marks in the flesh forward of the genital slit.

· · ·

"Pull!" Tall Man said. He and Amanda brought the rope in hand-over-hand. Looking overboard, they could see the top of the cage as it cleared the bottom of the boat. The shark was a gray form, hovering nearly motionless beneath the cage. Tall Man dropped down onto the swimstep and held the rope out over the stern. "Another five feet and we've got—"

"No!" Amanda screamed, pointing.

There was a flash of a scythelike tail, a rush of water, and the conical head of the shark broke the surface. The mouth barely opened; it struck the swimstep, skidded, and fastened on the rope. With a single shake of its head, the shark tore the rope from Tall Man's hand and sheared it from the cage. Tall Man fell backward into the stern.

The shark swam away; the cage began to fall.

. . .

Chase lurched to his feet, grabbed the air valve on the intact flotation tank and twisted it all the way on. There was a hiss of air, and the cage's descent slowed. But it was still falling.

Chase inflated his buoyancy vest and Max's, hoping that removing their weight and adding buoyancy would stop the cage, make it neutral, until Tall Man could lower a rope to them.

The cage continued to fall. Chase looked at the depth gauge on the tank: the needle passed thirty feet, then thirty-five, forty. . . .

He looked quickly in every direction. The shark had vanished.

Fifty feet . . .

Chase knew he had no choice, they could not ride the cage to the bottom. They would both run out of air, probably before they reached the bottom, certainly before Tall Man could reach them.

He pulled Max to his feet and pushed open the

hatch. He put his hands on Max's shoulders and looked into the boy's eyes, willing him to recall the lessons he had learned, praying that the boy had listened. He took his mouthpiece out and shouted the word, "Remember!"

Max understood.

Sixty feet . . .

Chase propelled Max up through the hatch and followed immediately. He took the boy's hand, and faced him so he could monitor Max's breathing.

They were rising too fast, faster than their own bubbles; the air in their vests was expanding, seeking the surface, dragging them upward. They *had* to slow down; if they kept rising at this pace, they were risking a ruptured lung or an embolism or the bends.

Chase vented the vests, and they slowed. Now their bubbles were preceding them. Good.

Chase looked at his depth gauge: forty feet . . . thirty-five . . . He didn't look down, he kept his eyes on Max's face. He didn't see the shark rising beneath them.

Twenty feet . . . fifteen . . .

Suddenly there was a splash above them, and a roil of water, and Tall Man swam down at them, carrying a speargun.

Now Chase did look down, and he saw, rising

like a missile through the gloom, the yawning mouth and the prolapsed jaw of the great white shark.

Tall Man pulled the trigger. There was a puff of bubbles from the carbon-dioxide propellant, and the spear shot from the gun. It struck the shark in the roof of the mouth, and stuck. The shark hesitated, shaking its head to rid itself of the annoyance. It bit down, bending the spear, crushing it.

Chase broke through the surface, pulled Max after him and shoved him onto the swimstep. Amanda grabbed Max and hauled him into the boat as Chase swung his legs up, rolled onto the swimstep and reached down for Tall Man's hand.

But Tall Man stayed just beneath the surface, watching. At last, he kicked upward and, in a single motion, flung himself onto the swimstep.

Chase shrugged out of his harness, dropped his tank on the deck and crawled forward to Max, who lay on his side as Amanda helped him out of his tank. "Are you okay?" Chase asked.

Max's eyes were closed. He nodded, managed a faint smile and said, "Jeez . . ."

"You did great . . . you followed the rules . . . you didn't panic. You did *great!*" Chase felt guilty and stupid and relieved and proud; he wanted to express all those feelings, but he didn't know how, so he simply took one of Max's hands in his, rubbed it and said, "What a hell of an initiation to open-water diving." He saw Tall Man walking forward, toward the cabin, and said, "Hey, Tall . . . thanks. I wasn't looking, I didn't see it coming."

"I know," Tall Man said. "I thought I better give the bastard something else to chew on other than you. That was our shark, y'know. She's still got the tag in her."

"I've never *seen* behavior like that, never *heard* of it. She was berserk! It's weird, like the blue sharks, only opposite: the white was nuts with aggression instead of fear." Chase paused. "But whatever's causing this behavior, it's the same creature: there were five slashes on that white shark's belly."

· · ·

They raised the anchor, turned to the west, heading for home. Chase stood at the wheel on the flying bridge; Max lay on a towel behind him, warming himself in the high afternoon sun. Amanda was feeding the sea lions. When she had settled them in the stern, she climbed the ladder to the bridge.

The low silhouette of Osprey Island was just coming into view when Tall Man appeared at the foot of the ladder and said to Amanda, "Your pilot's on the radio; he's got whales."

"How far away?"

"Not far, couple miles to the east."

Amanda hesitated. She looked at her watch, at the sea lions, then at Chase.

Chase said to Max, "How do you feel?"

"Fine," Max replied. "I'm fine. Let's go; I've never seen whales."

Chase turned to Amanda. "It's up to you," he said. "Do you think the sea lions will work?"

"Sure, till they're tired, then they'll stop."

"They're not spooked?"

"No, I don't think so. If they see the white shark, they'll get out of the water, just like before. Besides, sharks usually stay away from pods of big, healthy whales."

"Uh-huh," Chase said. He swung the wheel to the left and headed east. "I wasn't thinking only about the white shark."

24

"I CAN'T hear them," Max said.

Two hundred yards ahead, a pod of humpback whales was moving leisurely northward.

"You might if you were underwater," said Chase. "You could hear them for miles."

"But if they sing . . ."

"It's not really singing, we call it that because we don't know how else to describe it. They don't actually have voices. They make sounds with a mechanism inside their heads. And they don't do it all the time."

They stood on the flying bridge. The boat was idling in neutral, bobbing slowly in the long ocean swells.

The great gray bodies rolled through the sea, displacing mountains of water with their huge bulbous heads, displaying vast flat tail flukes fifteen or twenty feet wide, spouting geysers of misty breath into the warm air. There were adults and young, males and females, but it was impossible to count them, for every so often one or two would slap the surface three times with their tails and then disappear in a deep dive, to reappear long minutes later in some unpredictable position among their fellows.

"What does their song say?" Max asked.

"For a long time, nobody knew; all they knew was that the whales were communicating, maybe talking about where they were going or where there might be food or if they sensed any danger. All whales communicate; I've heard that blue whales can keep in touch with each other over a thousand miles of open ocean. Humpbacks, though, are the only whales that sing in such a complex series of sounds and tones. Now scientists are pretty sure that the song of the humpbacks is sexual, that the males sing to attract the females." Chase smiled. "I like to think they're wrong, that the song is still a mystery."

"Why?"

"Mysteries are wonderful things. It would be boring to have all the answers. It's like the Loch Ness monster, I hope they never find him, either. We need dragons to keep our imaginations alive."

"Max!" Amanda called from the stern. "Come on down and get Harpo ready."

Max walked aft on the flying bridge and

climbed down the ladder into the cockpit.

Three of the sea lions had been fitted with harnesses, and secured to each harness was a video camera whose lens pointed forward. The fourth animal shifted nervously from side to side as if confused.

Amanda handed Max the fourth harness and showed him how to fit it around the sea lion's shoulders, along its belly, behind its flippers and over its back.

As Max slipped the leather straps over the silky skin, the sea lion nuzzled him with its icy nose and tickled him with its whiskers.

Amanda attached the camera and called up to Chase, "All set."

Chase looked out at the ocean. Everything seemed normal, peaceful. And yet . . .

"Are you sure you want to do this?" he asked. "We have three months."

"Yeah, but we won't get whales every day. Let's go."

"Okay, it's your call. How close do you want me to get? I don't need to break federal laws about harassing whales."

"Not too close. The important thing is for us to get in front of the whales so the sea lions don't get pooped trying to catch up with them."

Chase put the boat in gear and accelerated, keeping well away from the whales so as not to alarm them with his engine noise. On a day this calm, there would be no problem keeping the whales in sight; their tail flukes and spouts would be visible for a mile or more, so he traveled what he judged to be five hundred yards in front of them before throttling back and letting the boat idle.

In the stern, the four sea lions were poised behind one another like schoolchildren lined up for lunch. Amanda spoke to each one and made a series of gestures before switching on the video camera and sweeping her arm toward the opening in the transom. Max stood behind her, mimicking her gestures.

One by one, the sea lions waddled to the stern and flung themselves into the ocean.

When they had all surfaced behind the boat, Amanda raised both arms and pointed at the approaching whales, and swept her arms downward.

The sea lions barked, turned and vanished beneath the surface.

"How long can they stay down?" asked Max.

"About ten minutes on each dive," Amanda said. "Not as long as the whales, but they can dive over and over again, and they can go to six or seven hundred feet."

"Deeper than a person."

"Much. And they don't have to decompress, they don't get bends, don't get embolisms."

From the flying bridge, Chase said, "You want the boat to follow them?"

"No, we'll stay here. I don't want the whales to think the boat's chasing them. You can shut the engine off if you want. The ladies know where we are."

"But how can you be sure the sea lions will come back?" Max asked.

"Because they always have," Amanda said, and she smiled.

Chase came down from the flying bridge, turned off the engine and took a glass from a cabinet in the galley. "Come on," he said to Max. "Let's see if we can get lucky."

"Where to?"

"These aren't breeding grounds, and humpbacks usually sing only on their breeding grounds. But maybe, just maybe, we can hear a little concert."

He led Max below, into the forward cabin. He lifted a corner of the carpet and rolled it back a few feet, then dropped to his knees and put an ear to the cold fiberglass deck, motioning Max to do the same.

"What do you hear?" Chase asked.

"Water," Max said, "sort of slopping around, and . . . wait!" His eyes widened. "Yeah, I do! But it's really weak."

"Here," Chase said, and he lifted Max's head

and placed the bottom of the glass under his ear, the open bell against the deck. "Better?"

Max grinned, and Chase knew what he was hearing: the ghostly hoots and avian chirrups, the whistles and tweets, the lovely, lilting conversation between leviathans.

"Cool!" Max said, beaming.

"It sure is," said Chase, and he thought: being a father is too.

The whales passed a few hundred yards to the east of the boat and continued on their way. Gradually their sounds faded until, at last, even with the glass, Max could hear only faint echoes. He and Chase went topside and opened the cooler Mrs. Bixler had packed for them.

· · ·

The first of the sea lions returned after half an hour.

They were sitting in the stern, eating, when they heard a bark and looked over the stern and saw the animal ride a little swell onto the swimstep.

"Hello, Groucho," Amanda said.

Chase shook his head. "I don't know how you can tell."

"Live with them night and day for three years, you'd be able to tell, too."

The sea lion raised itself up onto its long rear flipper and heaved itself through the door in the transom.

As Amanda removed the camera and harness, the sea lion barked excitedly and swung its head from side to side.

"What's she saying?" asked Max.

"She's telling me what she saw," Amanda said. "You know, like, 'Hey, Mom, get a load of this!' "

Chase said, "And what do you think she saw?"

Amanda held up the camera. "We'll look at the tapes on the way in," she said. "As soon as the others come back, we can try to catch up with the whales again." Then she said to Max, "Why don't you give Groucho some fish while I dry this off and reload it?"

Max lifted a hatch in the afterdeck, brought out a bucket of mullet and dangled a fish before the sea lion. It didn't snap at the fish, didn't lunge for it, just extended its neck, accepted the fish and seemed to inhale it.

The second sea lion, Chico, returned ten minutes later, the third, Harpo, a few minutes after that. Max fed them both, and when they had eaten, they waddled across the deck and lay down in a heap with Groucho, and the three of them slept in the sun.

· · ·

Amanda checked her watch; Chase knew this was the tenth time in the past five minutes. Then she shaded her eyes and looked out over the flat water, straining to see any movement on the surface.

"You said they can keep diving all day," he said.

"They can. But they don't, especially after a workout like they had with the sharks." She looked at her watch again. "None of them has ever stayed out for two hours. They're trained to come back in under an hour. Besides, they *want* to: they get tired, hungry." She frowned. "Particularly Zeppo. She's the lazy one. She's late. Very late."

"Maybe she just decided to take off."

"Not a chance," Amanda said flatly.

"I don't know how you can be so certain. She's a—"

"They're *my* animals," she snapped.

Chase raised his hands in a gesture of surrender, and said, "Sorry."

"Where are the binoculars?"

"There's a set up top and a set down below."

Amanda started to climb the ladder to the flying bridge.

"We can go look for her," Chase said.

"No, she knows where we are. We're staying here till she comes back."

If, Chase found himself thinking. *If.*

25

AS IT had moved into deeper water, scouring the sloping sands in search of things to kill, the membranes in its head had sensed new sounds—unfamiliar, high-pitched, far away. It had tracked the sounds, feeling them grow ever louder and more pronounced.

Finally, in water that had lost its gray-green gloom and become clear blue, it had come upon the sources of the sounds: animals larger than it had ever seen, certainly too large to attack, dim shadows that rose and fell with ease, showing no vulnerability, no fear.

It had been about to turn away, to resume its hunt elsewhere, when it had noticed other things among the large animals: smaller, quicker things, things that might be prey. It had waited in the distance, moving just enough to keep pace.

Once, one of the new things had wandered

close, and it had tried to catch it from behind—lunging forward with swift kicks and sweeping strokes—but the thing had sensed its approach and had fled, too fast to pursue.

Eventually, it had fallen behind, and soon the living things were out of sight, leaving only a tantalizing trail of sounds.

Now it hovered in midwater, its eyes glowing like white-hot coals as they probed the fathomless blue.

A sudden pressure wave startled it; it looked up, and it saw a black blur receding upward toward the light: one of the smaller living things had returned, swooping by and continuing on its way.

Instantly alert, it willed adrenaline into its veins and lactic acid into its musculature. It stayed as still as possible, moving its limbs barely enough to keep from falling.

Another animal passed by, slowing briefly but not stopping.

It did not give chase, sensing that any attempt at pursuit would be futile. It waited, feeling strength suffuse its body.

Another animal appeared, and this one came close, circling slowly and gazing curiously.

The creature hung motionless, wanting to appear harmless, dead.

The animal drew closer, shaking its head, expelling a stream of tiny bubbles.

The creature waited . . . and waited . . . and then there came an instant when the neurons in its brain formed a conclusion that possibility had become opportunity.

It struck, lashing out with steel claws. The claws found softness. They plunged deep into adipose flesh and curled in upon one another, fashioning a grip.

The other arm sprang forward, and its claws, too, found pinguid tissue.

The animal lurched backward. Its mouth opened with an explosion of bubbles. Its appendages thrashed, its body contorted as it struggled upward.

The creature expected the animal to retaliate, to defend itself, but it did not. Now the creature knew that the animal was an alien here, could not survive here, so success could be achieved simply by holding it here.

After a few moments, the animal stopped struggling. Its head lolled, and blood gushed from its torn flesh.

The creature began to feed. The animal was covered with a thick layer of fat—nourishing, energizing, warming fat—and so it was positively buoyant, it would not sink. Predator and prey were bonded together in still suspension.

As it ate, its peripheral vision detected other animals—larger animals, predators—attracted by the scent of blood and oil drifting in the current.

It surrounded its food and consumed it ravenously.

Most of the animal was edible. Bones fell away into the abyss, and were surrounded by scavengers; bits of flesh escaped and were swarmed upon by schools of little fish. There was a hard inedible object, which the creature tore free and cast away. It floated upward, toward the surface.

26

"HOW LONG till dark?" Amanda asked. She sat on the bulwarks, stroking the heads of the three sea lions.

The late-day sun cast long shadows on the sea, and as she turned her head, Chase saw shadows on her face as well—in the lines of grief that etched the skin beneath her eyes.

"An hour," he said, "but we don't need light to get back. We can stay here all night if you want."

"No," she said softly. "There's no point."

They had not talked much during the past couple of hours; they had sat and watched until their eyes were red with strain and fatigue. Max had tried to entertain the three sea lions, had tried to feed them, but they seemed to sense something was wrong, and they had refused to respond.

Chase had offered no more theories, though he had one. Theories wouldn't help, especially if the one he harbored was correct.

"Okay," he said finally. He stood up and looked to the west, at the silhouette of Block Island. They had drifted at least two miles. He walked forward to start the engine as Tall Man climbed to the flying bridge.

"It could've been the white shark," Amanda said, as if continuing an interrupted conversation.

Chase started, for that had been his theory, the only one that made sense. The sea lions had escaped from the shark before, but they had been near the refuge of the boat. Alone in the open ocean, a sea lion—especially one tired and distracted—might well be ambushed by a big, fast great white shark.

"Yeah," he said. "It could've." He pushed the starter button and flicked the switch that turned on the boat's running lights. He rapped the overhead with his knuckles, to tell Tall Man to head for home.

"Maybe the others picked up something," Amanda said. "Let's look at their tapes."

As Tall Man swung the boat around to the west, Amanda took a video monitor from one of her boxes, placed it on the table in the cabin and switched it on. She connected a VCR to the monitor and inserted one of the tapes. When she had rewound it, she pushed the "play" button, and sat on the bench seat. Max sat across the table from her; Chase stood at the end of the table.

She fast-forwarded through a couple of minutes of blank ocean blue, then slowed the tape as the first image of a whale came onto the screen.

"The whale looks so small," Max said.

"It's a wide-angle lens," said Amanda. "It has to be, or all you'd see would be a lot of shots of blubber."

As they watched, the whale grew until it filled the frame.

"How close is she now?" asked Max.

"Sixty, seventy feet. She'll close in, then she'll stop at about thirty feet."

The image continued to grow, traveling along the side of the whale, passing an enormous fin, then slowing as it reached the head. When the eye came into view, Amanda pushed the "pause" button, and the image froze.

"Look at that eye," she said to Max. "Tell me that's not an intelligent being."

"It's different from a shark's eye," Max said. "It's . . . I don't know . . . just different. Not as flat."

"Richer, deeper." Amanda smiled, enthusiasm for the moment erasing her loss. "You know why? Humpbacks have a brain the size of a basketball. They say the eye is the mirror of the soul. Well, there's a heck of a soul behind that eye."

She pushed the "play" button, and the image moved again.

There were shots of the whale from all angles, as the sea lion had swooped around it, playing with it, riding in its slipstream. The whale had ignored the sea lion, never altering its predestined course.

Amanda fast-forwarded through ten or fifteen minutes of tape, until through the jiggly scan lines she saw the whale begin to undulate more vigorously and plunge into a deep dive. She slowed the tape then and watched the image grow dimmer as the sea lion had followed the whale down into the benthic darkness.

When the whale was no more than a dark blob against the inky blueness, the camera angle suddenly swung upward and rushed toward the light far above.

"She broke off," Amanda said, "I'd guess at about five hundred feet."

The tape ended, and she replaced it with another.

The second sea lion had followed a large female humpback, and as the image on the screen grew, Max suddenly shouted, "Look! A baby!"

A calf, probably twenty feet long, was nestled under its mother's left pectoral flipper.

"They always ride there," Amanda said.

"Why?" asked Max.

"Partly to learn. Watch, you'll see that he does everything she does, imitates every move."

Indeed, the calf duplicated exactly his mother's every movement. When she rose to breathe, he breathed; when she dove, he dove; when she rolled on her side to look up at the sea lion, he rolled with her.

"See her looking?" Amanda said. "She's protecting him, too. If there's a big shark around, we'll see her snuggle him really close and get pretty agitated. She'll probably take him down into the deep."

But the mother didn't get upset. Evidently satisfied with her identification of the sea lion, she rolled back onto a level plane and continued her leisurely journey near the surface.

"Nothing," Amanda said, and she fast-forwarded through the rest of the tape.

Two minutes into the third tape, Amanda laughed and said, "This is Harpo's."

"How can you tell?" Max said.

"She's a chicken. Look"—she pointed at the screen—"she comes up behind a whale, and as soon as the tail flukes flap, she skitters away." The image on the screen went to empty blue, broke the surface and angled down onto another whale. "It takes her about ten minutes to figure out that they're not gonna eat her. She's learning, she's just not as quick as the others. They've all got quirks."

"Like what?"

"Groucho likes to get too close, so she gives me a lot of soft tape, out of focus. It's as if she doesn't feel she's made contact unless she touches the whale. Chico likes to hassle the whales, especially the small ones. She's just playing, but sometimes she upsets them."

"What about Zeppo?" Chase asked.

Amanda hesitated, as if abruptly yanked back to reality. "As I said, she's lazy. What worries me is, she's also the most curious. She'll swim right up to something, just to see what it is."

The image on Harpo's tape zoomed from whale to whale. There were a few good close-ups, and one spectacular shot of a whale breaching—roaring to the surface, exploding through to the sunlight above and crashing down again with a cataclysmic splash—but the last few minutes of the tape were blank ocean blue. Amanda fast-forwarded through it.

She had turned away from the screen to say something to Chase, when Max yelled, "Hey! Look!"

She returned to the screen. "What?"

"Go back."

Amanda scanned the tape backward, and after a few seconds she saw something—vague and blurry, but definitely something—on the upper right-hand corner of the screen. She passed it, pushed the "play" button, and the tape spooled forward.

Something was there, a shape, and then it was gone, and the image shuddered and zoomed away toward the surface.

"What the hell was that?" Chase asked, leaning forward on his elbows, staring at the monitor.

"I don't know," Amanda said, "but whatever it was sure scared poor Harpo. Did you see how fast she took off?"

Suddenly the engine slowed, and Tall Man's foot stomped three times on the overhead. Chase walked aft, out into the cockpit, and called up to the flying bridge, "See something?"

"A red blinker ahead," Tall Man said. "Like an emergency flasher. The light's so tough this time of day, I can't tell."

Chase leaned over the side and looked forward. It was almost dark, the water was like a sheet of black steel; against it, a tiny red light was blinking at one-second intervals. He grabbed the boat hook, braced his knees against the bulwark and waited for Tall Man to guide the boat to the light.

As the light slipped along the side of the boat, Chase reached for it with the boat hook. It was attached to something hard, about twelve inches square, and Chase twisted the hook till he snagged it, then brought it aboard and set it on the bulwark.

"It's a camera housing," he called to Tall Man.

"Ours?" Tall Man pushed the throttle forward and resumed his course for the island.

Chase heard footsteps behind him, then a short, sharp gasp.

"That's Zeppo's," said Amanda.

They took the housing into the cabin, dried it and set it on the table. The housing was undamaged, but the harness straps had been shredded. Sadly, silently, Amanda removed the tape from the camera and put it into the VCR. She rewound it, then pushed the "play" button.

The first few minutes of the tape were indistinguishable from the others: long shots of whales, close-ups of whales, whales cruising, whales rolling, whales diving. Then came an interminable shot of the surface, from just above, then from just below.

"She's basking," Amanda said, and there was a thickness to her voice. "I told you she was the lazy one."

The camera went underwater again and showed two whales in the distance, moving away. For perhaps fifteen seconds it pursued them, before turning away and showing nothing but blue.

Amanda said, "She gave up."

"But look," Max said, pointing at a minuscule

black figure in the center of the screen. "That's one of the other sea lions. Zeppo was following her, coming home."

The image roller-coastered up and down, as the sea lion had accelerated through the water, trying to catch up to its fellows. Then it slowed and broke through the surface—for a breath, presumably—and when it submerged it cruised slowly for a moment. Then, abruptly, it veered off.

Chase said, "Something's caught her attention."

Though there were no other animals visible in the blue vastness, speed and direction were discernible from rays of sunlight refracted by the surface into arrows that shot down into the darkness, and by the countless motes of plankton that glittered as they passed the lens.

"She's circling something," Amanda said.

"Why can't we see it?" asked Chase.

"Because she's above it, looking down, and the camera's on her back."

The sea lion had gone into a long upward loop—they saw the light from the surface flash by far away—and then had dived, turned and hung upright in the water, vertical and motionless. The surface shimmered in the distance above.

Amanda said, "She's looking at it; she's not afraid of it."

"Isn't she going to take pictures of it?" asked Max.

"She doesn't think she's supposed to; the only things she's supposed to tape are—"

Suddenly the camera jolted backward, and the blue water was clouded by a black billow.

Amanda screamed.

For ten or fifteen seconds, the image swung crazily, lurching left and right, dimmed by what looked like ink and then clear and then dimmed again.

Something shiny gleamed in front of the lens.

"Stop the tape!" Chase said, but Amanda was frozen, her eyes wide, one hand over her mouth. And so he reached forward and pressed the backward-scan button.

The image was fuzzy, for the shiny thing was too close for the lens to focus. But as he advanced the tape again, frame by frame, Chase had no doubt about what he was seeing: five claws, curved, pointed, razor-sharp and made of stainless steel.

27

"HIT ME again, Ray," Rusty Puckett said to the bartender at the Crow's Nest. He slid his empty glass across the bar and shoved a five-dollar bill after it.

"Enough's enough, Rusty," said Ray. "Go on home."

"Hey! I put a fuckin' fifty down there, and said lemme know when I worked my way through it." Puckett pointed to the jumble of bills beside the ashtray. "I ain't halfway there yet."

"Watch your mouth!" Ray said. He put his hands on the bar, and leaned close to Puckett. "Happy hour's come and gone, Rusty; there's people here for dinner, they're not interested in hearing your cock-and-bull stories. Do us both a favor: pick up your change and head on home."

Puckett turned around on his stool and gazed glassily at the room. Ray was right: the bar had filled up, and there was a line of people waiting for tables in the dining room. When had all this happened? He looked at his watch, closing one eye to sharpen the numbers on the dial. Christ! He'd been here three hours.

He noticed a few people staring at him, and guessed they'd been listening to him while he was telling Ray about what he'd seen. To hell with them, he didn't care, it was true, every bit of it. He winked at one of them, a not-bad-looking woman, and saw her blush and turn away. She was probably interested; maybe he'd go have a talk with her.

Something funny popped into his head. He turned back to Ray and said, loud enough for everyone to hear, "You don't dare shut *me* off, Raymond; the fuckin' place'd go broke."

Ray didn't laugh, in fact he looked kind of pissed off, and all of a sudden he raised the fold-back panel in the bar, came through and grabbed Puckett by the scruff of his shirt.

Puckett felt himself lifted off the stool, felt Ray's hand jam a wad of money into his pants pocket and found himself being frog-marched out the door.

"You can come back when you sober up and stop hallucinating," Ray said. "I'd worry if I was you, Rusty. You're in the grip of the goddamn DTs."

Puckett heard the door close behind him, and Ray's voice saying, "Sorry, folks."

He stood on the street, bewildered, swaying slightly. A couple got out of a car and gave him a wide berth as they made their way toward the restaurant.

He put a hand on the side of the building to stop the swaying. Then he started down the street, keeping his eyes on each foot as it landed in front of the other.

What the hell did Ray mean, "cock-and-bull stories"? Ray knew him well enough to know he didn't make up fairy tales. And he wasn't in the grip of any DTs, either. He knew damn well what he'd seen, what had almost killed him, and he hadn't exaggerated anything.

It sounded stupid, impossible. But it was the truth. He'd seen a fuckin' monster.

PART FIVE

▲ ▲ ▲ ▲ ▲ ▲ ▲

THE
BLESSING

28

"ARE YOU sure you don't want to wait for Amanda and me?" Chase said. He held the bow line of the Whaler while Max started the motor and stowed his camera under the steering console. "She'll be ready in half an hour, eleven-thirty at the latest."

"I can't," Max said. "The Blessing of the Fleet starts at noon; if I don't go now, I'll never get a decent spot."

"You sound to me like a young man who has a date." Chase smiled.

Max grimaced. "Dad . . ."

"Okay, sorry. . . . Now: you know where the anchor's stowed, you've got two life jackets aboard, you—"

"We've been through all that."

"Right." Chase sighed and tossed the bow line

into the boat. "Park the boat at the club; beach it if there're no slips."

"Okay." Max put the boat in gear, turned the wheel and moved slowly away from the dock.

"Remember," Chase called after him, "no stopping on the way . . . for *any*thing . . . no matter what you see."

Max waved and shouted, "See you!"

Chase stood watching as Max accelerated, bringing the boat up onto a plane.

At first, Chase had resisted letting Max take the Whaler; the boy had never been out in the boat alone. Though the channel into Waterboro was well marked, there were rocks to hit if you were careless. Though the outboard motors were meticulously maintained by Tall Man, all outboards harbored gremlins and could seize up and stop at any moment for no apparent reason. Though Max had shown that he was a careful boatman and a fine swimmer, what would happen if he had to go overboard and swim for shore?

But for the past three days, the weather had been lousy: the wind had blown from the northeast, a relentless fifteen to twenty knots, sometimes gusting to forty, and a chill rain had soaked the coast from New Jersey to Maine. There had been nothing for Max to do, except for an occasional trip to town with Chase or Tall Man, during which the boy had disappeared into the warren of back streets and tiny houses and, Chase hoped and assumed, made friends with some of the local children. Max had looked forward to the Blessing of the Fleet, had been caught up in the town's enthusiasm for the celebration.

Now that the day had arrived and the weather had at last turned fine, Chase wanted Max to enjoy it, and so he had relented.

He almost wished the weather had gotten worse. The good thing about bad weather was that it kept people out of the water, boats had stayed ashore and nobody else had been hurt. Whatever was out there, wherever it was, it had had nothing to prey upon. Chase hoped that fair weather wouldn't bring on a feeding frenzy.

The morning after the sea lion had been killed, he had taken the videotape to the police station and shown it to Gibson. He had suggested postponing or even canceling the Blessing until they could determine what the animal on the tape might be.

Gibson's reply had been brusque. "Forget it, Simon," he had said. "I'm not gonna cancel the biggest event of the summer because of two seconds of crappy videotape that doesn't look like diddly . . . or on the testimony of some drunk."

"What drunk?"

"Rusty Puckett. He got himself sauced to the gills last night, started telling everybody that he'd seen some mutant zombie from hell. He made such a nuisance of himself, got thrown out of the Crow's Nest and two gin mills, that I locked him up."

"He's here? Can I talk to him?"

"Nope, not till after the Blessing. Then you can talk to him all you want, till you both come down with bullshit poisoning." Gibson had paused. "Have you shown this tape to anybody else?"

"No."

"Good. I think I'll just keep it here for the next few days. We have all the rest of the summer to get hysterical."

"I wish I thought you were right, Rollie," Chase had said. "But something's out there."

"Then let it stay there, Simon, or let it go to hell away. Either way, I don't imagine it's gonna come ashore and start hassling tourists."

• • •

When the Whaler was so far away that it was invisible against the contours of the mainland, Chase walked up the hill and down the slope to the sea lion tank. He could see Amanda standing on the concrete apron, using fish to try to lure the sea lions out of the tank. They were shaking their heads, refusing.

"They won't do it," Amanda said when Chase arrived. "It's like every day since we got back from the whales: no matter what I do, they will not leave that tank. It's as if they're receiving warning signals from the water."

"What signals . . . electromagnetic?"

"I guess so. All I know is, something is telling them to stay out of the sea. And they're behaving like they're scared to death."

29

MAX SAW her as soon as he rounded Waterboro Point, and he felt his heart jump.

Though he still had to cross the entire harbor—a quarter of a mile, at least—there was no mistaking her: a slender, delicate figure standing alone at the end of the club dock, wearing blue, as always. In the ten days he had known her, he had never seen her wear anything but blue: blue sweaters, blue shifts, blue skirts with blue blouses. It was as if she knew how much blue became her, reflecting the blue in her eyes and complementing the shining gold of her hair.

He waved, though he was sure she couldn't see him, not through the maze of sailboats that clogged the harbor, all bedecked with multicolored flags and pennants and burgees in honor of the Blessing of the Fleet. Even the fleet vessels themselves—dark, rust-spotted behemoths laden with nets and outriggers and radar domes and enormous winch drums—displayed rainbow pennants as anniversary finery, as if eager on this once-a-year day to live up to their absurdly precious names: *Miss Eula, Miss Daisy, Miss Wendy.*

Max wanted to ram the throttle forward and zip between the boats, but he didn't, for he knew the marine police were on the prowl, and the last thing he needed was a speeding ticket. He had no Connecticut license to drive a boat, he was underage to be alone in a motorboat, and even if he were to be let off with a warning, the news was certain to get back to his father, who would have no choice but to ground him.

So he forced himself to putter slowly down the harbor, checking, whenever he came into an open space, to be sure Elizabeth hadn't left, given up on him and gone off to watch the Blessing on her own.

Every time he looked, she was there, waiting. Not reading a book or checking her watch or pacing. Just waiting, as she had promised she would.

When Max passed the last of the big boats, a hundred yards from the dock, and began to thread his way through the club's small fleet of moored Bluejays, he waved again. This time she saw him, and she raised a hand and smiled.

He was confused by the feelings rocketing

around inside him. He had known girls all his life, had been around them daily since nursery school. He had been to parties with girls, and to movies, though always in groups, with other boys. He had friends who were girls.

But he had never had a girlfriend. He had never suffered the awful aches of jealousy and longing. He had never kissed a girl, and though he had seen a lot of kissing on-screen, and had often fantasized about doing it and more, he wasn't sure he would know how to go about it. Movie kissing looked easy and fun, but then, movie kissers weren't twelve years old.

Max wasn't even sure that what he was feeling for Elizabeth were boyfriend-girlfriend feelings. He knew only that they were different from any feelings he had ever had for a girl, and that Elizabeth was different from any girl he had ever known.

She was pretty—beautiful, even—but she behaved as if she didn't know it . . . or, if she did, she didn't use it as a weapon the way some girls did. She was smart, she had read ten times as many books as Max had, including a lot of adult books, but she never showed off. She was shy, but it wasn't a reclusive kind of shyness, not self-conscious or ashamed of something; rather, it was a sweet shyness, serene and nonjudgmental, as if she were simply happy with herself.

Maybe it had to do with being deaf—surely, a major handicap like deafness had to be a determining factor in someone's life—but Max didn't know enough about deafness to guess how it could affect a personality.

She was always glad to see him, and he found that he was feeling a kind of emptiness when he wasn't with her, which led him to conclude that this probably *was* the beginning of a boyfriend-girlfriend thing. The prospect alarmed him because it meant that a time would come when he'd have to kiss her—or try to—because that was what boyfriends and girlfriends did.

It frightened him, too, because he didn't trust his own perceptions. He was already suffering from sensory overload: the myths he had created about his father were being dispelled, replaced daily by new realities—not in a bad way, for the truths about his father were quite as fine as the fictions he had fashioned, it was just that everything was new.

He had never doubted the stated circumstances of his parents' divorce, but he had recently come to realize that the fact that he had been living with his mother all these years was implicit criticism of his father. Why had he never lived with his father? Were money and private schools and tennis lessons and summer homes really better for him than peanut-butter-and-jelly sandwiches and swimming with sea lions?

Then there was Amanda, about whom Max's feelings were, as best he could describe them, weird. She wasn't his mother and didn't pretend to be, and she treated him more like an adult than his mother ever had, which made him feel closer to her than to his mother.

He didn't know what his father felt about Amanda, or Amanda about his father. They liked each other, that was for sure, they were friends.

It was all too much for Max to cope with, and it made him question his itchy feelings about Elizabeth.

Maybe he was going crazy, he thought as he motored slowly along the floating docks in search of an empty slip. Maybe everything would sort itself out when he went back West.

On the other hand, he wasn't sure he wanted to go back West.

He found a slip and stopped the engine and tossed Elizabeth the painter.

"Hello," she said, and she beamed.

"Hi." He reached back and raised the engine so the propeller was out of the water, and locked it in place.

"Hello," she said again. There was a studied deliberateness to the word. "Hello."

Only then did it strike him: she had spoken to him, aloud, out in the open where anyone could hear.

"Hey!" he said, smiling as he turned to face her, speaking clearly so she could read his lips. "Good for you. That sounded real good."

When they had first met, she had not spoken at all, though he recalled the eerie feeling that some sort of communication had taken place. When he had found her again, after seeing her picture in the paper, she had written notes on a pad she kept in her pocket, with a ballpoint pen that hung on a chain around her neck, and had taught him to read a few rudimentary hand signs. As they had seen more and more of each other, she had confessed that her speech embarrassed her. Since she couldn't hear it, she had no idea what it sounded like to others, but she could tell from people's faces that it sounded strange.

By now, there were times when she seemed to know what Max was thinking before he said a word. When he asked her about it, she dismissed it as a simple skill, no big deal, that had developed over the years since the strange fever had made her deaf. She likened it to a dog's ability to hear sounds that humans can't, and explained that a doctor had told her that when a person loses a primary sense like hearing, often other senses will become much more acute. She said it didn't work all the time, or with most people.

Max grabbed his camera and hopped up onto the dock. "Did you find a spot?" he asked.

"Cool," Elizabeth said, and she grinned and took Max's hand and led him up the road toward the borough. She was barefoot—she never wore shoes, at least he had never seen her in any—but she didn't flinch even on the roughest stretches of the pebbly pavement.

The high school band was assembling in the boat-storage yard at the foot of Beach Street. Drum majorettes in sequins and spangles practiced tossing their batons in the air; trumpeters and trombonists blared cacophonous bars of nameless tunes; two boys were attempting to hoist a tuba onto the shoulders of a girl built like a linebacker; an old gray dog sat in the dirt and barked randomly.

Masons, Elks and Rotarians gathered in cadres behind the band. Members of the Holy Ghost Society, decked out in colorful Portuguese costumes, admired one another as they smoked their final cigarettes and, a few of them, shared a paper bag containing a flagon of sustaining elixir.

The road into town had been closed to automobile traffic, and hundreds of pedestrians swarmed over it and up toward the Catholic church on Settlers Square, from which the bishop would emerge to lead the procession through town and to the docks for the ceremonial blessing.

Elizabeth led Max past the crowd, across the square and down Oak Street, where throngs jammed the sidewalks. Little children sat on the hoods of cars; teenagers perched in the branches of trees.

Max stopped Elizabeth and gestured at the people and said, "We'll never see a thing."

She winked at him and touched her chest—trust me, she was saying—and dragged him onward.

A little saltbox house stood on a corner. Elizabeth led Max behind the house, opened a gate into the yard and ushered him through. She pointed to a hole in the base of the fence on the far side of the yard—a big dog had probably dug it—and darted across the grass, dropped to her stomach and squeezed through the hole. Max followed her, and when he stood up on the other side of the fence, saw that they were in the courtyard of what had once been a church but was now a private house. The belfry or clock tower or whatever it had been loomed high over the roof of the house.

Elizabeth scampered up the wide steps to the front porch and stood before the massive double door. She gestured to Max, cupping her hands in front of her and bending her knees.

"Hey," he said, "I don't—"

"Away," she replied.

"Yeah, but—"

"Okay," she said, and again she touched her chest. "Really."

Max shrugged and cupped his hands, bracing his elbows on his knees.

She put a foot into his cupped hands, braced one of her hands on his head and hoisted herself up until she could reach the top of the lintel over the door. She felt along the shelf, then jumped down.

Smiling, she held a key up to Max's face, and said, "Cousins."

She opened the door, let Max and herself in, then closed the door and locked it. She led Max to the left, through a door and to a staircase that spiraled up the tower. They climbed for what seemed to Max an hour, until at last the stairs ended at a single door, bolted top and bottom. They slid back the bolts, Elizabeth pushed the door open and Max stepped out onto a narrow walkway.

His breath caught, and he heard himself say, "Wow . . ."

It was like being in a plane or a helicopter, like soaring above the town without moving. They were higher than any tree or building; the borough lay beneath them like a diorama, and beyond, Max believed, he could see practically forever. To the east were Little Narragansett Bay and Napatree Point and the gray-green shapes of Osprey and Block. To the south, sailboats and oceangoing freighters were framed against the low silhouette of Montauk Point. In the west he could see hints of Stonington and Mystic, and in the north the ribbon of highway leading to Rhode Island.

"Cool?" Elizabeth said.

"*I'll* say." Max opened the lens of his camera and looked for sights to shoot.

Far below, they heard the first ragged bars of "The Stars and Stripes Forever," and a cheer went up from the crowd.

Max zoomed his lens and shot pictures of the bishop and the drum majorettes and the band; he immortalized the Holy Ghosters and the Elks and the Rotarians.

And then suddenly the parade was by them and heading for the point, and Elizabeth was tugging at his arm. He followed her down the stairs and out of the house, boosted her up to return the key, then let her lead him through a maze of back streets and alleyways paralleling the parade route.

As they neared the point, the noise grew louder, and the onshore breeze was laced with the aroma of frying fat.

The town of Waterboro tapered to an end, like the tip of a pencil, in a gravel parking lot that overlooked Fishers Island Sound and was occupied, usually, by sightseers during the day and by teenaged revelers at night. Today, cars had been banned, and replaced by pickup trucks and minivans and aluminum specialty wagons purveying T-shirts, pennants, mugs, buttons, pins, posters and food . . . fried, boiled, broiled, grilled, skewered, frozen, raw and alive, served on sticks and spits, in napkins and newspapers and folds of flaky bread.

Along one side of the parking lot, behind a rickety fence, lay the town's only public beach, a small strip of sand fronting the harbor.

Though the day was fine and already warm, the beach was practically deserted: a baby-sitter, wearing an Indigo Girls sweatshirt, divided her attention between a copy of *People* magazine and a two-year-old who toddled along the water's edge, gathering shells. Beyond, in the harbor, sailboats hung on moorings, bobbing gently from the wakes of launches that ferried yachtsmen to and from the town docks.

As Max followed Elizabeth through the crowd that waited for the parade to arrive, he was entranced, imagining that he had been transported to a Middle Eastern bazaar. Though he recognized only a fraction of the foods piled high on folding tables, and though he had eaten breakfast only a couple of hours earlier, he was tantalized by the rich, exotic aromas.

He stopped before a van selling plump sausages in doughy rolls, and he fished in his pocket for money.

Ahead of Max, threading her way among couples and families and men discussing the downfall of the Red Sox, Elizabeth sensed that she was alone, and she turned, retraced her steps and found Max smiling sheepishly at her as he chewed on a sausage sandwich, red grease drooling down his chin.

She started to speak, then took her pen from inside her blouse and her pad from her pocket, scribbled a note and passed it to Max.

He read aloud, "Do you *like* eating greasy dead things?" Then he grinned, and said clearly, "Sure . . . doesn't everybody?"

30

IT SWAM back and forth erratically . . . confused, tormented, tantalized. It could see very little in the foul and weed-clotted shallow water; its brain registered a cascade of sounds and impulses, but none was discernible, none appeared to hold promise.

Some of the impulses were threatening, and although it did not know fear, it had been programmed to preserve itself and thus to defend itself, so signals of threat triggered reflexive alarms. And yet none of the threats materialized.

Its store of energy was nearly exhausted; it had eaten nothing since the fat, sleek thing that had wandered close in the deep.

It had searched near the shores and far from them, over sandy bottoms and among clusters of big rocks. Living things that had once patrolled the shallows were gone, or hidden. None of the vulnerable things, the easy prey, had appeared above; none of the clumsy things had entered the water from the shore.

It had noticed changes in temperature and turbulence, but could not connect them to the lack of food.

Now, suddenly, it knew there was food nearby, but it could not find it. The water seemed permeated with the fragrance of flesh, but there was no flesh to be found.

Slowly, carefully, it thrust itself upward and let its head break through the glassy film of the surface.

Its olfactories were assaulted by aromas that tripped a flood of gastric juices in its belly.

Its eyes, once their lenses cleared, saw living things . . . not just one, but a host of living things, all gathered in a herd, all taunting it with their smells. Adrenaline pumped renewed energy through its veins.

But then its alarms took control, warning it that the living things were *too* many, and too far from the safety of its world. It could not feed on them and survive.

Except for two . . . smaller ones, apart from the rest, alone at the border between the worlds.

But to take even those two would require a complex decision, a decision it had been programmed to make but never had, a decision that could end its life instead of preserving it.

Conflict tore at the creature's primitive brain and incomplete conditioning. Survival had two paths, which warred with each other.

And so it swam back and forth erratically, and the urgency within its body grew into frenzy.

31

AS THE parade made the turn around the point in front of the parking lot, band members ducked out of line and grabbed cans of soda from friends among the onlookers; Elks took hits from proffered paper bags; Holy Ghosters accepted linguisas from their awestruck offspring. Even the youngsters in the bishop's entourage were not immune to cajolery: one accepted a lighted cigarette from a compatriot in the crowd—like a relay runner taking a baton—and took a deep drag on it before tucking it under his robe.

Max photographed it all, until, just when he had the pirate smoker in his frame and pushed the shutter release, he heard from within the body of his camera the whirr of rewinding film. He watched the counter click swiftly back to zero, then said, "Damn."

Elizabeth nudged him and raised her eyebrows: what is it?

"Out of film," Max said, pointing at the counter. "D'you know where I can buy some more?"

Elizabeth nodded. She pointed at Max, then at the parade, and said, "Follow." Then she pointed at herself and used two fingers of one hand to portray a running figure. She said something else, something that sounded to Max like "ketchup."

"But how'll I find you?" he said. "How—"

She put her hand on her chest, then took his hand and put it on top of hers, and she winked at him.

"Okay," he said, laughing.

She turned away and darted through the crowd.

It took only a couple of minutes for the final stragglers in the parade—two boys leading a gargantuan Saint Bernard caparisoned like a clown—to round the point and head down Beach Street toward the commercial docks.

The concessionaries were already shutting up shop, extinguishing fires and bagging trash, hurrying to move to another parking lot on the other side of the borough, where they would reopen for the post-blessing feast.

Max bought a candied apple from the last open stand, then ambled behind the Saint Bernard.

As he passed the fence surrounding the public beach, he saw a little child with its face pressed against the wire mesh. Its mouth and hands were filthy, as if it had been eating dirt, and its soiled diaper sagged on one hip. Behind the child, a teenaged girl lay on her back on the sand, a magazine held above her face.

The child's stubby fingers clutched the wire, and its big eyes followed Max.

Max looked at the child, then, impulsively, stepped to the fence, leaned over it and offered the candied apple. "Here y'go, buddy," he said with a smile.

The child beamed, reached up with both hands, grabbed the candied apple by the stick, tried to jam the entire apple into its mouth . . . and fell backward. The apple tumbled into the sand. The child rolled over, clutched the apple and licked at it, gurgling gleefully.

Max turned away and started down the street.

· · ·

As soon as the last food truck had departed, two volunteers from the Holy Ghost Society appeared on foot and began to clean up the parking lot. The gravel was littered with cigarette butts, paper cups, sparerib bones, half-eaten hotdogs and sandwiches, and sausages that had burst in the cooking and been shoved off the fire. There were eggshells and vegetables, squid rings and octopus tentacles, chicken wings and scattered bits of random entrails. A sickly sweet odor of olive oil and salad dressing and grease hung like a gas over the parking lot.

The volunteers wore gloves and carried camp shovels, and they scooped the offal into plastic bins.

"People're worse'n pigs," muttered one. "Fuckin' place looks like a slaughterhouse."

"And stinks like a morgue," agreed the other.

Fifty-gallon barrels had been placed around the parking lot to collect trash, and the volunteers lugged a loaded bin to the nearest barrel. It was full, as was the second, and the third.

"Well, shit . . . *now* what're we s'posed to do?"

"What about that one?" The volunteer pointed at a barrel on the beach.

His partner shrugged. "Let's try it. I'm not takin' this crap home with me, for sure."

Carrying the plastic bin, they opened the gate to the beach and crossed the soft sand.

The barrel was empty. As they dumped the bin, they noticed a small child sitting nearby, happily gnawing on something, and even over the rank stench of garbage, they could smell the child.

Ten yards away, a woman lay on her back with a magazine covering her face.

"Hey!" one of the volunteers called. "You this kid's mother?"

The woman lifted the magazine, and they saw that she was in her teens.

"That'll be the day," she said.

"Well, you know how to change a diaper?"

"What're you," the girl said, "the poop patrol?"

Offended, the volunteer said, "Listen, you . . ." and he took a step toward the girl.

His partner stopped him with a hand on his sleeve. "Leave it, Lenny. The kid's carrying a load, so what? You mess with the girl, next thing you know you're in court for sexual harassment."

"I'd sooner harass a sheep," he said, loud enough for the girl to hear.

"I bet you do, too," the girl said, and she let the magazine fall over her face again.

"Leave it, Lenny. Just leave it."

The volunteers filled the plastic bin twice more and dumped it into the barrel on the beach, shouldered their shovels and walked home to wash their hands and have a drink.

32

IT LAY prone in the shallows, only its eyes and nose out of water.

Most of the living things had gone, and the percussive jumble that had thundered on its tympanic membranes had faded into a distant pattering. Only two living things remained, and they emitted no threat signals, so its alarms were silent.

But the tantalizing odor persisted, a lush stew of flesh scents, stronger than ever, closer than ever. And perplexing, for it did not seem to be associated with the living things.

It inched forward, pulling itself with its claws. Its gills opened and closed rapidly, pumping vigorously; the oxygen content of the surface water was weak and corrupted with impurities.

The strongest spoor of prey came from an alien object near the living things.

Its capacity for making decisions was poor, its

sense of options undeveloped. It craved everything, but sensed that it had to choose.

And then, as if a gate had suddenly opened in its brain, it received a message telling it that it could have everything. It must only decide what to have first.

It willed its gills to close, it rose up on its powerful arms and sprang forward.

33

THE GIRL had fallen asleep, though she hadn't meant to; it was the cardinal sin for a baby-sitter with a two-year-old near the water. Her sleep was light, barely deep enough to accommodate a fluttery dream about Princess Diana asking her to be her roommate and help care for the two little princes. All of a sudden, out of nowhere, one of the princes was crying—shrieking, actually.

She bolted upright, knocking the magazine off her face, and turned to look for Jeremy.

He was there, sitting on the sand where he had been, and she was flooded with a rush of relief.

He was howling—head thrown back, mouth gaping, eyes closed—and she knew kids well enough to know that this wasn't a howl of temper or anger, but one of pain or terror, as if he had burned himself or cut himself or been bitten by a dog.

She went to him, and stood over him, and said, "What's wrong . . . you hurt?"

He didn't answer, not even with one of his dumb baby words, he just shrieked louder.

"Jeremy . . . don't be a wuss . . . tell me where it hurts."

He opened his eyes and raised his arms, begging to be picked up, which surprised her because he never wanted her to pick him up, he didn't like her any more than she liked him. Their association was based on mutual tolerance, the tacit recognition of a bad situation that neither of them wanted but both had to endure.

"Forget it," she said, shaking her head. "You think I need poop all over my clothes?"

He howled again, even louder, and stretched his arms up to her.

Flustered, she said, "Jesus . . . shut up, will you?" She looked around to see if anyone was watching. "What *is* it?" An idea occurred to her. "Asshole burn, that what it is? Yeah, that must be it. Well, if you wouldn't poop in your pants all the time, your asshole wouldn't hurt."

She half expected her logical conclusion to provide consolation, to shut him up, but it didn't. He still sat there like some yowling little Buddha.

"Fuck!" she said, and she bent over, put her hands under his arms and lifted him up and, holding him as far away from herself as possible, walked toward the water.

He squirmed and kicked and screamed, and the closer she got to the water, the more violent he became, as if whatever it was that had frightened him or hurt him was out there in the water.

She fought to hold on, probably gripping him too tightly but not caring, and when she was in the water up to her knees, she dunked him to his waist and peeled off the adhesive strips that held the diaper on and let the diaper float away. Then she swirled the child around, hoping the water would clean his bottom.

After a minute or so, she hauled him out of the water and, still holding him at arm's length, walked back up the beach and set him down on his feet.

His crying subsided into breathless, staccato sobs, but still he begged for her to hold him, and when she wouldn't, he grabbed her leg.

"Let go, goddamnit!" she said, and she raised a hand to slap his arm away from her leg. But the instant she felt the impulse to strike the child, her anger vanished, replaced suddenly by fear, fear of herself, of her power over the little child and the damage it could do . . . to him and to her.

Fear quickly transformed into sympathy. "Hey," she said, "hey . . . it's okay." She knelt down and let him wrap his arms around her neck, and put an arm under his bottom and lifted him up. "Let's go watch TV, what d'you say?"

As she crossed the beach back to where she had left her towel, she noticed something awry, something missing. Then she saw tracks in the sand, as if a heavy object had been dragged into the water, and she realized that the trash barrel wasn't there anymore.

She looked out into the harbor and saw— maybe twenty-five yards out, no farther than she could throw a stone—the black neck of the empty barrel as it floated on the surface.

"D'you *believe* it?" she said, soothing the child with the sound of her voice. "Those guys fill that trash can with all that crap, and then they go and throw it in the harbor so it can wash up on people's lawns. I tell you, Jeremy, the bottom line of life is, people stink."

She gathered up her towel and tote bag and, with the child settled on her hip, made her way through the gate and onto the sidewalk . . . talking nonsense to keep the child quiet, and vowing to herself that next summer, no matter what, she would find an easier way to earn five crummy bucks an hour.

34

ENRAGED, IT flailed through the shower of dispersing garbage, grabbing random bits of flotsam and gnashing at them, as if violence would somehow force them to yield nutrients they did not contain. A few pieces were nourishing, but very few, only enough to make it yearn for more. Most were worthless, and there was no way it could tell one from another.

Its gills labored, clogged with alien things that lodged in the flaps and impeded motion.

It had chosen wrong, following scent rather than instinct.

It propelled itself slowly to the surface and waited for its eyes to adjust their focus on the shore.

Empty. The living things had gone.

They were there, however, somewhere, in company with many more. It knew that.

It knew, too, that they could be brought within reach.

But another decision would be required, a decision for which it had been programmed, but one for which the implementation was—or so the creature sensed—beyond its abilities.

It allowed itself to drift downward again, and it rested on the mud bottom, lolling like a corpse among the ribbons of kelp while it probed the recesses of its brain for long-lost keys to long-hidden locks.

Its brain was dim but not slow, out of condition but not disabled, and the more it demanded of the brain, the more the brain responded.

One by one, the keys appeared.

At last, it knew what it must do, and how to do it.

Energized by new promise, it crawled along the bottom that sloped up into the shallows. When its back was nearly out of water, it crabbed sideways into the shelter of some boulders, and it waited, scanning the shore until it was confident it was alone. Even then, it waited a few moments more, rehearsing the steps it must take, reluctant to leave the safety of the world it had known—for how long? Forever, as far as it knew—but certain that its life depended on the course it had chosen.

It ducked down, immersing its head and gills, and pumped water through its system, flooding its blood with oxygen like a diver preparing for a record plunge.

It raised its head, pulled itself to its feet and began to walk. The muscles in its legs were weak—they had not borne weight for half a century—but they supported it, and with each step they gained an iota of new strength.

It needed shelter for the exercise it was programmed to perform, and it needed it soon. Because it had no sense of time, it did not know what soon was, but it knew that its blood would tell it: as oxygen was consumed, more would be demanded, and the brain would lapse into crisis.

Soon.

. . .

The streets were empty, doors closed and windows curtained. Still, it felt exposed, and so it lurched for the comfort of the shadows between two buildings. Its ears could hear now—they did not only record pressure changes—and they heard raucous sounds not far away.

It passed more closed doors, turned down another dark street, saw more closed doors and was about to turn again when, in a niche near the end of this street, it saw an open door. It staggered toward the door, trailing a smear of slime, beginning to feel the first alarums from its brain, demanding oxygen.

The door was large, and broad, and the space

inside was dark and empty.

The creature looked upward and saw what it needed: large crossbeams supporting the roof.

It could not leap up to the beams, and there was no rope or ladder for it to climb; it probed one of the walls with its claws. The wood was soft—from age and rot and humidity—and its claws pierced it as if it were wet clay.

Its claws sank deep into the wood, and it scaled the wall like a panther.

The effort sucked oxygen from its blood, and by the time it reached the first crossbeam the alarums in its brain were urgent. It swung its legs over the beam and hung upside down, a dozen feet above the dirt floor, its arms dangling beneath its head. Out of its mouth a trickle of liquid oozed and dripped to the floor.

It waited for a moment, monitoring the metabolic change: The metamorphosis was too slow: before its system would be cleansed, before its motor could be stopped and restarted, the brain would have begun to die, starved for oxygen.

And so, as it had been taught to do fifty years before, as it had done once in practice, it balled its fists beneath its rib cage and snapped them upward.

Green liquid gushed from its mouth like vomit. The first spasm encouraged a second, and a third, until a cycle of convulsions began that pumped water from the lungs and flushed it through the trachea.

A fetid pool of green fluid formed in the dirt below, a miniature swamp.

It took only a few seconds for the lungs to empty and the chest cavity to contract.

When it was done, the creature hung motionless, its eyes rolled back in its head, eggshells of perfect white. Droplets of slime made their way down its steel teeth and fell like emeralds.

Its life as a water-breather was over.

Clinically, it was dead. Its heart had not begun to beat; the fluid in its veins lay still.

But the brain still lived, and it commanded itself to send one final burst of electricity across the synapses that would restore life.

The body convulsed once more, but this time it expelled no liquid.

This time it coughed.

35

ELIZABETH SLAMMED the door behind her, hopped down onto the sidewalk and stood still, trying to sense where the parade was. She couldn't hear it, of course, but she could feel it, as a pulsing on her eardrums and a faint tympany on the soles of her bare feet. The drums and the tuba sent pressure waves through the air, and the pounding of hundreds of feet shocked the concrete sidewalks for blocks in every direction.

It had taken her longer to find the roll of film than she had expected, and she guessed that by now the parade was close to the commercial docks. She wanted to get the film to Max before the parade actually arrived at the docks, for the arrival and the Blessing itself were the most photogenic parts of the ceremony.

She took a breath, and held it, and closed her eyes, turning in the direction of the feelings she was receiving. She was right: the parade was two thirds of the way down Beach Street, only a hundred yards or so from the docks. She could still beat it, though, if she took several shortcuts.

She dropped the film into the pocket in her skirt and started to run.

She knew Max would be there, he wouldn't have gotten impatient and gone off on his own to look for film; she was sure he trusted her as much as she trusted him, liked her as much as she liked him. It had never occurred to her to wonder why she liked him more than other boys she knew, for she wasn't an analytical person, she was an accepting person. She took every day as it came, knowing there'd be something new in it and something old, something good and something bad.

She just liked him, that was all, and when he went away—as he would, for nothing was forever, her fever had taught her that—she would continue to like him. If he came back, that would be good; if he didn't, that would be too bad. At least she would have had someone to like a lot for a period of time, and that was better than not having had someone to like a lot.

For the moment, all she wanted to do was get the film to him and see his face light up when she gave it to him, and to watch his amazement at all the carryings-on of the Blessing.

She vaulted a fence, traversed a yard, vaulted

the fence on the other side and dashed down a back street. She turned a corner, squirmed between some garbage cans and crossed an alley. She was only a block away from Beach Street now, and she could feel the thump of the drums in her ears.

The street she was on was narrow. Cars were parked on both sides, except in front of an open garage. As she neared the garage, she smelled a strange odor—salty and rotten-sweet—and saw a trickle of green liquid seeping from the garage into the gutter.

She slowed, for the garage belonged to friends of her parents, and if the liquid seeping into the street was something important—fuel oil or sewage, something that might suggest an emergency—she should find the people at the Blessing and tell them.

She bent down and sniffed the fluid. It was like nothing she had ever smelled. As she straightened up, she looked into the dark garage and saw a huge pool of it, and as she looked, more drops fell. No question, something was broken and dripping.

She stepped into the garage.

· · ·

Hanging like a giant bat, it sucked air into its lungs, and felt life return to its tissues.

Suddenly it smelled prey, heard it. It willed its eyes to roll forward, and looked down.

· · ·

Elizabeth sensed a change in the surrounding air pressure, as if a great animal had taken a great breath. Unable to hear, unable to see into the dark recesses of the garage, she felt a spasm of fear.

She turned and ran.

· · ·

The creature's arms twitched, the long webbed fingers of its huge hands flexed; it straightened its legs and somersaulted to the floor. This prey was small and fragile . . . an easy catch, an easy kill.

But as it hit the floor, its legs, too weak from bearing too little weight for too long, buckled, and the creature tumbled onto its side. It pushed with its arms, raising itself into a crouch, and moved awkwardly toward the light.

The prey was gone.

It roared in frustration and fury, a guttural, mucous growl. Then, abruptly, it sensed danger, recognized the possibility that it might be pursued. It knew it must flee. But it did not know where to seek safety.

It had no choice: it had to return to the world it knew.

It moved out of the shadows and onto the street.

It had no recollection of how it had gotten here or of what route to take for its return. Surrounded by buildings, it could not see the sea, but it could smell it, and it followed its nose toward the scent of salt.

It had traveled for less than a minute when, from close behind, it heard a sound it recognized as signaling aggression. It wheeled to face the threat.

A large animal covered with black hair was crouched in a dark space between buildings. The hair on its neck had risen, its lips were drawn back, exposing long white teeth, and its shoulders hunched over the large muscles of its forelegs. A rumbling noise came from its throat.

The creature appraised the animal, thinking less about food than about flight. It sensed that the animal would not permit flight, that it was intent on attacking.

So the creature took a stride toward the animal.

The animal sprang, teeth bared, claws extended.

The creature caught it in midleap and drove its steel teeth deep into the animal's throat. Immediately the rumbling noise changed to a whine, and then to silence, as the creature held the animal and let it die.

When it was dead, the creature flung it to the pavement, knelt beside it and slit the animal's belly with its claws. It reached into the warm body and tore away the entrails.

Then it continued toward the safety of the sea.

36

"STOP WORRYING, Max," Chase said. "From the sound of it, the band's gonna turn the corner up there in about ten seconds, so relax and enjoy the show. She'll find you."

"But not where I said I'd be," said Max. "I shouldn't have—"

"Hey, Max, what have you got going here?" Chase grinned. "You wouldn't by any chance—" He stopped when he felt Amanda dig her elbow into his ribs.

"She'll find you, Max," Amanda said, putting an arm around his shoulders, "and she'll understand. Really."

Max had been following the parade, trailing the Saint Bernard, when he had glanced at the space between two shorefront houses and seen Amanda and his father cruising slowly by in the Institute's Mako. He had sprinted down to the rocks and waved, and Chase had nosed the boat ashore and urged Max to jump aboard. They had rafted the Mako to a sportfisherman tied up at one of the commercial docks, and stepped ashore to await the parade.

The bishop appeared first, followed by his entourage and the drum majorettes. As the first of the musicians turned the corner and entered the straightaway to the dock, the band struck up the "Colonel Bogie" march.

Max looked down at his empty camera.

"I've got one," Amanda said, and she pulled a tiny camera from her pocket. "I'll make copies for you."

Roland Gibson made his way through the crowd behind Chase and stopped beside him. The police chief's uniform was freshly pressed, his shoes shined. "Two thousand tourists, Simon," he said, smiling. "And you wanted me to cancel it."

"I'll grant you," said Chase. "But it's not over yet. When are you letting Puckett out of jail?"

"As soon as the last visitor leaves his last dollar . . . around six o'clock. Then you can hear all about Rusty's monster."

The radio on Gibson's belt crackled, and a voice said, "Chief . . ."

Gibson unhooked the radio, spoke into it, listened, then said softly, "Shit."

"What's up?" asked Chase.

"Tommy didn't say, just said there was something I should see." Gibson replaced the radio and stepped out onto the dock. "See you later."

All of a sudden Chase heard, behind him and over the blare of the approaching trombones, Max's voice shouting, "Elizabeth!"

He turned and saw Max sprinting along the edge of the crowd toward a barefoot girl in a blue dress who was running beside the band as fast as she could.

Max and the girl met; the girl was trembling, and Max was reaching for her, to calm her. As Chase drew near, he heard the girl try to speak, but all that came out of her mouth were incoherent sounds. Her hands fluttered like hummingbirds before Max's face, and Max was shaking his head and saying, "Slower, slower."

"What's she saying?" Chase asked.

"I can't tell," Max said.

Amanda came up beside Chase, knelt down, took Elizabeth's hands in hers and said, "Are you hurt?"

Elizabeth shook her head.

"Scared?"

Elizabeth nodded.

"Of what?"

"Something," Elizabeth said thickly. "Something big."

Then Chase heard his name being called. He looked up and saw Gibson beckoning to him from the end of the dock. "Be right back," he said to Amanda.

Gibson's face was grim with anger. "Something just killed Corky Thibaudeaux's guard dog, Buster," he said. "Tore out his throat and gutted him, right up on Maple Street. Tommy found this."

He held out his hand, and Chase saw a stainless-steel tooth. Two of its edges were serrated, and there were tiny barbed hooks on each end of the third, thicker side.

Chase's breath stopped; he stared at the tooth. Then he looked up at Gibson and said, "It's here, Rollie. It's come ashore."

37

IT ENTERED the water at the same place it had emerged—it saw its own tracks in the sand—and, staying in the shelter of the boulders, made its way slowly down the sloping mud bottom until it was immersed up to its shoulders.

It emptied its lungs of air, ducked underwater and, as its brain told it to do, generated motion in its gill flaps, opened its mouth, expanded its trachea and breathed in.

It choked.

It sprang instantly to the surface, gasping and coughing. Pain seared its lungs and knotted the muscles in its abdomen.

Enervated and off balance, it slipped and began to sink. Water seeped into its gill slits, and again it choked and gagged. It reached for an outcropping on one of the boulders, grabbed it and clung, wheezing, until at last its lungs were clear.

Twice more it tried to submerge, following each step of the ancient program. Twice more it failed.

It did not know what had happened, or why, for its brain could not ask itself such questions and thus could provide no answers. It knew only that it could no longer exist underwater, that survival depended on breathing air.

But it also sensed that it could not survive among the air-breathing things.

If it could not live underwater, still it would have to live *in* water.

It drew a breath of air, clamped its gill slits closed and ducked down. This time it did not choke. It could see, for the lenses surrounding its eyes were intact, and it could move. Tentatively, it swam forward.

But when it attempted to dive, it noticed a difference: diving was no longer simple, fluid, natural; diving had become difficult, and a pressure within drew it up toward the air.

There was another difference; very quickly its lungs began to ache, there was a pounding in its ears, and its brain commanded it to find air to breathe.

It arced upward, broke through the surface and gasped. As it breathed in and out, its buoyancy changed, and it had to kick slowly to maintain its position.

Its simple brain was challenged. The changes

required adaptations if it was to survive.

After a few moments, it felt comfortable enough to swim gradually away from shore. Across the water it saw land.

Staying underwater as long as it could, surfacing only to breathe, it swam toward the land. There, it sensed, it could find safety.

There it could hunt.

PART SIX

▲ ▲ ▲ ▲ ▲ ▲ ▲

THE
WHITE SHARK

38

"SAY HEY, Ray," Rusty Puckett said as he pulled out a stool and slapped a twenty-dollar bill onto the bar.

"Seven-and-Seven?" asked the bartender.

"Make it a double; I got a terrible thirst." Puckett glanced around; the room was less than half full. It was seven-thirty, the early drinkers had gone into dinner, the late ones hadn't arrived yet.

Ray mixed the drink, put the glass in front of Puckett and took the twenty. Smiling while he made change, he said, "I hear you been on a holiday, courtesy of the borough."

"Bastards," Puckett said. He drained half the glass and waited for the warm feeling to pool in his stomach. "They didn't even apologize. I got half a mind to sue Rollie Gibson."

"For what, drying you out? You look pretty

good to me; never hurts a man to take a day or two off."

Puckett finished his drink and signaled for a refill. The truth was, he did feel good, and not only physically: he felt vindicated. Gibson and the others hadn't believed a word he'd said, thought he was lying or hallucinating, and then all of a sudden this afternoon they'd gotten real interested, wanting to hear his whole story from the beginning. But he'd shown them, he'd stonewalled Gibson and that Simon Chase, claimed he couldn't remember. Why should he give anything away for free when there might be money in it? Some of those TV shows—what did they call them? Docudramas—paid big bucks for exclusive interviews, and he was pretty sure he was the only one who'd seen that thing, whatever it was. All he had to do was wait, the word would get out and they'd be coming to him. He could be patient; he had all the time in the world.

"Nate Green was in here before," Ray said. "Looking for you."

"I bet he was." Puckett smiled. "What'd you tell him?"

"That I hadn't seen you."

"You still haven't, okay?" To hell with Nate Green, Puckett thought. There were bigger fish to catch, lots bigger, than the Waterboro *Chronicle*.

"Sure, Rusty," Ray said. "No skin off my nose."

Puckett finished his second drink. Now he was feeling really good. Even Ray was treating him with respect.

A man entered from the street, sat at the far end of the bar and ordered a glass of wine. As Ray poured it for him, the man said, "Do you know a man named Puckett, a Mr. Rusty Puckett?"

Puckett froze and pretended to read the menu on the blackboard over the bar.

"Uh-huh," Ray said, without glancing Puckett's way. He returned the wine bottle to the cooler and resumed slicing limes.

"Have you seen him?"

Puckett heard an accent in the man's voice, not American, foreign, like from somewhere in Europe.

"Might have," Ray said. "You got business with him?"

"Possibly."

Puckett chewed on an ice cube and reflexively scrolled through his brain for potential trouble. He didn't owe anybody money; he hadn't poached anybody's lobsters recently; he hadn't cut away any buoys, hit any other boats or struck anybody with his truck . . . as far as he knew. Then he searched for potential good news. Maybe the guy was from a big magazine or one of the docu-drama shows, and wanted to make a deal.

When he had sorted through all the possibilities, he felt safe enough to turn to the man and say, "I'm Puckett. Who wants to know?"

"Ah," the man said. He smiled and rose from his stool, carrying his glass of wine, and as he passed the bartender, said, "Very discreet of you."

Puckett watched the man approach. He was tall, a couple of inches over six feet, broad-shouldered and narrow-waisted, a guy who took care of himself, probably worked out. Puckett guessed he was in his late forties: hair that had once been blond was light gray, and swept straight back from his forehead. He wore a gray suit, a white shirt and a dark tie. His skin was pale . . . not sickly, just pale from never seeing the sun. Puckett decided he looked like an undertaker.

"May I join you?" the man asked.

Puckett gestured at the stool beside him and thought: European, no question. *Join* came out *choin.* German, maybe, or Dutch, or one of those pissant countries that kept breaking apart over there.

The man said, "There is a gentleman outside who would like to meet you."

"Why?"

"He has heard of you . . . of things you have said."

Puckett paused, then said, "Okay, so bring him in."

"I'm afraid that's not possible."

"Why?" Puckett laughed. "Too big to get through the door?"

"Something like that."

Some*sing* . . . some*sing* like that. German. Had to be. "Hey, Ray," Puckett said, "you got no rule against fat guys, do you?"

Ray didn't laugh.

"Would you please come outside?" the man said. "I think it would be worth your while."

"Worth my while how?"

"Financially."

"Well, hell, why didn't you say so?" Puckett stood up. "Keep my seat warm, Ray. If I'm not back in ten minutes, call nine-one-one."

A van was parked across the street. It was black, its windows were tinted so no one could see inside, and Puckett noticed that its license plates were New York handicapped permits.

"Fuck is this?" he said. "An ambulance?"

The man slid open one of the side panels and gestured for Puckett to climb in.

Puckett leaned over and glanced inside. It was dark and, as far as he could see, empty. For no good reason, he felt a chill. "No way," he said.

"Mr. Puckett—"

"Look, Hans, I don't know who's in there, I don't know you, I don't know nothing. All I know is, I'm not gettin' in there. Tell him to come out."

"I told you—"

"Forget it. You want to do business, we do it in the sunlight. End of story."

The man sighed. "I'm sorry," he said.

"Yeah, well . . ."

Puckett never saw the man's hands move, but suddenly he was spun around, his feet were off the ground and he felt himself flying into the darkness of the van. He hit the carpeted floor and lay there, dazed, listening to the side panel slam and the engine start, and feeling the van begin to move.

39

CHASE PULLED the last page of the fax from his machine, read it quickly. "Another *oid,*" he said disgustedly.

"Which one this time?" asked Tall Man.

"*Elasmobranchoid:* manifesting the characteristics of the cartilaginous fishes." He tossed the paper onto his desk. "Some of these guys must take advanced degrees in covering their asses. They're geniuses at stringing together sentences that sound great and say nothing."

For the past forty-eight hours, Chase had faxed every marine scientist he had ever met, sent photocopies of Polaroids of steel teeth and claw marks on dead animals, described every incident that had happened since the discovery of the Bellamy brothers and pleaded for opinions—guesses, speculations, *any*thing; he had promised to keep them confidential—about what kind of creature they might be dealing with.

The few scientists who had deigned to reply had been vague and guarded, none venturing to identify a specific animal, all hedging their bets by attaching the suffix *oid*, which told Chase nothing he didn't already know.

"So now," he said, "we've got *carcharhinoid*—it could be a class of sharks; *ichthyoid*—it could be a fish; *pantheroid*—it could be a seagoing lion or tiger; and *elasmobranchoid*." He stared for a moment at the pile of faxes, then thumbed through them and selected one. "You know the only one that makes any sense to me? This one, from the cryptozoologists."

"The sea-monster people?" said Tall Man. "But they're—"

"Fringe. I know. Pseudoscientific, nobody takes them seriously. But they're the only ones with the guts to use the *oid* I like: *humanoid*."

"Come on, Simon." Tall Man shook his head. "You know the stats better than I do. The thing that killed the sea lion was at least two hundred feet underwater; there were no bubbles on the tape, so it wasn't wearing scuba gear. And nobody free-dives two hundred feet, not long enough to kill and eat a sea lion."

"I didn't say it *is* a human, I said it may be human*oid* . . . a kind of human . . . humanlike. Hell, I don't know."

"You're beginning to sound like Puckett. Has anybody found him yet?"

"Nope, he's gone, disappeared, nobody's—"

The phone rang; Chase picked it up. He sighed, covered the mouthpiece with his hand, said, "Gibson," then closed his eyes, leaned back in his chair and listened to the litany: the chief's budget was out of control; he was running police boats twenty-four hours a day, keeping his officers on double shifts; the press was hounding him; Nate Green's story in the *Chronicle,* headlined MONSTER EATS DOG, in which he had alluded to the unsolved deaths of the Bellamys and Bobby Tobin, had drawn reporters from every news service in the land; a producer wanted to do a TV movie called *The Fiend from the Deep;* real-estate brokers, restaurateurs and the town's burgesses were keeping the police station's phones lit up like Christmas trees.

As always, Gibson's litany ended with the accusatory question: Chase was supposed to be the big honcho scientist around here; what was he going to *do* about it?

"What d'you expect me to do, Rollie?" Chase said when Gibson had finished. "Run around the great big ocean in my little tiny boat? I don't even know what I'm supposed to be looking for. Did the lab boys come up with an analysis of the slime on the floor of the garage?"

"Yes and no," Gibson said. "I think they've got their heads tucked. I told 'em I wouldn't give 'em the time of day till they get the final DNA results."

"Why? What do they think?"

"They say it comes from a kind of mammal."

"What kind?"

"They think . . ." Gibson hesitated, as if embarrassed to utter the words. "They say it looks like it could be from a human being. Crissakes, Simon . . ."

Chase hung up, stood and said to Tall Man, "Where's our resident mammal expert?"

"Where she always is, down with the kids and the sea lions."

· · ·

As Chase and Tall Man started down the hill, they could see Max and Elizabeth in the pool, playing with the three sea lions, and Amanda watching from the concrete apron.

The sea lions had grown increasingly fearful; Amanda said they seemed clinically neurotic. They were avoiding the water, all water—not just seawater. For two days they had adamantly refused Amanda's command to enter their pool.

In desperation, Amanda had called a colleague in Florida who worked with dolphins, and had learned that the intelligent mammals seemed to respond extraordinarily well to children, especially children afflicted in some way, communicating with them in some inexplicable, evidently extrasensory fashion. Amanda had asked Elizabeth to help her with an experiment, and the results had been amazing.

When the animals would no longer obey Amanda directly, they would permit Elizabeth to approach them, stroke them and, somehow, convince them to follow her into the water and play with her and Max.

Amanda had been so excited by the success of the experiment that she was relaying more and more instructions through Elizabeth and encouraging her to make up instructions of her own, in an attempt to stretch the limits of interspecies communication.

When she heard Chase and Tall Man behind her, Amanda pointed at the children and the sea lions and said, "This is fabulous."

"I need to talk to you for a couple minutes," Chase said. "It's about Gibson's lab tests."

"I've been meaning to come up and see you, too, but it didn't seem important enough to stop this. I figured there was nothing we could do about it."

"About what?"

"I just got a call on the radio in the shed from

the pilot of the spotter plane."

"I thought you'd paid him off and let him go," Chase said, "since the sea lions wouldn't work anymore."

"I guess he got interested in what we're doing here. Anyway, he was out spotting swordfish for the commercial boats, and he saw a sportfisherman this side of Block, setting out a humongous chum slick. He said he thought we'd like to know. He said it looks like the guy's baiting up white sharks."

"The guy must be certifiable. With all the publicity about the trouble around here, why would anybody go out on the water and spread a chum slick?" Chase frowned. "Anyway, there's nothing I can do about it, there's no *law* against chum slicks."

"No," Amanda said, "but there's a federal law against using juvenile bottlenose dolphins for bait. And that's what the pilot says he saw."

"Dolphins!" Chase said. "He's sure?"

"Positive. But I thought by the time we called the Coast Guard or the EPA or whoever—"

"Did he recognize the boat?"

"Yes, he said it's from Waterboro . . . the *Brigadier*."

"Can't be . . . he's gotta be wrong."

"Why?"

"It just can't." Chase started for the shed.

"What did you want to talk to me about?" Amanda called after him.

"In a minute," Chase replied.

Tall Man followed Chase into the shed. *"Sammy?"* he said. "I can't believe it." They had known Sammy Medina for fifteen years; he was a successful, responsible charter-boatman who had led a recent campaign to restrict fish catches by commercial and sport fishermen.

"That is, if it *is* the *Brigadier*," Chase said. "Hard to tell from a plane. But we'll find out soon enough. Cindy'll be straight with me." There was a phone on the wall of the shed, and Chase picked it up, dialed a number, spoke for a moment or two, hung up and said to Tall Man, "I'm a son of a bitch."

"That was Sammy?"

"Himself." Chase nodded. "At home . . . taking the day off, tying flies. He says he got an offer, bare-boat charter, not including him or his crew, just rent the boat, no questions asked . . . for ten thousand dollars a day!"

Tall Man whistled. "What kind of fishing's worth ten grand a day?"

"That's what I wanted to know." Chase paused. "Guess who rented the boat from him."

"Donald Trump?"

"No. Rusty Puckett."

"Puckett?! Puckett doesn't have that kind of

dough, nobody around here does. Besides, what does Puckett want with—"

"He's not fishing for great whites, Tall," Chase said. "Sammy says the stupid bastard thinks he's found a monster . . . or at least he's convinced some big-hitting sucker that he has. Or can."

40

IT LAY in a clump of bushes, listening to the sound of its own breathing, and to the sounds of life in the surrounding woods. It received the sounds and separated them, storing them for later identification.

It was tuning its senses.

Ever since it had emerged from the water, changes had been taking place within the creature, changes it could feel but not understand. The longer its vascular system, its heart and its brain were infused and nourished with the blend of oxygen and nitrogen that was air, instead of hydrogen-dominated water, the more it seemed to comprehend and to remember, and the greater were its abilities to innovate.

As its chemistry altered, so did its life.

It knew, for example, what it had once been. Its mind could put names to various objects and animals, though its voice could not yet articulate them. Words of all kinds caromed around in its brain, words that generated memories of emotions as diverse as anger, hatred, pride and elation.

It sensed the magnitude of its own strength, and recalled—however dimly—the pleasure it had derived from using that strength. It recalled other pleasures, too, from wielding power, inflicting pain and causing death.

It had built itself a shelter by digging a shallow trench and covering it with leaves and branches. So far, it had remained undetected, except by a curious dog, which it had killed and eaten.

It had learned that it could not pursue and catch most of the animals with which it shared the wild, but it was beginning to teach itself how to trap them. Still, it was not able to feed itself enough to satisfy its enormous, and growing, need for energy. As its strength grew, so did its demands: the more energy it expanded, the more it needed; the more it needed, the more it had to expend to fill the need.

It had become actively, not reflexively, cautious, knowing what to avoid and what to confront, what was harmless and what dangerous.

Though past and future remained fog-bound landscapes, patches of the fog had begun to lift, and it now had a goal: to fulfill its mission of annihilation.

It rested now, hearing the calls of birds and squirrels, footfalls of foxes and deer, the rustle of wind through the trees, the slur of little waves on the nearby gravel strand.

Suddenly, new sounds: clumsy treads, heavy and careless, through the underbrush. And voices.

It rolled to its knees, then onto the balls of its feet, and looked through the bushes toward the sounds.

· · ·

"Hell's bells!" shouted a young man named Chester, rubbing his leg. "I like to broke my foot in that chuckhole."

"Then look where you're walkin'," said his friend Toby.

"I still don't see why we hadda come alla way out here."

"Like I told you: it's where the critters are."

"It's private property, too."

"I been here a million times, they don't give a shit."

"Yeah? Then why's all them 'No hunting, get your ass outta here' signs?"

"Insurance," said Toby, who had already turned seventeen and thus possessed two months' more wisdom than Chester. "They gotta have 'em."

"Well, they sic the cops on us, it's you stole that friggin' thing, not me . . . don't think I won't tell 'em."

"You helped."

"I watched."

"Same difference."

"Anyhow," Chester said, "I don't know what makes you think you can hit a friggin' raccoon with a friggin' crossbow."

"It said on the box: accurate to fifty yards. 'Sides, maybe we'll see a deer instead."

"Oh, no, you don't. You shoot a deer, it's outta season and I'm outta here."

"Don't be an asshole."

They walked on for a few more yards, until they came to a big tree growing amid a tangle of thick foliage.

"Perfect," Toby said, and he stepped into the foliage and made his way around to the far side of the tree.

"That's poison ivy," said Chester.

"You got long pants on."

"What's perfect about it?"

"Chestnut tree. They'll come right to it, they love chestnuts."

"What does?"

"Critters . . . all kinds."

"A lot you know."

"Shut up."

They knelt behind the tree. From a quiver at his waist Toby took a steel-pointed graphite bolt, eighteen inches long. He set the butt of the cross-bow on the ground, pulled back the drawstring, cocked it and fitted the bolt into its slot.

"How's that thing fly true with no feathers?" asked Chester.

"The slot here makes it spin like it's rifled."

"The tip's not even barbed."

"Neither's a bullet, shithead. A thing's got enough force behind it, it'd prob'ly kill a rhino."

"Or a jogger. That'd be a fine one to explain to the—"

"Shut *up,* I tell ya!"

Chester stayed silent for a moment, then whispered, "So, whadda we do now?"

"Whadda hunters always do? We wait."

. . .

There were two of them, one fatter than the other, both slow and vulnerable . . . but apparently armed, though with what it did not know. It watched, waiting to see what they would do.

They did nothing, only squatted in the bushes.

The bird noises had stopped, and the squirrel sounds.

It moved slowly to its left, until it had a clear path toward them. It would take them easily, first one then the other, and drag them both back to its den.

The fat one first.

. . .

"What was that?" Chester said.

"What was what?"

"A noise, back of us."

Toby turned and looked, but saw only bushes. "Forget it," he said. "We're the hunters here, you think somethin's gonna sneak up on *us*?"

"I hate woods," Chester said. "I . . . *Toby!*"

. . .

The fat one had seen it, was looking at it, pointing at it, making a noise.

It sprang from the underbrush, took two swift strides and was upon the fat one. It dug one set of claws deep into the fat one's chest, the other into his scalp and eyes, bent his head back and, with its teeth, ripped at his throat.

The fat one died quickly.

It turned to the other.

. . .

"Oh God . . . oh Jesus . . . oh God . . . oh Jesus . . ."

Toby staggered backward. Something had Chester, something huge and grayish white, and blood was flying everywhere because . . . oh God, oh Jesus . . . the thing was *eating* him!

Toby's back struck the trunk of the tree.

Now the thing was turning toward him. It had

yellowish hair and steel teeth and eyes as white as cue balls, and it was bigger than Arnold Schwarzenegger.

Toby jerked the crossbow up and held it in front of him, and he tried to say something but no words came out. He pulled the trigger.

The crossbow bucked as the graphite bolt flew from its slot. He saw the bolt hit the thing and sink in, and there was a little squirt of what looked like blood.

But the thing kept coming.

Moaning in terror, Toby dropped the crossbow, wheeled around the tree trunk and ran.

. . .

It felt a burning sensation in its side, below its ribs, and looked down and saw something protruding from its flesh. It wrapped a hand around the thing, pulled it from its flesh and cast it away.

It was not badly wounded, none of its vital functions was impaired, but the pain slowed and distracted it. It stopped and watched the human blunder away through the bushes. It returned to the fat one, intent on dragging him back to its den.

Then, for the first time, it experienced foresight: the other human might come back, return to hunt it. With others. It was in danger, it would have to make a plan.

It sat down against the big tree, willing its brain

to work, to project, to sort, to innovate.

Its main priorities were clear: to staunch the flow of blood, to survive. From the floor of the forest it gathered leaves, and moss from the trunk of the tree, and it crushed them and packed them into the wound.

To nourish itself, it used its claws to cut strips of flesh from the fat one; it consumed them. It ate as much as it felt it needed, then forced itself to eat more, until it sensed that another bite would trigger regurgitation.

Now, it knew, it must escape, and find a different, safer place.

It arose and walked to where the trees ended at the shoreline. It stood in the shelter of the trees, to be sure it was alone, then it entered the water.

It could not submerge, but it could swim; it could not feed in the sea any longer, but it could survive until it reached different land.

As it had become aware of its past, now it was beginning to fathom a future.

41

THE SEA was flat, there wasn't enough breeze even to raise ripples, so the Mako rose quickly to a plane and cut through the glassy surface at forty miles an hour.

"I wonder who came up with the ten grand," Tall Man shouted over the scream of the outboard motor.

"Some TV producer, probably," Chase answered from the helm.

"Well, they better hope to hell they don't raise that critter."

A single boat was anchored in the deep channel southwest of Block Island; though it was still a quarter of a mile away, Chase recognized it instantly. "That's Sammy's boat," he said. "White with a blue stripe . . . tuna tower. . . outriggers."

The sun was behind them, lowering in the western sky. Tall Man shaded his eyes and squinted.

"They got two ass-kicker marlin rigs off the stern," he said. "Wire lines. Only a couple guys in the cockpit."

"Is one of them Puckett?"

"Yeah." Tall Man paused, looking. "The other's a big dude, big as me. Looks like he's cradling an AK-47."

"Cradling," Chase said, "not aiming."

"Not yet."

Chase kept a hundred yards from the bigger boat as he passed it. He saw no other crewmen, no cameras, no sound gear. "They're not making a movie," he said. "They're hunting." He swung the Mako around, took it out of gear and let it drift up alongside the fishing boat.

Puckett leaned over the side and shouted, "Beat it, Chase! Every time I get a break, you find a way to fuck it up. A man's got a right to earn a living."

"Not by slaughtering dolphins, he doesn't," Chase said. "You're looking to spend a lot of years in a little room all by your lonesome."

"You don't know shit." Puckett reached into his pocket, brought out a paper and waved it. "These dolphins died of a virus, them and a dozen others. We bought 'em from a lab in Mystic."

Chase hesitated. What Puckett said was possible, it even made sense. Over the past few years, hundreds, perhaps thousands, of dolphins of several species had washed up on the shores of the eastern seaboard, dead from viruses whose origins remained a mystery. Pollution was presumed to be the catalyst, but what kind of pollution—sewage, agricultural runoff, oil or chemical waste—no one seemed to know.

"So what're you doing, then, you and Rambo?" Chase gestured at the huge man holding the assault rifle across his chest. Before Puckett could answer, Chase felt Tall Man nudge him and look up, and he saw a video camera mounted on the lip of the fishing boat's flying bridge. It was moving, tracking them as they slid by in the Mako.

"Fishing for great whites, what else?" said Puckett. "A good white-shark jaw can fetch five grand, easy."

"Don't bullshit me, Rusty, I know what—"

The man with the rifle said, "We have broken no law. That is all that need concern you."

"No, what concerns me is, I know what you think you're looking for, but you don't have the faintest idea what—"

Suddenly, from a loudspeaker mounted somewhere above the cockpit came a disembodied voice, gravelly, unnatural—almost mechanical sounding—heavily accented and shouting, "Rudi! Get in here!"

The man passed the rifle to Puckett, turned and entered the cabin.

Chase's Mako had drifted past the anchored boat, and Chase reversed the motor and backed up until the two boats were once again side by side.

Puckett held the rifle at his waist, pointed at them.

"Put the gun away, Rusty," Tall Man said. "You're up to your eyeballs in shit already."

"Stuff a cork in it, Geronimo," said Puckett.

The man returned from the cabin. "Throw me a line," he said. "Come aboard."

"Why?" said Chase.

The loudspeaker boomed, "You!"

Chase looked up at the video camera and pointed to himself.

"Yes, you. You say you know what we are doing?"

"I'm afraid so," said Chase.

"Come inside . . . please . . . you and your friend. I think we need each other, you and I."

42

THE CABIN was dark; the glass in the doors was tinted, and curtains had been pulled across the windows. It was chilly, too, air-conditioned and dehumidified.

As their pupils adjusted to the dark, Chase and Tall Man saw that all the furniture had been removed from the cabin and replaced with what looked like a portable intensive-care unit. In the center of the room was a motorized wheelchair, and in it sat a man. A rubber tube led from a digital monitor through a hanging bottle and into the veins in the crook of one of the man's elbows. His other hand held the end of a hose attached to a tank of oxygen. Behind him were more machines, including an electrocardiograph and a sphygmomanometer, and on the overhead in front of him was a television monitor showing a color image of the stern of the boat.

The man was old, certainly, but how old was impossible to tell, for his head was shaved and he wore sunglasses. The breadth of his shoulders suggested that he had once been large but had shriveled; a blanket covered him from knees to chest.

The man raised the hand holding the oxygen hose, nudged aside the folds of a yellow ascot and pressed the hose to his throat. His chest expanded as he filled his lungs.

Then he spoke, and Chase was startled to hear the words come not from him but from a box behind him, an amplifier of some kind.

"Where is he?"

"He," Chase thought, what "he"? "I don't know," he said. "Now *you* tell *me: what* is . . . it?"

Again the man touched the hose to his throat, and again he spoke. "Once he was a man. He became a great experiment. By now, there is no way to know. A mutant, perhaps. A predator, definitely. He will not stop killing; that is what he was made to do."

"By who? And what makes you think you—"

"I know what he needs. If I can deceive him into . . ." The man slumped, he had run out of breath; he waited, as if to regain the strength to breathe.

"What d'you mean he was an experiment?" Tall Man said. "What kind of experiment?"

The man took a breath. "Sit down," he said, and he gestured at the open deck by the door.

Chase glanced up at the television monitor and saw Puckett ladling fish guts and blood into the sea. The other man, Rudi, was sitting on the stern with the rifle in his lap.

The old man said, "If he comes, Rudi will shoot him."

"You can kill it, then," said Chase. "That's a relief."

"No, it is a question." There was a slight change in the tone of the man's words, almost as if he were smiling. "A good question: can you kill what is not really alive?"

Chase and Tall Man sat while the man gathered strength and, after a moment's silence, began to speak. At first, the words came in short bursts, but gradually he developed a rhythm of inhaling and exhaling that allowed him to express complete thoughts.

Chase closed his eyes—it was distracting to see the tube touch the throat and withdraw, to watch the chest expand and contract—and let the words wash over him and become pictures.

"My name is Jacob Franks," the man said. "I was born in Munich, and in the years before the war I worked as an apprentice in my father's pharmacy. We could have left, we were urged to leave, but my father refused, he was a man with an unfortunate belief in the basic decency of mankind. He could not believe the rumors about the Nazis' intentions for us Jews . . . until, one night, it was suddenly too late to get out.

"I last saw my parents and my two sisters as they were led away from a cattle car on a siding near a town no one had ever heard of.

"I was kept alive—I was young and strong and healthy—and put to work as a laborer. I could not know that what I was building were crematoria . . . essentially I was digging my own grave. My health began to fail, of course, from malnutrition, and in hindsight it is clear that I was only a few weeks or months away from being rendered into ashes, when one day a new doctor arrived at the camp. Because my papers indicated that I had some experience in pharmacology, I was sent to work for him.

"His name was Ernst Kruger, and he was a protégé, a friend and, later, a rival of Josef Mengele." He paused. "You know who Mengele was, I assume."

"Sure," Chase said. "Who doesn't?"

"*I* don't," said Tall Man.

"They called Mengele the Angel of Death," Franks said. "He was a doctor at Auschwitz; his joy came not from saving lives but from taking them, and in the most hideous ways possible. He enjoyed experimenting on prisoners, torturing them for no other purpose than to see how much pain they could endure, slicing open twins only to see how similar they really were, transplanting eyes only to see if they would function, freezing or boiling women and children solely to see how long it took them to die. He escaped at the end of the war and lived in Paraguay and Brazil."

"They never caught him?" Tall Man asked.

"No. He drowned, or so they say, a few years ago off a beach in Brazil. There is said to be forensic proof, but for me, Mengele will never die. The fact that such a man could exist, that God would permit it, means that a little bit of Mengele must exist in the darkest parts of each of us."

"And your doctor," Chase said, "this Kruger . . . was he like Mengele?"

"He was vicious like Mengele," said Franks, "and as brutal. But Kruger was smarter, and he had a stronger vision, warped as it was."

"Which was?"

"To usurp the power of God. He truly wanted to create a new species."

Tall Man said, "What the hell for?"

"To some extent, to see if it could be done. But then, as he did more and more work and the impossible began to seem possible, as success followed success, word reached high into the Nazi hierarchy. Money, encouragement flowed back down to him. Kruger's vision became true megalomania: he decided to try to create a race of amphibious warriors."

Tall Man began to say something, but Franks cut him off.

"This was the nineteen-forties, remember. There were no nuclear submarines with infinite bottom time, scuba diving had barely been invented, man was still a stranger to the sea. Imagine a creature with the intelligence, the knowledge, the training and the brutality of man, but combined with the capacities of an apex marine predator."

"Jesus," Chase said, "Nazi killer whales."

"Not quite. More versatile, even," said Franks. "Whales must breathe; Kruger's creatures would not. They would stay underwater indefinitely, dive to a thousand feet, set explosives, spy on shipping. His dream was for them to have the potential for unlimited mayhem."

"Meaning he was nuts," Tall Man said.

"Not necessarily," Chase put in. "I remember reading about a professor from Duke who tried the same thing during the sixties. He started with mice, got them to breathe liquids without drowning and found that liquid-breathing eliminates the possibility of getting the bends. One time he decompressed a mouse from thirty atmospheres to surface pressure in three seconds, which would be like a diver going from a thousand feet to the surface at seven hundred miles an hour. The mouse survived. He saw no reason the same thing couldn't work with humans. He only stopped experimenting because of a lack of need: robots came on the scene, ROVs, submersibles; they could do a better job in deep water, with no risk to people. But he was convinced he could have created an amphibious human."

Franks nodded and said, "In theory, creating a water-breathing human being should not be very difficult. We come from water-breathers, after all; fetuses survive on liquid, and in various stages of development they show evidence of flippers and even gills. And we are all liquid-breathers already, in the sense that our lungs contain fluids without which they couldn't function."

"So you're saying Kruger succeeded?" Chase said.

"Almost," said Franks. "If the war had gone on longer, he might actually have done it. What held him back was the quality of his subjects; they were weak, sick, malnourished—slaves. Many developed infections from the initial tracheotomy surgery, and because there were no antibiotics then, they died. Some failed to survive the flooding of their lungs with saline solution and fluorocarbons. But Kruger had an inexhaustible supply of patients, so he pressed on.

"And then, from somewhere high in the chain

of command, perhaps Hitler himself, came a gift: a perfect subject. Heinrich Guenther was the Aryan physical ideal, six and a half feet tall, muscled like a Greek statue. He had won medals in the nineteen thirty-six Olympics in the shot put, the javelin and the hammer throw, and he became something of a national hero. He joined the SS, secured a commission and, when the war came, seemed destined for a brilliant future. He was fearless and ruthless. He was utterly without conscience. He was a killer.

"He was also not quite sane, though that wasn't evident at the time. A solitary man, he lived alone, and apparently he had been murdering people—prostitutes, lowlifes for the most part—for years. That only came out after he went berserk in a beer hall one night and killed three people. Today I suppose he would be diagnosed as a sexual psychopath or a paranoid schizophrenic; in nineteen forty-four he was labeled a homicidal maniac. He was sentenced to be shot, and was about to be, when someone decided that he could perform one last service for the Reich. They sent him down to us."

"You worked with the guy?" Chase asked.

"Worked *on* him. With Kruger. For months. He was treated like a tiger. He was caged between surgeries, fed raw meat and vitamin injections, anesthetized and programmed in ways that are sophisticated even for today: biofeedback, subliminal conditioning. He was almost finished, Kruger had only one last step to go, when the Allies closed in on the camp. But Kruger was obsessed; he refused to abandon the experiment. He took Guenther with him when he fled . . . like most of the Nazis who knew they would be branded war criminals, Kruger had been given an escape route to South America.

"So we flooded Guenther one final time, packed him in a bronze box full of concentrated fluorocarbons and enriched saline solution and loaded him onto a truck. Kruger left on foot, he headed north toward the sea. I never saw either of them again."

"What about you?" Chase asked. "What happened when the Allies arrived?"

"They freed me . . . they freed all of us."

"And that was that?"

"Why should it not be?"

"Because you hadn't just survived," Chase said. "You'd worked side by side with that monster while he killed people."

"Well . . ." said Franks, again with what sounded like a weary smile, ". . . perhaps they thought I had suffered enough."

He leaned forward in his wheelchair, and the glow from the television monitor fell on his face. He removed his sunglasses. One of his eyes was normal, but the other was a deep, egg-yolk yellow. Then he touched the tube to his throat, but this time after he had inhaled he used his fingertips to pluck away the ascot around his neck.

There were three diagonal slashes on either side of Franks' neck, healed decades ago into ridged purple scars, and in the center of his throat was a black and ragged hole that led down into his gullet.

"My God . . ." Chase said. "Are they . . . you've got . . . *gills?*"

"I was an early experiment . . . and a failure," Franks said. He replaced the sunglasses. "And I am the only survivor. My lungs were too weak to absorb the fluorocarbons; over and over again, I drowned . . . to the brink of death. Kruger could have let me die, but he didn't; he would raise me upside down on a chain hoist and let gravity drain me, then restart my lungs with what passed in those days for CPR. He kept bringing me back to life because, he said, he needed me." Franks leaned back, out of the light. "I never recovered fully, I never will. But I don't want to meet God without one last act of penance. I want to kill this . . . this ultimate abomination."

"If that's what it is," said Tall Man.

"It is, I'm certain of it. We know that Kruger never reached South America. The Nazi-hunters who tracked down Mengele and Eichmann and the others never found a trace of him. The U-boat he was traveling on was listed as missing."

"How do you know he got on a U-boat?"

"There are records. The Nazis were fanatics about keeping records. Kruger's work had a code name, and it was mentioned in the archives as having been loaded aboard U-165. The boat sank, or was sunk, I assume somewhere in the mid-Atlantic."

"How could the thing travel across a couple thousand miles of ocean bottom," Tall Man asked, "and survive all this time?"

"Kruger had slowed Guenther's metabolism to the edge of clinical death, a state way beyond hibernation. The chemicals in his box could sustain such basic life as there was, and his need for food would be nil, at least for a very long time. Eventually, like a bear woken by hunger in the spring, his body would have demanded food, and I guess he found something to eat."

Franks paused; Chase and Tall Man stared at each other.

"The answers are there," Franks said, "if you know what to look for. I stopped searching for Kruger long ago. All the evidence pointed to his having died. An uncle had brought me to America and put me to work in his chemical business; I built a new life, I had a son—Rudi—and I prospered.

"But I never forgot. A part of my mind was always looking for clues, hints that Kruger or Guenther had survived. And then I saw a newspaper item about a *National Geographic* photographer disappearing from a research vessel near Block Island."

"We heard about that," Chase said.

"The story said that a bronze box the size of a big casket had fallen overboard and disappeared . . . a box the researchers had brought up from the wreck of a submarine in the Kristof Trench . . . a German U-boat."

"You said Guenther's programming hadn't been finished, there was one step to go. What was that?"

"Kruger's ambition was to create a truly amphibious killer," Franks said. "A half-human weapon that could survive equally well in air or water, could go back and forth between the two. He conditioned Guenther to breathe water, then taught him how to drain his lungs and breathe air. What he had not had time to teach him was how to reverse the process when he wanted to return to the water. Once on land, Guenther would become what is called an obligate air-breather. He would be trapped there. So, you see, it is very urgent that we destroy him before—"

"Christ!" Chase said suddenly, and stood up. "Puckett didn't tell you? The thing's already been ashore! It killed a dog in Waterboro." He turned to Tall Man and said, "Get on the horn to Rollie Gibson, he keeps the radio in his office tuned to sixteen. Tell him what the thing is, and it may be loose in town, or maybe in the woods."

Tall Man climbed the steps to the wheelhouse while Chase opened the door and went out onto the stern. He ordered Rudi to cut away the baits and Puckett to start the engine, then he returned to the cabin.

"This thing is partly human," he said to Franks, "or used to be. So it should be able to be killed like a human being, right?"

"I wish I knew for certain," Franks said. "Kruger altered the central nervous system, so he—it—lives on a very primitive level. I would say he would be as hard to kill as a big shark . . . which reminds me, Mr. Chase, I never told you his code name. The Nazis referred to it as *Der Weisse Hai* . . . 'The White Shark.' "

Tall Man returned from the wheelhouse. "I couldn't get through on the radio," he said, "but it doesn't matter, Rollie'll be on the case by now . . . we're too late."

"What d'you mean?" Chase said.

"The radio's like a friggin' Chinese fire drill, everybody yakking. Some kid was killed over on Winter Point. His buddy swears the kid was killed by a yeti."

"A yeti?" Franks said.

"The Abominable Snowman." Chase turned to Tall Man. "Let's go." He started for the door. "The Mako can get us to town in—"

"Simon . . . the thing may not be in town."

"What d'you mean?" Chase said.

"The kid, the survivor, said he saw it dive into the water and start swimming eastward."

"Eastward? What's to the east of Winter Point? There's no land out there except . . . oh my God." The only land to the east of Winter Point was Osprey Island. "Call Amanda on twenty-seven, tell her to take the kids and—"

"I tried," Tall Man said. "There was no answer."

43

"COOL," SAID Elizabeth.

"Awesome," said Max.

The children stood on the rocks seaward of the sea lion pool, watching Mrs. Bixler's vintage speedboat zoom out of its cove and approach in a high-speed turn. As the boat banked, the late-day sun glittered on the polished mahogany hull and the stainless-steel fittings; it looked like a fantasy spaceship.

Max loved the boat, had begged Mrs. Bixler to let him drive it. "Not till you get to be my age," she had said with a smile. "Only an old fool like me drives an old boat like this one."

Amanda stood behind them; behind her, the sea lions rocked back and forth on their flippers, barking for their supper.

In the shed ten yards beyond the pool, a voice came over the speaker of the VHF radio. "Osprey

Base, Osprey Base, Osprey Base . . . Osprey Mako calling Osprey Base . . . come in, Osprey Base."

The voice echoed off the cement walls, unheard.

Mrs. Bixler was wearing an orange life jacket, sunglasses and a baseball cap turned backward so the bill would shelter her hairdo from the wind. She slowed the boat as she neared the rocks, and the roar of the big GM V-8 engine lowered to a growl. She picked up an ancient megaphone from the seat beside her and called through it, "I'm going to town for Bingo; probably spend the night with Sarah. I'll get hold of the police when I get to shore, make sure Simon reported in. They probably already sent a backup boat. I'll call you if there's any news."

Amanda and the children waved. Mrs. Bixler pushed the throttle forward, and, like a racehorse suddenly given its head, the boat leaped forward, banked around the point and headed west toward the mainland.

In the shed, the voice said again, "Osprey Base, Osprey Base . . . come in, Osprey Base . . ."

"Time to feed the girls," Amanda said, and she stepped back toward the pool. "Then we'll go up to the house and I'll fix us some supper." She took Elizabeth's hand, faced her and said, "I'm glad your mom said you could spend the night."

Elizabeth nodded and said, "Me too."

Max stayed on the rocks, looking out to sea. "I

wonder where Dad is," he said. "It's getting late."

"On his way home." Amanda hoped her voice carried more conviction than she felt. "We'll set places for him and Tall."

They fed the sea lions, returned the leftover fish to the refrigerator and stowed the plastic balls, rings, triangles and other training tools in the shed. Elizabeth was the last to leave the shed. As she pulled the door closed behind her, she felt a faint vibration in the air, similar to that of a voice. She looked around, but couldn't locate the source, so she shut the door.

The sound was muffled now, nearly inaudible: "Osprey Base, this is Osprey Mako . . . come in, Osprey Base . . ."

When they reached the top of the hill, Max looked down and saw the heron standing in its tidal pool. "I should go feed Chief Joseph," he said.

"Tall will do it," Amanda said.

"But he may not get in till late. I can—"

"No," she said curtly, and she realized she was nervous . . . not afraid, for there was nothing to be afraid of, but apprehensive, anxious . . . but about what? She didn't know. She smiled at Max and softened her voice. "Tall likes to do it, it's his ritual."

They continued on toward the little house where Amanda lived.

. . .

Mrs. Bixler was perched on the back of the front seat of the boat, steering with her bare feet. The sea was oil calm, and the planing boat left a blade-straight wake in the flat water. She felt young and free and happy. This was her favorite pastime, her favorite time of day, cruising into the setting sun. Already the water tower and white houses of the borough were turning pink; soon they would turn blue-gray; by the time she reached shore, they would be the flat gray that was the harbinger of night.

Something in the water ahead caught her eye. She dropped her feet from the wheel, stood in the seat and held the wheel with one hand.

A dorsal fin, tall and perfectly triangular, zig-zagged through the water; behind it, a scythelike tail slashed back and forth.

A shark? What was a shark doing around here this late in the day? A big shark, too, probably fifteen feet long.

She turned the boat and followed the fin. The shark seemed to be behaving erratically. Though she was hardly an expert, she knew enough from listening to Simon and Tall, and from watching videos, to know that this shark wasn't just travel-ing; it was feeding, or about to. It was hunting.

As she drew near, she saw a glint of metal be-hind the dorsal fin: a tag. One of the Institute's tags. This was Simon's great white shark.

At the approach of the boat, the shark submerged and disappeared. Mrs. Bixler waited for a moment, but the shark did not surface again, and so she turned back toward shore.

She couldn't wait to tell Simon; he'd be fascinated—excited, even thrilled—to know that his shark had shown up again. Now that he had recovered the sensor head, he could locate the shark and . . .

Something else in the water, dead ahead. A man. Swimming. At least, it looked like a man, though it was bigger than any man she had ever seen, and it was swimming like a porpoise, arching his broad back out of water and kicking with his feet together.

The damn fool, she thought. Swimming out here alone, at twilight.

She realized that the man was what the shark was hunting.

She accelerated toward the man, praying she could reach him before the shark did, praying she'd be strong enough to haul him aboard, praying . . .

Suddenly he was gone, too. Submerged, just like the shark. She stopped the boat and looked around, waiting for him to come up. He'd have to surface, he'd have to. He'd have to breathe.

Unless the shark had already gotten him. Or he

had already drowned. What could she do then?

The man didn't reappear, and fear seized Mrs. Bixler. It was a vague but profound terror of something she couldn't identify.

She put the boat in gear, jammed the throttle forward and aimed the bow of the boat toward the mainland.

44

IT FILLED its lungs and dived. When the motor noise had receded, it turned and searched the darkness for the shark.

The cells of its brain were recovering like explosions of sparks, and with each explosion it knew more and more about itself.

And so it was not afraid; it was galvanized. It felt not threatened, but challenged. This was what it had been created for, programmed for—to fight, and to kill.

It knew its limits and its strengths. In the water, it was vulnerable only on the surface. Underwater, it had no equal.

It felt the shark first, a surge of pressure in the water. Then it saw the gray shape, the conical head, the gaping mouth.

Still, it was not afraid, for it knew it had an advantage; it had a brain that could innovate.

As the shark charged, relentless but unthinking, the creature ducked away and blew air from its lungs. Confused by the blast of bubbles, the shark hesitated; it rose up, exposing its white belly.

The creature flexed its fingers and lunged forward, driving its claws deep into the soft flesh, pulling downward. The flesh separated. The claws pushed deeper, and now blood billowed from the ten slashes in the belly.

The body of the shark twisted, contorted, and each movement tore more of its flesh. Viscera swelled and oozed through the wounds.

The claws withdrew. The shark hovered for a moment, then began to sink away.

A searing ache suffused the creature's lungs, but it forced itself to watch until the shark was consumed by darkness.

Then it surfaced, drew a deep and nourishing breath and savored its triumph. It felt fatigue, but fatigue relieved by elation. It was back, whole again. It was *Der Weisse Hai.*

Now it must seek land, where it could hide and hunt. Using its webbed hands, it turned in a slow circle, until it located its goal: a single light on a lone island, not far away.

45

IT WAS nearly dark when Chase and Tall Man reached the island; a sliver of pink still lit the western horizon, but the sky overhead was a blanket of blue-black, broken by the golden dots of the evening's first stars. The only lights on the island were in the windows of Amanda's little house.

The tide was high, so Chase could drive the boat close to shore without fear of hitting submerged rocks. Tall Man stood in the bow and shone a powerful flashlight on the passing land.

Everything seemed normal, undisturbed. The flashlight's beam fell on a raccoon feeding on a fish on a flat rock, and the animal froze, its eyes glowing red. A fox fled the light, scampering away into the underbrush. Only the sea lions seemed agitated, huddled together by the mouth of their den, rocking back and forth.

"Maybe it turned north," Tall Man said. "Napatree would've been closer for it than here."

"I hope," said Chase. "I still want to get Amanda and the kids into town . . . just in case."

"She won't want to leave her sea lions."

"I don't plan to give her a choice." Chase had made up his mind on their way from Block: if there was a chance, even a remote possibility, of that thing coming to Osprey, he would evacuate the island. They could return tomorrow, in daylight, with the police and as much heavy weaponry as they could muster, and scour the island from end to end.

When he had circled the island and seen nothing out of the ordinary, no dead animal or fresh trail, Chase returned to the dock and swung the Mako into its slip. He turned off the motor, and stepped onto the dock. "Stay here," he said, looping the bow line over a cleat. "I'll go get them." He started up the path.

Tall Man stood on the dock, listening to the sounds of the night: crickets, birdcalls, the lap of lazy waves on the shore. Suddenly he sensed that something was out of place, or missing; it took him a moment to realize what it was. The heron. Where was Chief Joseph? Normally, by now the bird would be standing in the water by the dock, demanding food with its irascible glare. He looked over the side of the dock, but the cove was completely dark, he couldn't see anything, so he returned to the boat, fetched the flashlight and shone it on the tidal pool.

The bird wasn't there. Where had it gone? He swung the beam up to the boulders, then to the shore.

Amid a tangle of brush he saw a feather: long, blue-gray. He walked up the path, stepped into the brush, parted it with his hands. The brush felt sticky, and when he shone the light on his fingers, he saw blood.

He yanked a clump of brush out by its roots, clearing a space. There, in the dirt, was the heron's head. It had been torn from its neck, and its eyes were gone.

A rush of panic flooded Tall Man's chest. He turned and ran toward the house.

46

"BECAUSE THERE *aren't* any guns," Chase said to Amanda. "I don't like them, I've never kept any around."

They were in the kitchen. Max and Elizabeth sat on the floor; they had been playing War with two decks of cards.

"I can't leave the sea lions, Simon," Amanda said. "They're like my children. I couldn't do it."

"You *have* to. We can't defend ourselves here. If that thing comes ashore here—"

"I won't go. You take the kids to town, leave Tall Man here with me. We can bring the big boat to the dock, I'll try to get the girls aboard, and—"

The kitchen door flew open. "It's here!" Tall Man said, stepping inside and locking the door behind him.

Max started, and repeated Tall Man's words for Elizabeth.

"Where?" asked Chase.

"I don't know, but it killed Chief Joseph. It's here, Simon. Somewhere."

Chase looked at the children. "We can't leave, then."

"Why not?"

"We don't dare take the chance. It could be anywhere. Suppose it's in the bushes by the dock."

"It would've jumped me," Tall Man said.

"Maybe not, maybe you're too big, but it'd sure as hell go after one of the kids."

Amanda started for the door.

"Where are you going?" Chase said.

"To get the girls, bring them up here."

"Are you *nuts*?"

"They'll follow me. I'll be quick about it."

"I don't care. It's pitch black out there. Three hundred yards each way. You'll never make it."

"I have to." Amanda unlocked the door. "I'll stay out in the open, I'll be able to see it coming."

"They're animals, Amanda!" Chase said.

"Not to me." Amanda gestured at Max and Elizabeth. "Not to them."

"I won't let you."

"You can't stop me."

"Yes, I can." Chase took a step toward her. "If I have to, I'll tie you down."

"Stop it, Simon," Amanda said, and she

opened the door and darted out into the night.

Chase ran to the door and looked out, but Amanda was already rounding the corner of the house and running down the lawn.

"Well, shit," Tall Man said. He picked a butcher knife from a rack over the sink, slipped it into his belt and took the flashlight from the counter where he had put it.

"What do you think you're doing?" Chase said.

"Maybe you were right, Simon, maybe it won't go after six foot of redskin Terminator." Tall Man stepped through the door and was gone.

When Chase had locked the door, he looked at Max and Elizabeth. They had stopped playing cards and were sitting side by side, ashen, holding hands. He knelt beside them, put a hand on theirs and said, "This'll be okay. It's probably hiding somewhere. We'll get the police here at first light, and—"

"But Dad . . ." Max said. "What if . . . " He let the rest of the thought go unspoken.

Chase didn't answer, for he had no answer. Instead, he forced a smile and said, "Hell, Max, can you imagine *any*thing getting the better of Tall Man?" His mind raced, flitting between possibilities like a mosquito in a crowd of people, trying to decide where to land. If the thing found Tall Man, or Amanda, if Tall Man didn't kill it, what could they do? They couldn't shoot it, couldn't stab it, couldn't flee from it.

There were no answers, and yet Chase knew one thing for certain: he would do anything, including sacrifice himself, but Max and Elizabeth were going to survive.

He stood up and turned, and as he glanced through the door into the living room, his eyes fell upon the steel cylinder bolted to the floor.

Max saw him looking at the cylinder and said, "What about the decompression chamber . . . you called it Dr. Frankenstein?"

"What about it?"

"We could get inside and lock it. The thing could never get in."

"It doesn't lock from the inside," Chase said. "The only way—" He stopped, for an idea suddenly appeared in his mind, inchoate, like a cloud. He didn't rush it, but let it slowly take shape until it became a possible answer.

47

TALL MAN caught up with Amanda halfway down the hill. He had shouted to her, told her he was coming, and why, and she had stopped running. As they walked, he swung the flashlight from side to side.

They heard a bark, then several more—quick, high-pitched, frantic.

"No!" Amanda yelled, and she started to run. Tall Man reached for her, to stop her, but she was lighter than he, and quicker, and on the downward slope the best he could do was maintain a distance between them of ten feet.

She reached the pool area first; he stopped beside her. They could hear the sea lions barking, a cacophony of shrieks, but they couldn't see them. Tall Man shone the light toward the sounds.

Two of the sea lions were huddled against the side of the equipment shed, rocking on their flip-

pers, their heads bobbing as they barked hysteri-
cally. He swung the light to the right.

Something was crouching by the rocks on the
far side of the pool, something huge and grayish
white. They could see only its massive back, for its
head was bent out of sight. But as the light fell on
it, it rose and turned.

Amanda screamed. Tall Man felt his heart
jump and adrenaline surge through his arms and
shoulders.

It was as large as an ape and as gray as ash.
Through the blood that covered its face they saw
the glitter of steel teeth, and through the gore that
dripped from its hands, long steel claws. Its body
was hairless; the sinews in its arms and legs stood
out like whips; where once there had been geni-
tals, now there was but a crudely stitched patch of
mottled hide. Its eyes, as the light struck them,
gleamed like reflectors.

Behind the thing lay the partly eaten carcass of
a sea lion.

The thing opened its mouth, uttered a glottal
roar and took a step forward.

"Go!" Tall Man said to Amanda.

"I . . . but . . ." She stood frozen.

"Go! For crissakes, go warn them! Go!"

Amanda took a step backward, turned and ran.

Tall Man didn't move. He glanced up toward
high ground. Behind the thing lay nothing but

water, and he wasn't about to tangle with this thing in water. Not after what he'd heard about it.

He took his knife from his belt, bent his knees and held the knife before him, waving it slowly back and forth.

The thing hunched its shoulders, rolled forward onto the balls of its feet, raised its arms and spread its webbed fingers, baring claws as long and sharp as scalpels.

If man made you, Tall Man thought as he moved in a slow circle, man can unmake you.

48

CHASE REMOVED the last of the screws from the long mirror, pulled it away from the back of the bathroom door and set it on the floor. He measured the mirror against himself, and guessed that it was five feet tall and two feet wide. He carried it into the living room, and set it beside the open hatch of the decompression chamber.

"It should fit," he said. "Just."

Amanda slumped in a chair beside the far wall, still shaking, her color still pasty. "You're wasting your time," she said. "That'll never work."

"I've gotta do *some*thing. You have a better idea?"

"What do you use to put animals down?"

"Anesthesia."

"Well?"

"You think you can get close enough to that thing to give it a *shot*? Christ, Amanda, for all I know, it just . . ." He stopped, for he saw the children standing by the living room window, trying to see down the hill, and he didn't want to frighten them. But his mind couldn't shake the image that had clouded it ever since Amanda had burst through the door, an image of Tall Man sprawled dead among the rocks. "Give me a hand, will you?" He turned to Max. "See anything?"

"Not yet," Max said.

Amanda rose from the chair. Chase bent down, stepped into the chamber and turned to take the mirror from Amanda as she slid it through the hatch. He carried it to the far end of the chamber and stood it upright against the steel wall. Then he backed away, checking his reflection; he crouched just inside the hatch, beside the opening. "What do you see?" he asked Amanda. "Remember, the light'll be dim."

"It's okay," she said. "But, Lord, Simon, a six-year-old child could—"

"It isn't a child; it's a thing."

"Dad!" Max shouted. "Dad, it's Tall!"

Chase crawled out of the chamber and stood. Max was pointing out the window. Elizabeth stood beside him, shading her eyes from the light inside the room, straining to see through the darkness.

Chase expelled a huge breath of relief. "About

time," he said. He walked toward the window.

"Thank God," said Amanda.

Far down the lawn, by the crest of the hill before the sea lion pool, Chase saw a figure moving toward the house. The movement was erratic, yawing.

"Tall looks like he's hurt," he said. He was about to turn away, to go to the kitchen and out the door and down the lawn, when he suddenly saw color in the figure, a hue of lightness against the dark trees.

"Jesus Christ," he said. "That's not Tall."

49

IT HAD been wounded, it could tell from the burning sensations in the flesh of its face, from the fact that one of its legs was responding slowly to signals from its brain, and from a numbness in one of its hands. It looked at the hand and saw that a finger was hanging by strands of sinew. It tugged at the finger until the sinews snapped, then it cast the finger away and scooped up mud, which it packed around the bleeding stump.

It did not feel weakened by the wounds, it felt strengthened, invigorated by an elation born of triumph. It had met an enemy worthy of it—not merely prey but an adversary—and had conquered it.

Its wounds were nothing; it would survive and recover.

It no longer perceived the need for defense, no longer felt caution, for from somewhere deep within itself had come a conviction that it was now invincible.

It saw a light in the distance, at the end of this sloping ground. Light meant shelter, and perhaps more opportunities to destroy more enemies.

Leaning into the hill, it dragged its sluggish leg up the slope—moving slowly, veering this way and that, not concerned with time. Time meant nothing to it; it was immortal.

50

"WHY CAN'T we just *run*?" asked Max. He was pale and fidgety, and he seemed about to cry. "It can't catch all of us, not if we spread out."

"No, Max," Chase said, putting one arm around his son, the other around Elizabeth, who trembled slightly but seemed impassive, as if prepared to accept whatever would happen. "I don't want it to catch *any* of us, especially not you two."

He went to the window, shaded his eyes and peered out into the darkness. He could see the thing more clearly now, a ghostly shape against the black. How much time did they have? Chase couldn't tell, for the thing was moving slowly, veering left and right, almost aimlessly . . . almost, but not quite, for with every brief tack it advanced a few feet closer to the house.

"Let's do it," he said. He turned to Amanda. "Are you sure you've got the sequence down?"

"Positive. But I still—"

"Good." Chase took the children's hands and led them to a small closet behind the decompression chamber. "It'll be dark," he said, "but you can handle that, right? Amanda'll be with you."

Tentatively, the children nodded, and stepped into the closet.

Chase held his hand out to Amanda, moved close to her and whispered, "If anything goes wrong—anything—take the kids and head for the Mako. You should have plenty of time; the least I can do is stall the goddamn thing."

"Simon . . ."

Impulsively, Chase kissed her. "In you go," he said, and he ushered her into the closet and closed the door.

He went to the control panel on the wall, pushed the master button that activated the decompression chamber. There was a hum as the machinery engaged, and a hiss as the pressure tanks buried in the walls began to fill. He turned the lights out in the room, all except the pressure-shielded pink bulb inside the chamber.

Then he climbed through the hatch and crouched down, waiting.

51

IT WAS closer now, it could see movement in the house, dark figures against the light that shone through the windows. It was neither wary nor alarmed, but challenged. They might see it, they might not, but they could not stop it.

Then the light was gone, vanished as if sucked up by the night.

It halted, to assess the change, to reassure itself that the failure was not in itself.

No, it could see forms—the dark lump of the house against the black slate of the sky. As its eyes adjusted to the darkness, it even saw a faint pink glow from somewhere inside the house.

It resumed its march, and soon it was by the side of the building. It circled slowly, deliberately, seeking entry.

It found a door, a thin thing of wood and glass, and drew back an arm to destroy it.

52

OVER THE hum of the machinery, Chase heard glass breaking and wood splintering, then a low, guttural sound.

· · ·

It crossed the threshold into the large room, focusing on the faint pink glow.

It heard machine sounds, and saw a big rigid object in the center of the room. The glow came from inside it. It shuffled over to the object, moved to the end where a round door hung open and bent down.

In the dim light, it saw at the far end of the object a human, like the one it had recently vanquished, but slighter, weaker, frightened.

Prey. Easy prey.

It stepped inside.

· · ·

Chase smelled sourness and salt and rot, heard a footfall on the steel.

He didn't dare look down, didn't dare make any movement that would alter his reflection in the mirror.

The thing passed him, and now he could see the hairless ivory flesh of its legs and buttocks, the webbing between its toes, the curved steel claws clotted with blood.

Chase's legs began to cramp. He willed himself not to move, and begged the thing to keep going. Two more steps, he thought, just two more, then he could . . .

The thing stopped.

. . .

It was confused, something was wrong. The human was there and then not there, and it saw something else, something it did not recognize.

Suddenly it knew. It was seeing itself.

With a roar of rage, it turned.

53

CHASE HEAVED himself off the floor of the chamber and dove through the open hatch. He landed on his knees, turned and reached for the chamber door. It was heavy, heavier than he had remembered.

The creature took a step toward him, and lunged.

Chase swung the door and leaned against it. He saw a hand reaching for him, growing larger and larger.

The door slammed with a resonant clang.

"Now!" Chase shouted. "Now!" He spun the dogging wheel, and a red light blinked on, signaling that the seal was complete. He felt thumping against the steel door.

He heard the closet door open, and Amanda's footsteps as she hurried to the control panel. He had preset the dials; all she had to do was push the buttons.

There was a sound of compressed air rushing into the chamber through a dozen vents. Cold and dry, when it collided with the warm air already in the chamber, it became fog.

"Take it down," Chase said to Amanda, "as far and as fast as you can." He moved around to the side of the chamber and looked through the porthole.

. . .

It had abandoned the unyielding steel door, sensing that it had been trapped, searching for an escape. It saw a hole covered with glass, and drew back a fist to smash the glass.

Pain suddenly assaulted its head, pain such as it had never known, like fire, as if its brain were being crushed into a molten mass.

It pressed its hands to the sides of its head and shrieked.

. . .

Though they could see little through the fog swirling in the chamber, they heard the sound . . . a piercing yowl of an animal in agony.

"Its ears are going!" Chase said.

"No wonder," said Amanda. "I've pressurized the chamber to two hundred feet in five seconds; its ears can't equalize fast enough. It's gotta be hurting something fierce."

The shrieking stopped.

"Its eardrums must've busted," said Chase.

"Which means the pain's gone; it's deaf but it's equalized." Amanda looked at the gauge on the control panel.

Something slammed against the porthole. Tiny spiderweb cracks appeared in the glass.

"Hurry," Chase said. "Christ . . . it wants to break that porthole, and if it does, the chamber'll go off like a bomb." He turned to Max and Elizabeth, who stood beside Amanda. "Go outside," he said. "Fast."

"But . . ." Max seemed perplexed. "Go where?"

"Anywhere . . . just *go!*"

The children ran toward the kitchen door.

"It's at three hundred feet," Amanda said.

· · ·

As quickly as it had come, the pain had vanished, and now the creature perceived only a dullness in its head.

Though it could not know what was happening to it, it could identify the cause of its pain: the human staring at it through the glass. Its focus changed; no longer concerned with survival, now it sought vengeance.

One of its feet struck something hard. It bent down, picked up the thing, hefted it and lunged at the glass circle.

· · ·

"It's got a wrench!" Chase shouted, recoiling as the heavy head of the steel tool crashed into the porthole. New cracks appeared in the glass.

"Six hundred feet," Amanda said. "Six-fifty."

"We've gotta do it, we've gotta do it now."

"But we don't know—"

"It'll work," Chase said. "It's got to." He pressed his face to the porthole and strained to see through the fog. He saw the creature crouched, its arm cocked, the wrench held in its hand like a club. "*Do* it!" he shouted.

"Coming up," Amanda said, and she pushed a series of buttons. There was a deafening rushing noise, and the fog in the chamber swirled violently and began to dissipate.

Chase saw the creature tense, saw through the gray fog the white of its eyes and the silver gleam of its teeth.

It sprang at the porthole.

54

THE CREATURE seemed to stop in midair, as if struck by a bolt of lightning. Its body contorted, its eyes popped wide, it collapsed to the floor of the chamber and clawed at its own flesh.

"Five hundred feet . . ." Amanda said. "Four-fifty . . ."

"It's working," said Chase. He couldn't take his eyes from the porthole. "My God . . ."

With the chamber pressurized to six hundred and fifty feet, the squeeze on the creature—on its sinuses and lungs, on its stomach cavity and every other pocket in its body that contained air—had been nearly three hundred pounds per square inch. Now, as Amanda brought the chamber back to surface pressure, the air within the creature was escaping with the speed and violence of a balloon bursting.

. . .

It could not see, it could not hear, it could not breathe. Every joint and sinew felt aflame. Its stomach seemed to want to invade its chest, its chest to swell into its head, its head to fly to pieces.

It had no conception of what was happening, could not know that the air inside it was decompressing at a rate far faster than its body could accommodate, that bubbles of nitrogen were scattering throughout its tissues, lodging everywhere and growing inexorably, tearing the tissues apart.

Desperately it clutched itself, as if to force its misshapen body back into form.

. . .

Chase watched, fascinated, as the creature caromed from one side of the chamber to the other. Blood leaked from its mouth and ears; its eyes bulged, straining at their sockets, and it raised a hand as if to contain them. But before the hand could reach the face, one of the eyes launched itself from its socket—like a grape squeezed from its skin—and dangled grotesquely by red strands of muscle fiber.

The image was surreal—a writhing, pulsing, swelling figure that might have been created by a lunatic sculptor and controlled by a mad puppeteer.

"Two-fifty," Amanda said. "Two hundred . . . what's happening?"

"It's on its knees," said Chase. "It's . . . holy shit!"

The creature exploded.

A thick crimson mist filled the chamber; globules of blood and pieces of flesh struck the porthole, and stuck.

55

CHASE STOOD in the hospital lobby, waiting for an elevator, and looked at his watch. He was more than an hour late.

He had wanted to be there by two, but he had gotten stuck on the phone with Rollie Gibson and Nate Green, and had had to fulfill his promise to give Nate a detailed, exclusive story for the paper about what had happened on the island.

Then, when he had arrived ashore, Rudi Franks had been waiting for him, alone and bearing a gift: an old, cracked black-and-white photograph of Ernst Kruger and Jacob Franks operating on Heinrich Guenther.

Finally, there had been the confusion at the bank. He had stopped to cash a check, and one of the bank's officers had wanted to see him about something that made no sense whatever to Chase, something that had to be a mistake.

The elevator arrived; Chase got out on the fourth floor and walked to the nurses' station.

"You took your sweet time," said Ellie Bind-loss, a short, chunky woman with whom Chase had gone to high school. "We're not equipped to handle eight-hundred-pound gorillas around here, y'know."

"Sorry," Chase said. "Where is he?"

She pointed down the hall. "Can't miss him," she said. "You'll hear him before you see him."

As Chase approached an open door at the end of the hall, he heard Tall Man's voice shouting, "Sorry! What d'you mean, *sorry*? You just shafted me, and you did it on purpose."

Then Max's voice, laughing and saying, "Tough, chief. Move your man."

Chase paused outside the door, not sure what to expect, then stepped inside the room. "Hi," he said.

"Don't 'Hi' me," said Tall Man. "This vicious kid of yours has beat my butt four games in a row. We oughtta feed him to the fishes." He laughed, then grimaced and clutched the bandages that surrounded his chest and bound one arm to his side. "Christ," he said, "laughing's no fun. But it's better than coughing."

Max sat on the foot of the bed; between him and Tall Man was a board game littered with plastic cards and colored pieces. Amanda sat in a chair beside the bed, a newspaper in her lap.

Chase hadn't seen Tall Man for two and a half days, not since he had ridden with him in a police helicopter and brought him to the intensive-care unit in New London. Then, Tall Man had been covered with blood and dirt, his color a dusty gray, his breathing rattly and weak. It had taken the doctors two hours to stop the bleeding, suture and reinflate the collapsed lung and begin the first of many transfusions. They had shooed Chase away from the ICU and, that evening, when they were confident Tall Man would survive, had urged him to go home and sleep.

Chase still wasn't sure what had happened to Tall Man. He had started to search for him in darkness, but hadn't found him until nearly dawn, stuck between two boulders on the shore, unconscious. Tall Man claimed not to recall much, only that he had cut the creature several times, and then had felt himself stabbed in the right side and shoulder, lifted off his feet and thrown onto the rocks in the sea.

There was a purple lump on Tall Man's forehead, and a line of stitches extending from his left eyebrow across his temple.

"You don't look too bad," Chase said, stepping toward the bed. "Considering."

"Yes, I do, I look like a mile of bad road," said Tall Man. "And don't you even *think* about touching me; I feel like a train wreck."

Chase smiled. "Ready to go?"

"Damn right. If I stay here long enough, they'll starve me to death or stick me to death . . . or both." Tall Man leaned forward, swung his legs over the side of the bed and stood, leaning on the wall for support. Chase helped him on with his trousers and draped his shirt over his shoulders.

Ellie Bindloss appeared, pushing a wheelchair. "Sit down," she said.

"Never," said Tall Man. "I can walk—"

"Sit down before I knock you down."

Tall Man smiled, then laughed, then coughed. "You're a hard woman, Ellie Bindloss," he said, and he flopped into the wheelchair.

Max pushed the wheelchair down the hall, Ellie walked beside it and Chase and Amanda followed behind.

Chase told her about the photograph Rudi had given him, then said, "We've got to stop at the bank on the way back; I want to clear something up."

Amanda hesitated before saying, "Clear up what?"

"I don't know, the damndest thing. One of the officers told me the bank isn't holding my paper on the island anymore. He said they sold it."

"Really?"

"To a partnership. I thought for a minute

they'd screwed me, sold it to Finnegan or somebody else who'd want to take over the island. But then the guy said *I* was one of the partners."

Amanda didn't say anything, she just kept walking, looking ahead.

"You ever heard of something called the Pinniped Group?"

"It must be new," she said.

"What kind of name is that, the Pinniped Group? You know what pinnipeds are?"

"Sure."

"They're . . ." Chase stopped, and as the sense of what he was about to say hit him, the thought occurred to him that he had never felt so stupid in his life. "Sea lions. A pinniped is a sea lion."

Amanda smiled and took his arm. "We'll talk about the details later," she said. "We'll have plenty of time."

LARGE PRINT EDITIONS

Look for these at your local bookstore

American Heart Association, *American Heart Association Cookbook, 5th Edition* (Abridged)
Dave Barry, *Dave Barry Is Not Making This Up* (paper)
Peter Benchley, *White Shark* (paper)
Barbara Taylor Bradford, *Angel* (paper)
Barbara Taylor Bradford, *Remember*
William F. Buckley, Jr., *Tucker's Last Stand*
Leo Buscaglia, Ph.D., *Born for Love*
Michael Crichton, *Disclosure* (paper)
Michael Crichton, *Rising Sun*
E. L. Doctorow, *The Waterworks* (paper)
Dominick Dunne, *A Season in Purgatory*
Fannie Flagg, *Daisy Fay and the Miracle Man* (paper)
Fannie Flagg, *Fried Green Tomatoes at the Whistle Stop Cafe* (paper)
Robert Fulghum, *It Was on Fire When I Lay Down on It* (hardcover and paper)
Robert Fulghum, *Maybe (Maybe Not): Second Thoughts from a Secret Life*
Robert Fulghum, *Uh-Oh*
Peter Gethers, *The Cat Who Went to Paris*
Martha Grimes, *The End of the Pier*
Martha Grimes, *The Horse You Came In On* (paper)
Lewis Grizzard, *If I Ever Get Back to Georgia, I'm Gonna Nail My Feet to the Ground*
David Halberstam, *The Fifties* (2 volumes, paper)
Kathryn Harvey, *Stars*
Katharine Hepburn, *Me* (hardcover and paper)
P. D. James, *The Children of Men*
Naomi Judd, *Love Can Build a Bridge* (paper)

(continued)

Judith Krantz, *Dazzle*
Judith Krantz, *Lovers* (paper)
Judith Krantz, *Scruples Two*
John le Carré, *The Night Manager* (paper)
John le Carré, *The Secret Pilgrim*
Robert Ludlum, *The Bourne Ultimatum*
Robert Ludlum, *The Road to Omaha*
Cormac McCarthy, *The Crossing* (paper)
James A. Michener, *Mexico* (paper)
James A. Michener, *The Novel*
James A. Michener, *The World is My Home* (paper)
Richard North Patterson, *Degree of Guilt*
Louis Phillips, editor, *The Random House Large Print
        Treasury of Best-Loved Poems*
Maria Riva, *Marlene Dietrich* (2 volumes, paper)
Mickey Rooney, *Life Is Too Short*
William Styron, *Darkness Visible*
Margaret Truman, *Murder at the National Cathedral*
Margaret Truman, *Murder at the Pentagon*
Margaret Truman, *Murder on the Potomac* (paper)
Donald Trump with Charles Leerhsen, *Trump: Surviving
        at the Top*
Anne Tyler, *Saint Maybe*
John Updike, *Rabbit at Rest*
Phyllis A. Whitney, *Star Flight* (paper)
Lois Wyse, *Grandchildren Are So Much Fun
        I Should Have Had Them First*

The New York Times Large Print Crossword Puzzles (paper)

Will Weng, editor, Volumes 1–3
Eugene T. Maleska, editor, Volumes 4–7
Eugene T. Maleska, editor, Omnibus Volume 1